Snowfall Over Halesmere House

Suzanne Snow writes contemporary and uplifting fiction with a vibrant sense of setting and community connecting the lives of her characters. A horticulturist who lives with her family in Lancashire, her books are inspired by a love of landscape, romance and rural life.

Her first novel in the Thorndale series, *The Cottage of New Beginnings*, was a contender for the 2021 RNA Joan Hessayon Award and she is currently writing the Love in the Lakes series for Canelo. Suzanne is a member of the Romantic Novelists Association and the Society of Authors.

Also by Suzanne Snow

Welcome to Thorndale

The Cottage of New Beginnings
The Garden of Little Rose
A Summer of Second Chances
A Country Village Christmas

Love in the Lakes

Snowfall Over Halesmere House

Snowfall Over Halesmere House

SUZANNE SNOW

CANELO

First published in the United Kingdom in 2022 by

Canelo
Unit 9, 5th Floor
Cargo Works, 1–2 Hatfields
London, SE1 9PG
United Kingdom

A CIP catalogue record for this book is available from the British Library.

Print ISBN 978 1 80032 874 7
Ebook ISBN 978 1 80032 873 0

Cover design by Cherie Chapman

Cover images © Shutterstock

Look for more great books at www.canelo.co

Printed and bound in Great Britain by Clays Ltd, Elcograf S.p.A.

1

For Amy and Jessica, with all the love and sparkles

Chapter One

Ella Grant had never before been offered a job quite like the one at Halesmere House and she jumped out of her car to stare at the building. Was this it, really? It must be, it did match online images she had seen, and the imposing Georgian house seemed to be staring right back at her through the fading November afternoon, not a single light blazing or glimpse of family to welcome her.

As she scrolled social media a couple of weeks ago, the perfect-sounding stopgap had leapt out at her on an Instagram post. It seemed that Halesmere, deep in the Cumbrian countryside, required a person with energy and ideas to relaunch it as a holiday home in the New Year. She had applied at once, and after a few straightforward emails and a friendly Zoom chat, she had been excited to accept the position when it was offered.

She had never been made redundant before and this sudden change in her circumstances was partly voluntary. When the high-end catering company for whom she worked had been acquired by another larger one, some roles had become surplus, including hers; and although the new owners had wanted to discuss the potential for promotion, she'd taken the redundancy offer they were required to make and leapt back out into the world, unemployed for the first time ever.

A decision she still hadn't quite got her head around yet, a bit like the one that had drawn her to this glorious place. Evergreen ivy clung to stone walls and shutters were fastened across windows, barring her a view of the rooms. To her left was a snug cottage, attached to the house by an archway. She already knew from her research that the arch led to old stables and a barn set around a courtyard.

Thanks to the satnav trying to direct her to a dead end, Ella was fifteen minutes late, hoping someone was still there to meet her. She marched across the gravel drive and pressed an old-fashioned bell, not entirely surprised when a response wasn't forthcoming. She tried the cottage as well and although a dog barked inside, nobody came to greet her. There were no vehicles on the drive beside hers and she was beginning to think she had been forgotten.

She wasn't a person who sat still for long and locking herself in the car to stay warm didn't appeal. Maybe she'd squeeze in a run; it was one of the ways she liked to keep fit and she couldn't quite find enough peace in her days without it. She knew there was a tarn somewhere beyond the garden but heading down there now for a swim was hardly an option at this time of day, when it was getting dark. She fastened her coat and set off to explore. If she couldn't find anyone soon then she'd have to try to contact her new employer by phone.

As she walked around she saw that the courtyard was rather tired, some of the old stables boarded up, with clumps of weeds in places and patches of moss covering the cobbles. Ancient terracotta pots stuffed with winter bedding plants made the place more cheerful, and two pots sat at either end of a rusty metal bench. A black gate set into a low wall offered a glimpse of curving steps leading down to a door, a tiny sunken space that passed for a garden outside it. Another door was set in a high stone wall concealing the gardens surrounding the main house, and she heard a chicken squawking indignantly somewhere out of sight.

'Ella?'

'Oh!' Ella, who had both hands cupped to her face trying to see through a dirty window, spun round to find a woman she recognised from their Zoom as Noelle Bourdon. Noelle was even more attractive in person; willowy and elegant with grey curls escaping from a sheepskin Cossack hat, and lined, still-beautiful skin. An exquisite wool coat was tightly belted, a scarlet splash against the dull afternoon, a black scarf draped round her neck. Ella spent most of her life in sports kit or chef's whites and wished she could pull off such style with the same ease and elegance. Perhaps she'd need to be French to do that, like her new employer.

'Yes. Sorry, my hands are cold.' Ella held one out. 'It's lovely to meet you in person. I hope you don't mind; I was just having a wander as there wasn't anyone in the house. I wouldn't have minded a swim in the tarn but it's a bit dark for that.'

'*Pas du tout.* Not in the least, welcome to Halesmere.' Noelle clasped Ella's hand with both of hers, shaking it firmly. 'I am glad that you found us, it can be tricky if you do not know the way. I am sorry for not welcoming you when you arrived, I had forgotten to mention that I was collecting my grandchildren from school.'

Ella found the switch from French to English charming. It might be helpful, she thought, if she brushed up on her own very rusty French. Noelle drew two children forward and Ella offered them a reassuring smile.

'Hello, you must be Lily and Arlo. My name's Ella but I don't think it's as nice as yours.'

The children were both gorgeous, with identical honey-brown eyes and cautious faces dusted with freckles, and the little boy still possessed a childish roundness that his elder sister did not. Strands of red–gold curls were escaping from the plaits over Lily's shoulders and Arlo's floppy fringe nearly reached his pale red eyebrows.

'*Mes chéris*, remember I told you about Ella this morning? We are going to get to know her well over the next few months as she'll be working here and helping to take care of you.'

'Papa didn't tell us, Mamie. Does he know about Ella? I think he would have told us if he did.'

Lily's gaze was concerned, and Ella saw anxiety flit across Noelle's face. 'All will be well, *ma chérie*. Papa and I have spoken about your care and there is nothing for you to worry about.'

'If had to guess I'd say you're in Year Two, Lily, and Arlo is Year One,' Ella said to distract Lily from her moment of worry. 'Have I got that right?'

'Arlo's the baby, he's only four so he's in Reception. I'm in Year Two. I'm six, nearly seven. It's my birthday next month.'

'I'm not a baby, Daddy says you're to stop calling me that.' Arlo went to shove his sister, scowling as she skipped neatly out of his way.

'I'm going to tell Papa you pushed me!' Lily's voice was a wail as she gave her brother an angry glare and tried to poke him in the ribs.

'So am I! You started it!'

'*Faire taire maintenant*, no squabbling.' Noelle's tone was mild as she took a firm hold of Arlo's hand. 'It is not

4

necessary, you don't want Ella to think you are always fighting, do you? We want her to have a *bonne* impression of our *famille*.'

'You must be excited about your birthday, Lily.' Ella hoped to get her on to a happier subject than squabbling with her brother.

'I want to have a party, but Papa hasn't decided yet.' Lily gave an exaggerated sigh. 'I'm not allowed to invite the whole class, he said it's too many.'

'Okay.' Ella had little experience of children's events. Some of her former colleagues had children and they seemed to spend their weekends on a never-ending round of parties, watching their little ones slithering down slides or getting up close and personal with a range of interesting animals.

'Your hair is a pretty colour.' Lily was staring at Ella, and she laughed.

'Thank you, Lily, I'm glad you like it.' Ella smoothed her pixie crop from her face. She would need to find a new stylist before long; she could hardly keep driving back to her favourite one in Brighton to have her roots touched up. 'I like it lilac too, it's one of my favourite colours.'

'Mamie, may I have short hair like Ella's please?' Lily gave Noelle a hopeful glance. 'Then Papa won't have to plait mine for me.'

'Lily, you have naturally beautiful hair, do not rush to change it.'

'Ella, would you like to see our chickens? We have to make sure they're all in bed when we come home from school, so the foxes don't get them. We had foxes at home in London too.'

Ella was caught off guard when Arlo's small, warm hand found hers. She swallowed down the emotion

5

rushing into her chest as his fingers tucked trustingly inside hers. She couldn't remember when she had last held hands with anyone and was astonished to be so unbalanced by such a simple gesture. He was already tugging Ella, half-laughing, towards the garden as Lily grabbed her other hand. Ella was caught and there was nothing to do but follow, shrug off the sentiment she was so practised at hiding.

'What's going on?'

The words were fired at them like bullets and the children froze at her side. She glanced across her shoulder to see a man striding through the arch. After an incredulous stare at Ella, he turned his attention to Noelle.

'Maman? Who is this with my children?'

'Maxence! I wasn't expecting you back quite so soon.' Noelle clutched her hands together and a flash of guilt crossed her face. 'This is Ella, *chéri*. You remember we spoke about her position with us?'

'Is that supposed to be a question? I remember a discussion, but I made no decision.'

'You are quite right, we did have a discussion, and you didn't make a decision, I did.' Noelle had caught Ella up, the children still clutching her hands. 'I must apologise for my son's rudeness, Ella.'

'There's no need to apologise for me, Maman. I'm perfectly capable of doing it for myself when the need arises. And I'm still waiting for an explanation about what's going on.'

'Oh, Maxence, do you really have to be so difficult?' Noelle's voice was more placating as she lifted her chin.

Ella didn't appreciate his look, which had seemed to measure her and find her wanting, and his smile for the children was taut. His hair was an unruly, swept-back

6

strawberry blond and she couldn't miss the square jaw, and generous mouth possibly not given much to humour. His was a strong, handsome face and one that she would have found more attractive had he not been so sharp. He wore a practical navy waxed jacket above black jeans, his scarf a blue and heather check that suited his colouring. He dropped down to hold out his arms to the children and they let Ella go to run to him. He gathered them up, rising with one held on each side.

She was used to being underestimated, her heart-shaped face suggesting a fragility she'd never possessed, and she recognised it again in this man's cool expression. Her toughness had been honed over many years and sharpened by her competitive instinct and choice of career. No one rose to the positions she'd achieved in professional kitchens without being able to hold their own when necessary. She drew her shoulders back and walked towards him, making her smile dazzling on purpose. Her mum always told her it was one of her best features and that Ella didn't bestow it nearly often enough.

'Hi, I'm Ella Grant. Lovely to meet you. What a beautiful place you have here.'

For a second she thought he was going to be rude enough to refuse her hand, but he finally took it, shifting Arlo to offer a single bone-crunching shake that was over before she could be the first to relinquish her grip.

'Max Bentley.'

It was the very least he could offer, and she was certain he was doing it on purpose. His cool smile seemed sardonic, as though he'd recognised what she had been trying to do with her own. She offered a more natural one to the children still in his arms, gratified when they smiled shyly back.

'Maman?' Max's glare had softened a fraction, but his voice retained its edge. 'I'm still none the wiser as to who Ms Grant is or why my children were strolling across the courtyard hand in hand with a stranger. You were meant to be collecting them from school and giving them tea. We discussed this.'

'Papa, Ella's living here now and helping to look after us. Isn't that right, Mamie?' Lily glanced at her grandmother for confirmation and Noelle nodded firmly, ignoring Max's look of horror.

'I'd like you to tell me right now what you have done.' His voice had quietened, and Ella heard the ice in it.

'What have I done?' Noelle waved a fist in his face, her French accent becoming more pronounced as she shrieked. 'I will tell you what I have done, Max, and I would have explained earlier if you were not always so preoccupied with your work. I have done the sensible thing for this family and employed Ella to help us. You have enough demands on your time and you can't do everything yourself. Not with the children and your practice as well.'

Noelle's fist opened out into a palm she touched to his cheek, her temper subsiding as quickly as it had flared. 'I did this for all of us. You know we need someone but time and again you refused to make the decision. And Ella will help with the children, take care of them when we are both working.'

'She will not.' Max flicked a disdainful glance at Ella. 'You may have unusual methods of parenting, Maman, but mine are more conventional. And they include not employing a nanny without a thorough interview and careful assessment.'

8

'I'm not a nanny.' Ella was getting fed up with her new employers debating her position and seemed to be losing the feeling in her limbs as the temperature dropped. But she didn't want to stamp her feet, for fear of seeming petulant.

'Then what are you, if not a nanny?'

'I'm a chef.' Three little words that didn't come close to summing up her career or list of achievements.

'A chef?' Max laughed without warmth. 'I need a chef even less than I need a nanny.'

'Papa, are you angry with Mamie and Ella?' Lily was anxious now and Max was quick to reassure his daughter.

'A little frustrated with Mamie, Lily, that's all. She needs to understand you don't offer people jobs, especially when it's not your decision to make, without going through a particular process and being sure you know who they really are.'

'Mamie said Ella would be good for us, Daddy. Do you think she's wrong?'

'Lily, that's enough.' Some of the steel had returned to his tone. 'It's time I gave you some tea since your grandmother hasn't bothered.' He looked at Ella. 'It seems my mother has brought you here on rather false pretences, Ms Grant. I'll reimburse the expenses you've incurred. I'm sorry you've had a wasted journey.'

She stared as Max disappeared through the arch with his children. At a nod from Noelle, she hurried after him, and caught up as he opened the front door of the cottage.

'Excuse me?'

He turned and a glance was enough for Ella to recognise the tension lingering in the lines around his mouth and his refusal to meet her eye. 'Lily, go and play with Arlo, I won't be long. *Ça va?*'

9

'*Oui*, Papa.'

French sounded even more adorable spoken by Lily. Ella realised she'd left her phone in her car, and she needed it. She crossed the drive, retrieved it from the front seat and opened the most recent email from Noelle, wondering if her temporary and apparently straightforward new job was going to be considerably less straightforward and possibly a lot more temporary.

'Your expenses for today?' Max had followed with impatient strides and he produced a wallet from a pocket of his jeans. 'And of course, I'll compensate you for the inconvenience you've incurred.'

'I'm not sure it's quite that simple.' Ella jabbed her phone towards his face, making him blink. She wasn't expecting the vibrant, cornflower-blue eyes revealed by the flash of light. 'I was offered this job in good faith by your mother and have a written offer of employment to prove it. I accepted and have rented out my flat on the strength of her offer. Although I haven't yet signed a contract, I'm sure you're aware that one still exists. And I'm not going anywhere unless she withdraws the offer in writing with a proper period of notice.'

'My mother had no right to give you any sort of a job without agreement from me.' Max was forcing the words out through gritted teeth. 'Halesmere and all of its interests are run by me, and the decisions are mine to make.'

'And yet here we are.' Ella reverted to politeness. 'Noelle made it perfectly clear you need some help, at least temporarily.'

'What about my children?'

'What about them?'

'Does this offer,' Max glanced at her phone again, 'say anything whatsoever about taking care of my children?'

'Only that I would be collecting them from school and giving them tea a couple of times a week. Maybe some babysitting.' Ella had been looking forward to it. In a place like Halesmere she didn't expect to run out of things to do with them, even in winter.

'We'll come back to that.' He rammed his hands in his pockets. 'So what exactly does your job description say?'

'I haven't got one yet. Noelle said the family needed me and we'd, er, we'd make it up as we went along.' Ella knew this sounded too casual, and Max pounced.

'No job description? Humour me. Make up what as you went along? How do you expect to be spending your time here, time my mother presumably intends me to pay you for?'

Ella spotted a dog racing towards them, and opened her mouth, a fraction too late, to warn Max. It cannoned into him from behind, sending him staggering, and she had to leap out of his way before he knocked her backwards into her own car.

Chapter Two

Max righted himself and spun round to face the large, leaping dog, which was clearly ecstatic to see him. 'Get down,' he roared, but it completely ignored that instruction to hurl itself at him again, tail wagging madly. 'Lily! Who let her out?'

'Sorry, Daddy.' Lily was trotting across the gravel with Arlo not far behind. 'She saw you and ran off. I couldn't stop her.' Lily reached for the dog and tried to tug it from Max's thighs, but it was hopeless, like expecting a cat to take down a lion. 'Prim, you naughty girl. Daddy's cross with you again.'

'Here, let me.' Ella was enjoying seeing Max so disconcerted and called to the dog. Excited by a new person, it turned its attention to Ella and she ran a hand over its back as it leaned against her legs, staring up at her with a face that seemed to be grinning. At least it was warm and happy to see her, she thought gratefully.

'Who's this, Lily?' It didn't seem the right moment to ask Max, who was still furiously brushing short white hairs from his black jeans.

'This is Primrose because she's lemon and white. She's an English pointer.' Lily bent down to wrap loving arms round the dog's neck. 'She's only eight months old and very naughty sometimes. We've never had our own pet before and now we've got three chickens and we're getting guinea pigs for Christmas. We call her Prim for short.'

'And a few other things as well,' Max muttered. His gaze met Ella's over the dog and his daughter, and her lips flickered at the flare of amusement in his eyes. 'And you're going to have to write a very nice letter to Santa about the guinea pigs, I'm sure he's not decided yet.'

'Daddy loves Prim really, especially when she curls up with him after we've gone to bed. But she chewed up his favourite work boots last week and broke a tooth on the steel in the toes and had to go to the vet. Daddy said she'll have to live in a kennel in the garden if she doesn't stop misbehaving.'

'That seems a bit mean,' Ella murmured, still stroking the dog, so pale against the flash of Lily's red-gold plaits. 'Most dogs love to live with their families in the house.'

'That's what I said too, and Arlo told Daddy he'd sleep in the kennel with her if he made Prim go outside.'

'Right, enough, you two.' Max seemed satisfied he'd got rid of the dog hair on his jeans and gave the children a nod. 'Wait inside, Lily, I won't be long. And your brother too.'

'*Oui*, Papa.' Lily slipped a lead round Prim's neck. She stared up at her father, holding Arlo's hand as well, and her voice became defiant. 'Don't make Ella leave, Daddy, please. Mamie says we need her, and I think she's right. You're always working or cross, and you didn't used to be. I think you might be happier if you didn't have so much to do, and Ella can help with that.'

Max ran a weary hand over his face. He was very nearly beaten, and they all knew it. Bested by a six-year-old girl who'd shown him up to be bad-tempered and busy, a small boy, an unruly dog, and an eccentric French mother.

13

Unless he wanted to make them even more miserable than they apparently already were, it looked like Ella might be staying at Halesmere after all.

'It's not that simple, Lily.' Max frowned at his daughter. 'You don't just invite a stranger into your home without knowing lots about them.'

'Then they wouldn't be a stranger, would they?' Lily sounded perfectly reasonable. 'Mamie's very clever and she wouldn't ask someone to live with us that she didn't like, would she? I think Ella will be fun and I want her to stay. We all do, Daddy.'

'I'm warning you, Lily, go inside.' There was a chill in Max's tone that had Lily scampering off this time, Arlo running beside her with Prim leaping merrily, happy now she'd seen Max and made sure he was safely back on the premises. At the door Lily let Prim go and she ran straight back to flop beside Max.

'So.' Ella was shocked to find herself noticing that the stubble covering his jaw was more golden than blond, and she forced a level note into her voice. 'I think we've both been taken by surprise by the situation we're in. Wouldn't it be better to discuss my job rationally?'

'What, a proper interview, you mean?' Max sighed as he rubbed the back of his neck. 'Like normal people do before they employ new staff, unlike my interfering mother.'

'If that would help? And I think she means well.' Ella always preferred being direct. There wasn't room for indecision or hesitation in frantic kitchens, and she'd quickly learned to put aside her more natural, nurturing instincts. 'Is it really worth getting rid of me just to prove to your family that you are the one in control?'

'Touché.' He almost smiled at that. 'But I must warn you I'm yet to be convinced of any real value in the job my mother has offered you, despite what she may have led you to believe about our circumstances. She's always had her own way of doing things.'

'Then perhaps I can convince you. I've already done some research about the potential for your holiday business and how I might be able to help.'

'Have you?' One eyebrow was raised, and she sensed a glimmer of curiosity.

'Why don't you give me a month and if you're still not satisfied, I give you my word I'll leave by mutual agreement.' That would see Ella closer to Christmas with her family at least, and she'd have time to make other plans for the New Year. 'Who knows, I might be the one running for the hills before then.'

'I think you'll find you're surrounded by them.' He pointed to the darkened landscape beyond the silent house. 'The hills, I mean.'

Ella blinked, unsure if that was an attempt at humour. She'd become very good at reading people, and she was finding Max difficult. Granted, they'd only met a very short time ago, but he was giving away nothing more than impatience and frustration with those stunning blue eyes.

'What about my children? What relevant experience do you have?'

'Some.' Ella knew honesty was the best policy. 'I volunteered with a young people's adventure programme for two years and I have basic first aid and self-defence training.'

Working with young people had been a passion, so much more than a way to fill whatever time she had left over from her career, and she was going to miss her gang at the centre terribly. She'd loved seeing the children flourish as they gained in confidence and the possibility of volunteering up here was one of the reasons why this job had appealed to her so much.

'So no actual childcare then?'

'Not regularly, no.' She thought it couldn't hurt to throw in a little more detail. 'I spent my summers in between university terms in Chamonix, taking care of a family of eight, four of whom were children, and their guests. I babysat for them sometimes.'

'Okay.' Max seemed to be making an effort to be more pleasant. 'One month's trial, subject to a satisfactory interview and all the relevant checks. Nine a.m. tomorrow, in my office. You'll find it at the entrance to the back of the house in the courtyard.'

'Thank you.' She wasn't expecting the rush of relief at her reprieve. 'I'll do my best to make sure you don't regret it.'

'Right. And er, Ella, is it?'

'Yes.' She wondered if he really had forgotten.

'Where are you staying? I suppose it's too much to expect that my mother hasn't had a hand in those arrangements as well?'

'She has, she was kind enough to offer me the use of a flat.' Ella shook her arms to keep warm, ignoring the lurking anxiety at seeing where she was going to be living for the next month at least. She was dreading the evening ahead, trying to settle in the dark in a strange place so far from everything she knew. It was the one aspect of her new job she'd chosen to ignore. She'd promised to FaceTime her best friend Dylan tonight and he'd be drinking in some packed-out bar in the French Alps if she left it too late.

Max pointed to the arch separating his cottage from the house. 'There's only one place she can have meant for you to have. Through there, far side on the left.'

'You're not going to show me?' Ella swallowed worriedly. It was fully dark now and the night was icy, she could feel the cold rising around her feet. Christmas was only a few weeks away and there was nothing bright and cheerful in this place to suggest it was even coming. No lights strung outside the buildings, trees to offer some cheer or a merry plastic Santa on his way down one of the chimneys.

'Sorry. You're on your own unless you can find my mother. I have to take care of my children.' Max removed a bunch of keys from his pocket and separated one, offering it to Ella. She took it, feeling the welcome warmth of his fingers brushing hers. 'Up the narrow steps, yellow front door. You can't miss it. Be careful – you'll see why.'

'Thank you.' She heard the frightened whisper that passed for her reply. Noelle had vanished into the night and Ella knew she really was on her own. She had to force herself not to grab his arm and insist that he come with her. But such a thing would be foolish; he'd think she was incapable of caring for his two young children if she couldn't cross the courtyard alone in the dark.

'I have to go. Tomorrow, then.' Max nodded once as he picked up Prim's lead and turned away.

Ella made a conscious effort to ignore her spiralling alarm as she crossed the deserted courtyard, the key to her new home snug in her hand. She knew from Noelle and a bit more from Google that until a year ago the old stables had been a base for a couple of artists. But now the stables were empty, and Ella was trying not to see leaping shadows with every nervous step she took. Noelle over Zoom had been rather vague on details, suggesting there wasn't too much Ella needed to know beforehand and that she was more interested in finding someone prepared to get stuck in. This had suited Ella perfectly, keen as ever to make a decision and act on it.

It was impossible to miss the scruffy yellow door to her temporary new home, as Max had said. She wished it looked a bit more cheerful as she shivered in the frosted air. It sat proudly on the first floor of a small, narrow building, separate from the stables and the barn, with a set of steps leading up to it. A single window stared straight down into the courtyard; empty terracotta pots were plonked haphazardly on each uneven step. Another door, padlocked, was tucked beneath the steps and she climbed up warily, catching the welcome scent of a white winter-flowering honeysuckle in another pot, its stems wound around a flimsy wooden trellis tacked onto the door frame.

It took her two attempts to get the rusty old key to unlock the door, but she finally shoved it open, almost tripping on a thick mat as her eyes tried to adjust to the gloom. She fumbled for a switch and found one; anything to chase away the dark. She blinked rapidly as a bulb hanging from the ceiling without a shade lurched into life. Noelle had been even more elusive about the flat, only casually dropping in that it was 'tiny, *chérie*, a little outdated.' Ella saw now exactly what she had meant and leaned wearily against the door, wondering if she was on the wrong side of it. Perhaps she should be running for the hills after all.

She could see everything but the bathroom from where she stood. Two shabby red armchairs had been abandoned in front of an elderly black stove, separated by a coffee table, incongruously modern, with a tatty red and green rug on the wooden floor beneath it. A tall, thin bookcase in white stood to the right of the window, which was framed by faded, lime-green curtains, a colourful slash against walls also yellow, like the door.

It looked very much as though someone with a paint-brush and zero colour sense had let rip. Ella didn't want to hate it as much as she did, but she really couldn't help it when her gaze landed on the poky square at the far end that was her new kitchen. It couldn't have been more of a contrast from the kitchens she usually worked in. She crossed the room in six strides and glanced in cupboards, ran a hand along a beige Formica worktop, hoping for more daylight tomorrow through the small window at the back.

Sliding open the only other door bar the front one, she discovered her shower and toilet. Calling it a bathroom was definitely stretching things and she would really miss a good soak in a proper bath. Dylan would be concerned if he could see her now and she shook away a shiver of fright. She took a few images on her phone but decided not to send them yet. He might be working in France as a ski instructor for the winter, but she knew he'd come and scoop her up if he sensed she was unhappy here. She'd have to work hard to pretend; he knew her well. She had to try, to give it a go, however horrible this flat and Max's antagonism was.

She and Dylan had met at university when they were studying for their professional chef degrees. She hadn't liked him at first and had been determined not to fall for his charms the way everyone else seemed to do. Gorgeous and competitive, he seemed to collect new friends and casual girlfriends with effortless ease. Then one night in a bar they'd found themselves pushed together and had started chatting. Dylan had just broken up with another girlfriend and Ella had recognised how he wore his confidence as a layer, protecting himself from those things he didn't want the world to see, just as she did.

From then on, they'd stuck together and never minded their closeness confounding the general opinion that they must be a couple, instead preferring to play up to those assumptions if it suited them. They'd remained friends through differing placements, demanding jobs and, for Dylan, two years in a Barcelona restaurant and a beautiful Spanish wife. When his marriage had ended after six months and he'd returned to England devastated, Ella had suggested a role with her own employers to see him through. Dylan had accepted and until now, they'd shared her flat on the outskirts of Brighton.

She noticed a missed call from her mum and the voicemail icon. She'd ring her back later; her mum was probably just checking Ella had arrived safely and wanting to catch up on their plans for Christmas.

A ladder led to a mezzanine bedroom over the kitchen and half of the sitting room. She climbed up, noting the plastic rail for hanging her clothes. A pair of stumpy pine drawers either side of a metal-framed bed was the only other storage. It wasn't going to take much more for her to lock the door, toss the key back at Max and race to her parents' house. Maybe she wouldn't make it through his interview test tomorrow and she'd be on her way after all.

But first there was tonight to get through. Ella ran back across the courtyard to bring some basics from her car.

There didn't seem much point in fetching everything for what might turn out to be one night only. Back in the flat, she sank down onto the bed and stared at the silent and shadowed courtyard. The mattress was softer than she'd expected, lumpy too, and she had a pang of longing for her own comfortable flat. She slithered back down the ladder, swearing loudly when she slipped on a broken rung near the bottom. There was a sudden clatter at the window, and she spun round worriedly to look through it. Someone was standing at the bottom of the steps and there was no mistaking that hat. She opened the door, dodging another shower of stones she hoped were being aimed at the glass and not her.

'Ella,' Noelle hissed, glancing furtively over her shoulder. 'Are you alright?'

Yes? No? Both had an element of truth to them, and Ella shrugged. 'I'm okay,' she called down.

'*Bon*, I've brought you some supper, but Max mustn't find me here.' Noelle picked up a bag at her feet, waving it at Ella. She was still shifty but at least the hissing had stopped. 'Would you mind coming down to collect it, *chérie*, those steps terrify me. One day I will wake up and find myself at the bottom, my arms in pieces, and then how will I paint?'

Ella thought it was quite possible that she'd be in plaster too if that dodgy rung on the ladder had anything to do with it. She tried to avoid the empty terracotta pots, but one flew off and crashed to the cobbles, making Noelle shriek.

'Sorry.' Ella had already decided it would be better to get rid of them but probably not quite so dramatically; Noelle might prefer them intact. 'Did it hit you?'

'*Non*, I am fine.' Noelle shoved the bag at Ella. 'Here, your supper.'

'Thank you.' She took the bag, pleased to feel that whatever it contained it was at least warm.

'And how is the flat?'

She wasn't sure if Noelle was being sarcastic or not but what little Ella could see of her face beneath the hat seemed earnest. 'Well, it's small, as you said. A little old-fashioned.' Downright miserable and cold to boot, was what she really wanted to say.

Noelle's laugh was a throaty chuckle and she hastily checked over her shoulder again. 'There is no need for you to be tactful, *chérie*,' she whispered. 'The flat requires considerable improvement and I have a plan, but Max must not know of it. Bear with me and he will arrange it, you will see.'

'You think?' Ella wasn't quite so certain, whatever his mother might have to say about a plan, secret or not. 'He wants to interview me properly in the morning and then he'll decide if I can keep the job.'

'A mere formality, Ella, do not let the interview trouble you. You are a very bright young woman, and he will see the sense of my decision.' Noelle nodded, as though trying to convince herself. 'Max believes he must always be in control, and he would never admit it, but I know him, inside and out. All will become clear, and then you will understand. I am sorry but it is better that you eat alone in the flat tonight. I hope you sleep well, and I will see you tomorrow.' Noelle placed a gloved hand on her arm. 'I am sorry too for concealing you from Max and your lack of welcome from my son. But whatever he says, you are wanted, needed here. And Ella, you will come to know too that he is much more than the man you have met today. Welcome to Halesmere.'

She wasn't expecting the quick kiss from Noelle on either side of her face before the older woman hurried away. Ella could only stare as she disappeared into the darkness, gone as quickly as she had come.

Ella ate her meal curled up in one of the armchairs. The fire was laid, a basket of logs nearby, and storage heaters were puttering out a bit of warmth that was probably racing straight up to the eaves. Once done, she put the tray on the floor and called her mum, desperately wanting to hear a loving voice to make herself feel less alone.

'Ella, love, how are you? Hope the journey wasn't too bad, your dad was checking traffic updates and muttering about the M40 and hoping you'd taken the M6 toll, not the other one. You know what's he like. Is your flat lovely? What about the people, are they friendly? Have you seen the house yet, it looks gorgeous online, if a bit run-down. Ella? You there?'

She was, gulping back the emotion her mum's comforting and familiar chatter had produced. 'I am, it's all fine.' Not quite the truth but enough to let her mum think it was okay. Ella didn't want to worry her so soon into this new adventure. If her dad thought she was unhappy she knew he'd be straight in the car and would fetch her back himself, never mind how many employment offers she had in writing or keys to yellow front doors.

'It's just a long way from Brighton, that's all. And I didn't manage to get here in time for a run before it went dark.'

'Oh, Ella.' Her mum's voice had softened. 'There'll be other days, a rest would have been better for you anyway after that journey.'

'A run would have been better than a rest, Mum.' Ella hadn't meant to be sharp. 'Sorry, I am tired. How are you both?'

'We're fine, I was on the stall at the market again, it was really busy. And your dad's been online half the day, looking at flights.' Her mum paused. 'Actually, we've got a bit of news.'

'Oh?' Ella's heart bumped. She'd had a dread of news for years and the spike of anxiety wouldn't settle until she'd heard it, good or bad. 'Hurry up then.'

'Well, seeing as Jamie's going to Nick's family for Christmas and you're down in Cumbria, we thought we'd take up your Auntie Jenny's offer to spend a few weeks with them.'

'What, New Zealand?' Ella's voice rose in shock. Her parents had talked about travelling to see her dad's sister's family for years and still hadn't done it. 'And what's this about Jamie? He hasn't said anything to me about going to Nick's.'

'I think he tried. He left a couple of messages and said you hadn't got back to him yet.'

Ella felt a flash of guilt. She'd meant to call her brother and somehow hadn't found the right moment. Their conversations were snatched between her work and his, as an employment officer with a charity in London. Their hours rarely overlapped, and she knew they were overdue a visit.

'It's time, Ella.' Her mum's words were gentle, and Ella knew she was trying to soften the blow. 'We can't keep Christmas all to ourselves for ever and Nick's family want him and your brother to be with them for a change. It's only fair.' She paused. 'And now I know you'll be settled at Halesmere for a while, we thought it was a good time to go while we still can. You know your dad's always wanted to see the Tasman Glacier and national park.'

Ella did. As a recently retired geography teacher he loved to explore other countries, and he and her mum had always meant to travel more than they had. 'But that means I won't see any of you for Christmas.'

She'd been looking forward to the usual break with her parents, being gathered into the familiarity of family at Christmas when they were all together. Almost all together, she corrected herself. All together would never come again whatever they did, and a wave of hurt lurched into her heart. Christmas had long been a time of sadness overshadowing the joy and she only ever wanted to spend it with those who understood.

If her parents were away, then there would be no muted celebration or familiar traditions they'd managed to maintain in the face of their loss. No watching *The Snowman* every Christmas Eve or flopping in front of the old black and white classics her dad loved. No home-made Christmas pudding or the sherry trifle Ella could never better, eating turkey sandwiches for supper and helping her mum make the soup they all loved from leftovers. Ella adored that soup; she always took some back to Brighton and made it last for months in her freezer.

She was suddenly dreading the thought of the weeks at Halesmere stretching out in front of her. A winter stuck in Cumbria trying to keep a job Max didn't want her to have while she tried to plan for her future, one she couldn't picture yet. Only the outline of something different, hovering beyond reach unless her mind would allow her to follow her heart this time. And now Christmas on her own, for the first time ever.

'You could come with us if you wanted to?' Her mum's voice was gentle, probing, and Ella could picture her in the kitchen, chatting while she loaded the dishwasher or fed the dog. 'You'll surely be able to take some holiday even if you are only temporary.'

'Yes, but not long enough for weeks in New Zealand.' Ella let out a silent sigh she didn't want her mum to notice. 'It's fine, Mum. You're absolutely right, go while you have the chance, it's a brilliant idea.'

'But will you be okay?' There was anxiety there now too. 'They're nice people, are they, at Halesmere? You'll be all right, Ella, won't you?'

'Of course I will.' Her laugh was suddenly shaky. 'I'm a big girl now Mum, I'll be fine. Once I've settled in properly, you'll have to come. You'll love it, the landscape is incredible. I kept wanting to stop the car and stare on the way up.'

'I'm sure it is, sweetheart.' There was a clatter and Ella smiled as she heard the dog's bowl being dropped to the floor. 'We love you, take care. Don't push yourself too hard.'

'I will and I won't.'

'You won't and you will, you mean. Send us some pictures, I can't wait to come over.'

'Love you both too. Give Dad a hug for me.'

'Sure thing. Take care, speak soon.'

Ella tried calling Dylan as well, wanting to share that she wouldn't be going home for Christmas. No matter how flat out she was at work, she'd always made the trek to her parents, even if it meant barely staying a day because she had to get back. Dylan didn't pick up and she didn't bother messaging him. He was probably in a bar and fending off a few female tourists, if their usual nights out were anything to go by.

Of course, the Wi-Fi in here was non-existent, and no one had thought to give her a password anyway. She connected her phone to a Bluetooth speaker and got some music going. She liked noise, chatter, people around her. She loathed being alone and the moment she'd been able to afford to buy her flat she had lined up a friend from work to share it. When Dylan had returned from Barcelona and her flatmate moved on, she'd been only too happy to have him take the second bedroom. Only he knew how she hated silence, only he knew how she shivered at night, and more than once he'd crawled into her bed to hold her when she'd woken from a bad dream. Halesmere and this horrid little flat were certain to test her, but she'd make herself come through the night, whatever problems the morning threatened to bring.

Chapter Three

When Ella woke, low winter sun was pouring in through the green curtains, which were so thin she thought at first she'd forgotten to close them, and she fumbled for her phone. She'd set her alarm for seven a.m., planning a quick run before it was time to meet Max for the interview. She had had a more unsettled night than usual and had jerked awake several times, her heart racing in the dark and unfamiliar surroundings. She stared at her phone in disbelief, shrieking as she flung the quilt aside to leap out of bed.

She'd slept straight through the alarm and it was eight forty-five already. No time for a run now. She hurried down the ladder and pulled on a skirt with winter tights, boots, and a jumper from the case she'd left by the door. After brushing her teeth, she swallowed down a glass of water, wishing she could follow it up with a blast of caffeine to get her going.

She raced across the empty courtyard and almost fell through the open door at the back of the house, finding herself in a reception area. It only dawned on Ella it was Saturday when she saw Lily and Arlo either side of Noelle on a narrow sofa in front of a half-panelled, white-painted wall covered in art.

'Oh! I wasn't expecting everyone.'

Prim the pointer was lolling at Lily's feet, and she leapt up when she spotted Ella. Lily was holding Prim's collar and she tumbled to the floor with a giggle as the dog hurried across to greet Ella. Noelle reached out to haul Lily impatiently back onto the sofa.

'Lily, that dog is very disobedient. *Bonjour*, Ella, I hope you slept well.'

Ella didn't want to give a truthful reply to that and nodded vaguely.

'She's not really, Mamie, she's just very young.' Lily wasn't perturbed in the least by her grandmother's sternness over Prim. 'Papa hasn't had time to take her to training classes for a while. We're supposed to be going again after Christmas.'

Lily was stroking Prim's ears and Ella realised just how much she loved the big, friendly dog, who now had her large head on Lily's lap. 'She'll be much better soon, she just needs more walks.' Lily looked at Ella hopefully. 'Maybe you can help with that too?'

'That sounds like fun.' She loved the rush of pleasure her simple reply brought to the little girl's face. Back in Brighton, Ella would regularly meet people out running, some of whom with dogs attached to them by long, bendy leads. Perhaps she and Prim could run together, it might take the edge off the dog's exuberance.

'Papa is waiting for you, Ella, his office is just through there.' Lily pointed to a door on Ella's left.

'Right. Thanks.' She knew it was ridiculous to be feeling so nervous. Amongst the very best, she'd sailed through every test on the way to getting her previous jobs and had flourished under the pressure. But the thought of seeing Max again and facing that cool, blue gaze was making her stomach knot in ways she wasn't used to. She told herself firmly it was just the lack of her usual morning coffee.

'You're not all coming in, are you?' Ella's words came out in a rush. Her pixie crop was somewhat wilder than she would have liked for a formal job interview. The water was different here, her hair softer after a lukewarm shower last night, and it refused to stay in place. And Dylan always said the jumper she was wearing clashed with her hair's lilac colour. Oh well, it was too late to do anything about it now.

'*Non*, Max will not allow it.' Noelle pursed her lips.

'We tried,' Lily said glumly. 'Papa said he had to speak to you alone first.' Her red-gold curls were tamed today in a neat ponytail. Arlo had a toy tractor and a pop-up book about farming on his lap and Ella gave him a reassuring smile, which he cautiously returned. 'Then we do have some questions to ask you.'

'What, all of you?'

The door beside Ella flew open and Max appeared, giving her the briefest nod before glaring at his gathered family. 'You may as well all leave. I have no idea how long we will be.'

'We will wait, Max.' An array of bangles on Noelle's left arm rattled as she retrieved the book slipping from Arlo's knee. Her long hair was casually piled on top of her head and spilling to her shoulders. 'We would all like to get to know Ella better and I think your interview suggestion is an excellent one.'

'You might have thought of that before you offered her the bloody job,' Max muttered. He seemed to be having difficulty meeting Ella's eyes as he stood back to hold the door open. 'And stop trying to humour me or pretend you're going along with this as though it's all my idea, Maman. It doesn't suit you.'

'Daddy swore!' Arlo was both aghast and delighted, and Lily gave Max a sad look.

'That's a pound you need to put in Prim's box, Daddy,' she told him seriously. She turned her attention to Ella. 'Daddy swears a lot more now that we've got Prim, and he has to pay a fine every time he says a naughty word. We're collecting the money and giving it to the local dog shelter in case he ever sends Prim to live there. She only likes certain foods and a special bed.'

'That's enough, Lily.' Max seemed to be spluttering and Ella had to press her lips very firmly together to stop herself from laughing. Arlo was giggling and she heard Noelle chuckle as Prim's tail thumped on the ground. Max shook his head as he glanced at Ella.

'Let's get on with it, shall we?'

She nodded, breathing in so she wouldn't touch him by mistake as she passed through the door, conscious of his tall frame close to hers.

'You have a lovely office.' She had been expecting something more austere, not the huge, bright room she had just entered as Max snapped the door shut behind them.

'Thanks. It's a nice space to work in.' He sounded different this morning, more awkward with a shade less confidence in his voice.

She hovered uncertainly, waiting for him to invite her to sit. A large oak desk holding a laptop, huge monitor and mobile faced the garden, opposite a pair of two-seater sofas separated by a low coffee table, an iPad sitting on it. In the centre of the room stood a wide drawing board and stool, with paper, pencils and sketches placed neatly across it. The walls were also white and covered with landscapes, both paintings and photographs, with a few shots of the children and a vibrant watercolour of a beautifully planted garden. A pair of deep sash windows either side of French doors offered a glorious view of the garden, a tarn shimmering in the winter sun in the distance.

'Coffee?'

'Please.' Ella was still sluggish; sure the broken night's sleep must be reflected on her face. She wondered if she might be able to swap the mattress on her bed for something better; maybe Max would let her order a—

'How do you like it?'

'What?' She tried to drag her thoughts back to his question. Her eyes felt gritty, and she resisted the urge to rub them.

'Your coffee. How do you drink it?'

Was she imagining a note of sarcasm in his exaggerated patience? 'Oh sorry. Black please, strong.'

'Double espresso?'

'Perfect. Thank you.'

He still hadn't invited her to sit, and she wondered if he was doing it on purpose, trying to assert his authority. She edged towards the desk, a hand on the back of the office chair facing it. 'Noelle mentioned that you're an architect.'

Max was still busy with the machine, and he raised his voice over the noise of beans grinding. 'Landscape.'

'I'm sorry?' Ella's laugh was short as she tried to cover her confusion. 'I didn't sleep very well; the bed was a bit...'

'I'm a landscape architect. I design gardens, not buildings. Did she not tell you that part?'

Did he really have to keep butting in or speaking so slowly? 'Er, I think so.' Even to Ella the reply sounded feeble, and she decided to come clean. 'Actually, I'm not sure, she might have done. It's been a funny week.'

'Right.' Max was holding two cups and he nodded towards the sofas. 'Over there okay?'

'Of course.' Ella wasn't expecting that, assuming he would have wanted to keep the interview on a more formal basis and his desk between them.

She chose a sofa and sat bolt upright, hands on her knees. She had never been less prepared for an interview in her life and when Max passed a cup across, her hand rattled the porcelain on its saucer, almost sloshing the coffee onto her lap. She knew she wasn't presenting herself as the cool, efficient and capable person she normally was, her face now apparently competing with her tights for the brightest shade of pink.

'So what kind of gardens do you design?' Even her voice sounded different: high, nervous; she cleared her throat as silently as possible.

Max put on a pair of glasses from his shirt pocket and picked up the iPad. Ella blinked hurriedly when his gaze settled on hers, unprepared for how well the dark frames suited him, highlighting those cornflower-blue eyes and his casual, gold-blond hair. Her cup rattled again, and she gulped a mouthful of coffee, grateful for the hit of caffeine she knew would follow.

'We can talk about that later. I think I'm supposed to be interviewing you.' There was a trace of amusement in his voice.

'Right, yes, sorry.' She finished the rest of the coffee in a rush, sensing him watching as she put the cup and saucer safely on the table.

33

'So.'

She waited.

'I know almost nothing about you, Ms Grant, as my mother apparently declined to ask for your CV when you applied for the job she invented.' He drew in a breath and slowly let it out again.

'Could we drop the Ms Grant, please?' Ella was beginning to feel sharper and more like herself after the espresso. 'My name's Ella and I was hoping you'd let me call you Max. Mr Bentley seems so formal if I'm going to be working with your family. And you, of course.' She hoped that didn't sound as intimate to him as it felt to her, and a few seconds dragged by.

'Working together remains to be seen. But Max is fine. Whenever someone says Mr Bentley, I'm usually looking around for my dad.' Max attempted a smile, gave up and swallowed his coffee in one gulp. 'Could you give me a few career details, and perhaps anything else you think is relevant?'

'Like what? I don't mean to be difficult; I just want to be clear on what you wish to know.' She forced away a moment of alarm. Career details were fine, personal ones not so much.

'Right.' Max put his cup down to swipe at the iPad. 'Your education? Where did you go to university and what did you read?'

Ella began to relax; she could talk about her career all day if need be. 'I have ten GCSEs and four A levels, and I spent the summer before university working at an eco-retreat in Tuscany. I studied for my professional chef's degree at University College in Birmingham and waitressed in Pizza Hut to help with the fees. I have a master's in culinary arts management and did a six-month placement at a two-Michelin-starred restaurant in Malmö, where I was subsequently offered a job and stayed for a year.' The tension in her fingers was easing as she started to enjoy dispelling his assumptions about her being a nanny.

'I then went to work for Michelle Worthing at her Decoris restaurant in London and for the past three years I was a senior sous chef with a company based in Brighton who create high-end events and parties. The company was recently bought out and I accepted redundancy when it was offered.'

But it was too much. Ella had barely drawn breath. She knew she hadn't needed to give him a precis of her entire career, a list of achievements unnecessary for the job at Halesmere, which they both now knew she was well overqualified for. She saw his surprise and the doubts quickly following.

'Voluntary redundancy?'

'Yes.'

'So what exactly are you doing here, Ella?' Max put the iPad down and took off his glasses to rest a clear and determined gaze on hers.

'I saw the post online through a local shop and applied.' She hoped her smile was reassuring. 'I was very pleased to be offered the opportunity while I plan for the next stage of my career.'

'That's not everything, though, is it?' He was toying with a pencil, and she felt caught, trapped in his demand for the truth, as her fingers trembled in her lap.

'Whatever role my mother thinks she has dreamed up, if I allow you to stay then you will be working alongside me and my family. More specifically, around my children, and that concerns me. You're clearly very highly qualified, experienced and driven. What makes a person abandon that level of achievement to play around managing a holiday business that isn't even fully up and running yet?'

Ella had never been required to give an answer to a question like this in her life. She'd pursued the only career open to her, hadn't allowed anything to hold her back, not least her parents' concerns about her choices and why she'd made them. Now it seemed Max was forcing her to confront the reality of what she'd done in leaving her career, and whether or not he was going to allow her the opportunity at Halesmere she needed to go through with it.

'I wanted a change.' Her voice was low, and she had to force herself to keep her gaze steady on his. 'I took the chance when it was offered.'

'Because?'

'Because I just did, that's all.' She heard herself becoming defensive. 'Haven't you ever wanted to do something different, pursue a different dream?'

He ignored that. 'It's clear to both of us, I'm sure, that you won't stay here. Halesmere won't be enough for someone with your experience. So, what's the new dream?'

'I'm not really sure I have one yet.' A whisper this time, moisture gathering on her palms, thickened words forced from a dry mouth, wishing she wasn't having to confront her past in order to face her future. 'I'm hoping I might find out while I'm here.'

She dropped her head before he saw too much and prayed her reply would do. For all his antagonism she recognised his intuition and knew she was close to revealing her most private self, something she almost never did. He was pushing her in ways she wasn't used to, weakened as she was by the change in her circumstances, and she didn't yet have replies for all his questions.

'There are three people out there who don't want you to go, Ella.' Max pointed to the door, beyond which sat his family. 'And as you already have a written offer of employment from my mother, then our present situation is not entirely straightforward.' He paused. 'If you give me the truth about why you left your job then you're in for the three months my mother has promised you. We'll work it out, subject to the usual checks and references that any responsible parent would want.'

Ella felt dread running through her, the clutch of anxiety in her stomach at the thought of sharing her story with someone who was a stranger still. She pressed her palms against her thighs. 'And if I don't want to?'

His gaze was suddenly kinder, and she was shocked to realise he was offering to trust her, asking her to trust him with her truth. 'Then I can't let you stay.' He picked up the glasses and put them back on. 'My children come before everything, and I need to know.'

She nodded, she understood. It made perfect sense; she would be doing exactly the same if it were her sitting in his seat. She thought of her flat in Brighton, already occupied; pictured herself trailing Dylan around Chamonix or working in some pub for the winter, rushed off her feet preparing hundreds of bland Christmas dinners. But there was really only one choice and she made it. It would be part of moving on, a way to step forward. To continue with the healing that never quite ended. She was certain her parents would have cheered if they could have heard her.

Her voice was a croak, the words dredged up from somewhere deep inside. 'I lost my twin sister Lauren when

37

we were twelve. She only ever wanted to be a chef and I had to do it for her.' Ella's chin was trembling. 'I thought it was maybe time to try and find out what I want to be.'

She was not going to cry. Those days were over; there had been so many of them in the years following Lauren's sudden illness. Ella stared through the window, at her feet and the coffee table between her and Max as she fought the effort it took not to let new tears fall. And all of it was lost the moment she looked up and saw the sympathy, the understanding in his face, and her bottom lip quivered as a single tear trailed down her cheek.

'Here.' He reached across the table to offer a handkerchief she was still fumbling for in pockets she didn't have. 'I'm so sorry. It never really matters how long ago, does it? Thoughts of the people we've lost are never far away.'

Ella heard something catch in his voice and her damp eyes raced up to find his, bruised suddenly, unseeing on hers. 'You lost someone too?' She'd sat in enough bereavement counselling waiting rooms to understand that look, how he had instantly recognised her distress.

'Yes.' His voice was level, dulled. 'My wife Victoria, two years ago, when Arlo was two.'

Ella's breath caught. If she'd been different, more demonstrative, then she would have reached out, touched his hand perhaps and offered her own empathy through the gesture. Her fingers flickered, the thought hovering still, and she clenched them together, the moment gone. She and Max were very different and somehow the same, just two more people who lived with loss in their lives.

'Max, I'm so terribly sorry. I had no idea.' Poor Lily and poor little Arlo too, Ella thought wretchedly as more tears welled up for the children, their shattered family, and for Max. She felt a splinter in her boundaries, her defences slowly diminishing through their shared experience as his gaze refocussed on hers. 'Your mother mentioned that you were a single parent, but I assumed you were divorced, she didn't say anything else about your circumstances.'

'It's fine. Thank you.' Max picked up his cup, put it down again when he saw it was empty. 'Well, it's not but we're learning how to keep on living with it. I'm sorry for pushing you for a reply, I wasn't expecting something so difficult. I just thought maybe you'd had an affair with your boss or pinched the company silver— Sorry,' he added hastily. 'That was rather flippant.'

Ella's gasp ended up being one of laughter, and she appreciated his rather clumsy attempt at altering the direction their conversation had taken. 'Well… Not the silver, anyway.'

Her gaze shot to her hands, clenched on her pink knees. That hadn't been quite the right thing to say, even if it was the truth. But the brief affair with her charismatic and sexy former boss had ended the moment Ella found out he was not divorced, as he had said, but only recently separated from a wife who had no idea he was playing around and wanted him back. Dylan had warned her not to get involved and she'd ignored all her instincts and lived to regret it.

'More coffee?' Max leapt up, grabbing their cups, and knocked his over. A few drips of coffee trickled onto the table, and he ignored the mess as Ella swiped at it with his handkerchief, staining it brown.

'Yes please,' she croaked, leaving the ruined cotton in a crumpled heap. She wouldn't be washing that and returning it to him, it was going straight in the bin. She'd have to buy him another if he insisted on having it back.

But she did take his not throwing her out of his office after her little revelation to be a good sign. 'I don't usually, er, get involved at work, you know, like that. That was the first and only time. A mistake.' She faltered, knowing she was oversharing and probably making things worse.

'It's fine. I don't need to know.' Max was at the coffee machine and grinding noises soon followed. She wondered, in a moment of mild hysteria, if it was his teeth or the beans. 'And for the record, neither do I.'

And he hadn't been required to tell her that either, she thought as he returned with two more espressos and passed one across the table. Ella recognised a glimmer of the attraction that had flashed between them yesterday. She read the rules in his eyes, confirmed them with her own unflinching gaze, letting him know she understood, agreed. Never would they go there.

Chapter Four

'Thank you.' Ella's voice was steady again and she was grateful for the second coffee. She needed the boost after a most unusual twenty-four hours.

'Can you run me through the duties my mother wants you to carry out?' Max had also restored the crisp professionalism to his voice.

Ella was relieved to be back on safer ground, even if she wasn't certain what her role at Halesmere actually looked like yet. 'Noelle explained that you're ready to accept bookings now the house has been renovated and are considering ways to be creative in encouraging new guests. That's to be my main area of responsibility.'

'And my children?'

'She suggested it would be helpful if I collected them from school two or three times a week and looked after them until you were home.' Ella wondered if she would have accepted the job if she'd known that Lily and Arlo had lost their mum. Would she have wanted to become involved, however temporarily, with a family recently moved and at the beginning of a new life far away from their old one?

Max ran a hand across his jaw. 'That could be useful,' he admitted eventually. 'We walk to school every morning and I work after I've dropped them off. I often have client meetings on site and I'm still establishing my landscape team and building relationships with local suppliers and not always available at three p.m. My mother helps when she can, and they go to after-school club sometimes.'

'I understand. I'd be happy to help.' Another flicker of sympathy followed as Ella thought of him trying to balance his career with Lily and Arlo alongside his own loss. He must miss his wife immensely.

'Thank you. Only when necessary. I take care of my children myself.'

'Of course. I've done some research on ideas for the house if you're interested.' She hadn't fetched her phone in the mad dash from the flat earlier, and quickly improvised. It had been late after the Zoom with Noelle last week when Ella had scribbled down some thoughts and she couldn't remember all of them now. 'I could email you the notes I made if you like?'

'Please. I'd like to see them.' Max raised his eyebrows, the iPad once again on his lap. 'Is there anything else? I'm not entirely convinced what you've told me amounts to a full-time role.'

She knew it was a reasonable question. 'I'm not really sure. Noelle and I agreed that we'd sort out the hours and everything else when I arrived. Your mother was clear that you need some assistance and I'd be more or less full-time but not necessarily working regular hours over five weekdays. I have no other commitments right now and I'm happy to be flexible. It just seemed to fit, and we both thought it could work. How does that sound?'

Max let out a long breath as he settled against the back of the sofa. 'Helpful, if I'm the one being honest now.' There was a glimmer of amusement now, a growing acceptance of the circumstances Noelle had manoeuvred him into. 'How much has my mother told you about Halesmere? And us?'

'Not a lot, just that you moved here in February and would like to maximise the use of the buildings and plan to re-establish the holiday business. I've been exploring ways to bring the two together.'

'I actually bought it in a moment of madness and I'm still wondering if it was a mistake. It was supposed to be a new beginning for all of us, one where I'm less busy and have more time for Lily and Arlo now I'm working from home.'

'It is the most stunning location now I've seen it in daylight. I can appreciate why people would want to visit, even if it is a bit isolated.' Ella was picturing the quick charm in his smile and shook the thoughts away as she looked into the garden.

The borders were a sad jumble of overgrown shrubs and perennials gone to seed. She glimpsed stunted and gnarled trees in the grip of climbing roses bare of their leaves, the flash of yellow winter jasmine on bright green stems. An orchard and a meadow lay beyond, the landscape flowing into the distance until it met the rough fells soaring to the sky.

'Not much of an advert for my practice. I don't bring many clients here.' His tone was wry as his eyes followed hers to the garden. 'Another thing on my lengthening list of jobs to do next year.'

'Redesigning it?' Ella knew her mum would love the walled border with its old fruit trees trained across the stone.

'Yes.' There was a first flash of real enthusiasm in his face. 'I've already drawn a plan. The er, inspiration came

43

to me in the middle of the night and seemed to make sense.' The fleeting pleasure was already gone.

'I have nights like those too,' she offered quietly.

'And what do you do? When you can't sleep?' Max was busy with the iPad again and Ella guessed he was avoiding her gaze on purpose.

'Not design gardens, I wouldn't know my catmint from my clover,' she quipped, gratified to see his smile, head still bent. 'Walk sometimes, run if I need to go faster.' She knew her dad would flip if he thought she was running at night but thrashing around in bed never worked, she had to move. 'My hours were pretty unsociable, and I wasn't always ready to sleep when I got home.'

'And now, working here? How do you think you'll manage more ordinary hours?'

'I'll be fine. There's lots of places I can run or be on the water.'

'On the water? You sail?' Max lifted his head.

'Kayak,' she corrected. 'I've brought mine with me.'

'Oh? I didn't see one attached to the roof of your car.'

'It's inflatable,' she explained. 'It'll be perfect up here; I can't wait to try it.'

'Be careful.' His voice was quiet as their eyes held. 'I take it you won't be kayaking in the dark.'

'No,' she replied. She hadn't expected the concern she could see in his expression. 'I don't want to puncture it on some rock I can't see.'

His mobile over on the desk was ringing and he let it go to voicemail, swiping a finger across the screen on his iPad. 'So, a DBS. Do you have one?'

'Yes, for the activity centre I volunteered with near Brighton. I've applied for another enhanced one this week, but it hasn't come through yet.'

'Okay. Let me know when you have it. A scan copy via email will be fine.' Max checked his watch. 'The children are going to a party later and I'm seeing a client after I drop them off. We'd better get them in if they're to ask you their questions.'

'Seriously?' Ella's laugh, as she picked up her cup, was startled; she wasn't sure she was up to a grilling from Lily and Arlo quite so soon after the more emotional turn the interview with Max had taken. 'I thought they were joking.'

'Oh no, Arlo has some deadly serious questions to ask you and I think they're all to do with food. They've made a list. My mother just wants to know if you'll sit for her.'

'I'm sorry?' Ella was savouring the final drops of luke-warm espresso, wondering if she might be able to sneak into Max's office and help herself to coffee this good every day. She wasn't convinced the kettle in the flat would be up to heating water hot enough even for instant.

'I presume she's told you she's an artist with her own studio here?' His voice had risen a notch. 'But she paints nudes mostly, so watch out. She's famous for her persistence and she'll have you whipping your clothes off before you can say paintbrush. It's your eyes, the way they suggest a story you haven't told anyone yet.'

Ella spat her coffee straight back into the cup, frantically trying to turn her splutter into more of a polite cough. Max suddenly seemed to realise what he'd said as her incredulous stare met his, and he leapt up to cross the room and grabbed the door handle. Ella wondered if he was trying to run away from his own words as she swiped at her mouth with the back of her hand. The handkerchief was revolting now; she wasn't using that.

Lily and Arlo erupted into the room, crash-landing on the sofa, and were swiftly followed by Prim, who launched herself gleefully at Ella. Ella, happy for the distraction and still trying to get her pulse back under control, made a fuss of the dog, who was behaving as though she were a long-lost friend recently returned from some terrible adventure instead of someone Prim had met just yesterday.

'Budge up, you two.' Max plonked himself back on the sofa opposite Ella's. Lily and Arlo clambered onto his knee and he slid his arms round them, rolling his eyes at Prim, now lying on Ella's feet.

Noelle settled beside her, and Ella's worried glance darted across to the older woman. Last night she had been wondering how she was going to get through her time at Halesmere with Max not wanting her here. Now she was more concerned about avoiding Noelle and her apparently famous persistence for the next three months. Ella's heart tilted in a very strange manner at the sight of Max and his children and she was sharply reminded of what they had lost. Lily was consulting a handwritten list that, Ella saw, was surprisingly long, and the little girl gave Arlo a firm nudge with her elbow.

'How many kinds of pizza can you make, Ella?' His honey-brown eyes were wide, his tractor still held in one chubby hand, and she thought his shy little smile was adorable.

'Oh, lots, I suppose.' There hadn't been much call for pizza on the precisely planned menus at the sumptuous events she had cooked for. 'Once you have the base with the tomato sauce on top, you can pretty much add whatever you like.'

'So if I wanted cheese and chocolate on my pizza, could that work?'

'Absolutely not,' Max said firmly, ruffling his son's hair. 'That would be revolting, Arlo, and very bad for you.'

'But Daddy, Ella's just said you could add whatever you like.' Arlo had to tip his head back to find his father's exasperated gaze. 'And she's a chef, so she should know, not you. You promised to make pizza with us, and you still haven't done it.'

Ella's eyes met Max's and she saw the flash of guilt. 'Chocolate is tricky to heat up, Arlo,' she said quickly, hoping to distract him. 'The fats can separate if you don't get it right, and it wouldn't be very nice with cheese once it's cooked. As a professional chef I wouldn't recommend it.' She hoped he understood she was taking his questions seriously. 'What other things do you like?'

'Haribo? The fizzy ones,' he said hopefully, and she laughed, heard Noelle's chuckle beside her. Lily's scowl made clear her irritation with her little brother.

'Nice try, Arlo, I'm sure you know that's sweet as well. All that sugar would make a horrible gooey mess and would be awful with tomato sauce. What about vegetables or maybe some chicken?'

'I like small tomatoes, not the big ones, and sweetcorn. Mushrooms if they're sliced, not whole.'

'Perfect. Anything else?'

'Ham? I like it in sandwiches. Daddy makes good ones, better than Mamie's. We take them to school sometimes. Lily doesn't, cos she doesn't eat meat.'

'Yes, ham would be fine as well, we can ask Lily what other toppings she might like on her pizza.' Ella was enjoying this. Arlo clearly loved his food, and it wouldn't hurt to throw together a couple of pizzas with them while she was here. 'So have I got this right? Tomatoes, sliced mushrooms, sweetcorn and ham? But as I'm a chef,

Arlo, can I suggest trying another cheese as well, one like cheddar or Parmesan? Mozzarella is great because it's ideal for melting but it doesn't have as much flavour as the others. What do you think?'

'Yes!' Arlo scrambled off the sofa to face his father with imploring eyes. 'Please, Daddy, can we have Ella's pizza tonight?'

'Arlo, sit down.' Max went to grab him as Prim leapt up with a startled bark and shot over to the French doors. Ella saw her staring outside, searching for the source of excitement or harm about to befall her family. 'Now look what you've done, she'll be slobbering all over the glass. Prim, come here, you bloody idiot, there's nobody there.'

'That's another pound please, Daddy.' Lily didn't miss a beat and her face was expressionless.

'What?' Max stared at his daughter. 'For pity's sake, Lily, do you always have to keep count?'

'The dog shelter needs the money and Prim might, too.'

'Too right,' he muttered. He reached into his pocket and removed a blue note from his wallet. 'Here, have five. Might as well put the other three on account, you'll be needing them soon enough after what your grandmother's been getting up to.'

He placed the wallet on the table, his eyes shifting for a second to Ella's. 'And no, Arlo, Ella won't be making pizza for you tonight. Maybe another time when we're all more used to one another.'

'That's not fair.' Arlo stuck his bottom lip out and she resisted the urge to grin. He looked cute even through his sulk and she was glad she wasn't the one saying no to him. 'It's Saturday and you said yesterday that we could

48

have pizza tonight. Why can't we have Ella's? I don't want frozen pizza again, I want Ella's, made how she said.'

'Arlo.' There was a warning note in Max's voice along with weary resignation. 'Stop please, before I decide you have to wait outside until we're finished.'

'Max, *chéri*, if Ella is happy to make pizza this evening, then why not?' Noelle made it sound perfectly reasonable. 'It would be a simple way to get to know one another, as you said. Lily and Arlo will enjoy it and she will be collecting the children from school next week after all.'

'And she might not. I'm making no promises until I've seen the relevant paperwork.' Max's voice tightened as he attempted to regain control over the direction his mother was trying to take him. 'Besides, Maman, I hardly think that making pizza is what Ella came here to do. She probably wants to get away from the kitchen.'

His eyes found hers and Ella flushed, remembering how she had confessed her hopes for a new dream to him not fifteen minutes ago. Was he being kind because he knew she wanted something of her own in her life? Or was it a convenient excuse to prevent her spending time with his children, something she already knew concerned him? Or both? She was still trying to work it out when Noelle made the decision for him.

'Ella? Would you be happy to cook pizza for the children this evening?'

'If Max is okay with that?' She tried to keep a casual note in her voice, not wanting to thwart her new employer so obviously in front of his family. She could whip up the base and tomato sauce in the flat beforehand, help them spread the toppings on and leave them to it; she'd be in and out in no time.

Arlo squealed and it quickly turned into a roar as he toppled onto Lily and she shoved him away. Ella saw Max's quick scowl and wasn't sure if it was because of the children's behaviour, his mother's interfering over supper or being forced to accept Ella cooking pizza if he didn't want a riot on his hands.

'It's my turn to talk to Ella now,' Lily said firmly, picking up the list her brother had made her drop. 'Daddy will have to go to work soon, and you've had too much time, Arlo.'

'Yes, all right, Lily.' Max squeezed her shoulder but she ignored him, consulting her list. 'I think there's time for you to ask Ella one question.'

'Will you excuse me, my darlings, I also must work.' Noelle stood up. 'Ella, *chérie*, I would love for you to see my studio. Why don't you pop in later?'

'Oh, I, er, well, I suppose I'll be...' Ella was babbling, terrified that Noelle was going to entice her in and refuse to let her out again until she'd captured a reclining and quite possibly naked Ella on canvas for all to see. It certainly wasn't the right moment to glance at Max and see the smile hovering on his lips before he hastily looked away. 'I have to go shopping, see the house, and unpack. I've got so much to do. Max needs my notes on the business and...'

'You'll have plenty of time for all of that,' Noelle replied crisply. 'Max, I insist that you show Ella around properly, please do not leave her to find out everything on her own. Ella, I will be in my studio until suppertime. Come and see me this afternoon.'

'Mmm.' Ella hoped her fear didn't show. She resolved to make quite certain that Noelle didn't try to include life modelling in her new job description as she closed the door behind her.

'One question,' Max warned Lily, checking his phone. 'Then this interview is over. We have things to do, no matter what your grandmother says.'

'Daddy, that's not fair. Arlo asked Ella at least three questions.'

'I wasn't counting. Right, three questions,' he said firmly. 'And be quick about it.'

'How far can you swim without stopping, Ella?'

She laughed, completely unprepared for Lily's swift change of subject. She had still been thinking about pizza and whether Max or Noelle had all the ingredients Arlo wanted. If they didn't, where she was going to find them before tonight without a long drive into town? And when had she mentioned swimming in front of this clever and perceptive child?

'Hurry, Ella, please.' Lily shot Max a look and his hand went to her hair, gently smoothing the curls escaping her ponytail. 'Daddy's got to leave and I'm only allowed two more questions.'

'Right.' Ella thought rapidly. 'Well, my best stroke was the crawl, and I could swim two hundred metres when I was competing, so I suppose that's quite far. But I'm out of practice, I couldn't do it now, especially in open water in winter.' She dropped that last bit in before Lily had her down at the tarn with a stopwatch and a clipboard.

'Wow. You must be a really good swimmer.' Lily was entranced. 'My second question is, will you come to our school nativity, Ella, please? I'm one of the three wise men and Arlo's a sheep. He just has to stand there looking stupid so he's very good at it.'

'Lily, that'll do about your brother.' Max's voice was stern, but Ella saw the faint smile he was trying to conceal, and her own lips twitched. Thankfully Arlo was on the floor playing with the tractor and hadn't noticed his sister's remark.

'Will you be staying with us for Christmas, Ella? Mamie told us your family live far away.'

Lily's question seemed to hover between Ella and Max, and twenty-four hours ago she would have been able to say no quite truthfully. But after the conversation with her mum last night, Ella's plans had been swiftly obliterated, and Christmas was now looking very different and rather unwelcome.

'I'm probably going to be here, yes.' Unless Dylan would take her in for a few days. 'But I don't think I could come to see your nativity, I'm sorry, Lily. Those things are usually just for friends and family.'

'That's three questions, Lily.' There was a warning note in Max's voice, and Lily rushed on.

'Just one more, Daddy, please. Ella, are you married? Or do you have a boyfriend? Or girlfriend?'

'I'm sorry? Is that one question or three?' Ella was taken aback yet again, and she grinned, her gaze sliding over to Max and finding his somewhere else entirely.

'Lily,' he said sharply, lifting her firmly from the sofa to stand on the floor. 'That's private information and absolutely none of our business.'

'Why, Papa?' Lily shrugged. 'You said we needed to know lots about Ella if she's going to be living with us. I heard you tell Mamie that the flat was barely big enough for one, never mind two, and if Ella thought she was going to be bringing someone else here to live with her then she'd better think again, and Mamie might like to give

52

Ella her flat instead and take the other one seeing as all of this was her fault in the first place.'

Max closed his eyes, a hand going to his brow to cover his face, and Ella bit back a laugh. Lily was going to be keeping everyone on their toes and Ella didn't mind confirming her current relationship status. It barely ever changed, a dodgy boss being the rare exception.

'No boyfriend, husband, girlfriend or wife, Lily,' Ella replied, enjoying Max's discomfort a bit too much. 'Just me, so I think the flat will be fine.'

'That's good, isn't it, Daddy?' Lily was staring at him with an earnest expression. 'Then Mamie won't have to give up her flat for Ella and Ella won't be bringing anyone else here to live with her.'

'Lily.' Max's voice was firm, and it was Ella's turn to stare at the glorious view from the French doors. 'Time to go, this minute, and take Arlo with you. Wait for me at Mamie's studio and then we'll get you both ready for the party.'

'Okay.' Happy now, her questions answered, Lily skipped from the room, Arlo on her heels. 'Bye Ella, see you later.'

'Bye guys, great questions. Have fun at the party.'

Prim seemed to be considering whether to go with them but dropped at Max's feet with a sigh instead. The door clicked shut and he sank back into the sofa. 'Sorry about that, the personal stuff.' He took his glasses off and slid them into a messenger bag, along with his wallet. 'I had no idea what they wanted to know but clearly I ought to have checked.'

'It's fine.' Ella was still smiling. 'Have I passed the test, then? Can I stay?'

She meant her question to be light-hearted and suddenly it wasn't. She heard the catch on the last three words, the realisation that she wanted to be at Halesmere, to help take care of the children if she could. Her immediate future was in Max's hands right now, and she hoped he would allow her to make a temporary life here.

He stood up and Ella quickly followed as he offered a hand across the coffee table. 'Yes, you can stay, Ella Grant. I'm sure you're already discovering it's mostly a madhouse.' He hesitated. 'I apologise for being rude to you yesterday, I was taken aback to find a stranger holding hands with my children. I'm not a big fan of surprises or being backed into a corner, which is precisely why my mother invited you without telling me. Let's hope this works out well for all of us.'

Chapter Five

Max followed Ella out of his office, and she was relieved to find the reception room mercifully clear of any more people who might wish to interrogate her. He opened the door to the courtyard and Prim bounded away.

'Look, Ella, however much my mother thinks she's in command of my calendar, I can't show you around now.'

'I understand. And that's fine.' Ella didn't mind in the least; she'd be perfectly happy getting a feel for the place on her own. She wasn't sure she was ready for Max giving her the grand tour and trying to reconcile himself to the role his mother had brought her in to fulfil.

He found his phone, ran a finger across the screen. 'Let's plan a meeting for Monday morning after I've walked the kids to school. Then we can go over your notes and I'll explain where we're up to with the house. Other than being coerced into cooking pizza tonight, it's probably better you take the rest of the weekend to settle in.'

He glanced towards the yellow door sitting at the top of the steps across the courtyard. 'How's the flat? I haven't been in there for months and from what I remember it's not exactly boutique.'

Ella opened her mouth, wondering where to start.

'Oi Max, where've you been 'idin'? I need a word.'

She spun round to see a man strolling towards them, Prim walking happily beside him. He had a pencil tucked behind an ear, one hand deep in a pocket of his donkey jacket, its shoulders a bright orange splash against the black material. He grinned at her and slid his other hand, covered in a range of interesting tattoos, over the rough stubble on his jaw. He wasn't much taller than her, with broad shoulders and a barrel chest over stocky legs.

Max offered a smile that softened the lingering tension. 'I've not been hiding, Stan, just busy. Can it wait until later? I'm about to take Lily and Arlo out and see a client.'

''Spose so, it's only trees that want cuttin' down, don't 'spose they'll grow much bigger between now an' next week. So who's this, then?' His glance slid to Ella. 'You 'ere about one of them empty studios? Watch out for Max, 'e'll be chargin' you double if you're not careful. Comes up 'ere from London an' thinks 'e can pull the wool over our eyes. Thinks we was born yesterday.'

'Ella, this is Stan.' There was a wry amusement in Max's voice. 'He's the one you need to watch out for, not me.'

Stan snorted, wiping his hand on trousers covered in sawdust before taking the one Ella had proffered. 'Don't listen to 'im, young Ella. I'll look after you, any problems you come to me. Salt o' the earth I am. 'eart o' gold, too big for me own good. Accordin' to my missus, anyway. So it's a studio, is it?'

'Actually, I've just been appointed as the new house manager. It's great to meet you, Stan.' Ella hoped Max wouldn't mind the job title; it had been Noelle who'd suggested it. 'I'm definitely not an artist, I wouldn't know where to start with a painting or a pot.'

'You what? 'Ouse manager? What's all that about, then?' Stan aimed a suspicious glance at Max as he let go of Ella's hand and scuffed the ground with a worn boot.

'If you want the full story then you'd better ask my mother. And less of the cheek about me, thanks.' Max shook his head. 'Ella will have enough to do without you feeding her nonsense. She's going to be managing the holiday business and probably keeping an eye on you, heaven help her.'

She noticed Max hadn't mentioned his children and wondered if he'd avoided doing so on purpose, keeping her role here more professional and less personal.

'Well, things are lookin' up, even if you don't look tough enough to pull the skin off a rice puddin'. No offence, mind.'

Stan grinned again and Ella laughed. She'd met far worse than him in her career and wasn't bothered in the least if someone wanted to pull her leg. She could give as good as she got, and better when it suited her.

'And what do you do here, Stan? Are you an artist too?'

'Do I look like one?' He rolled his eyes. 'General dogs-body, that's me, came with the 'ouse when Max bought it. Been 'ere for years, came up to marry my missus an' never left. Anythin' broken, I'll fix it. Grass needs cuttin', I'm your man. Boilers, basic electrics, I can turn me 'and to anythin'. You get the picture, Ella.'

She did, and good handymen were very hard to find; she'd be looking after Stan and making sure to keep him on side. There was bound to be plenty she could find for him to do, starting with the broken rung she'd discovered on her ladder in the flat. And he looked like a man for whom the quickest way to his toolbox was through his stomach.

'You need anythin' doin', Ella, come an' see me. Not Max, 'e's too grand for us lot, what with 'is telly gardens an' all that malarkey.' Stan pointed a gnarled finger at Max.

'Now you know that's not true, Stan. I'd like a beer in the pub with the gang at the end of a long day as much as anyone, but I can't, not with Lily and Arlo to take care of.'

'Aye, well, my missus'll be down 'ere like a shot to look after them kiddies when you need 'er. Our Pearl's waitin' for our own grandkids to come along an' it's not 'appenin' quick enough for 'er. An' she 'as to knit for someone.'

'Yes, they love the Christmas hats she made, Stan. Even you might be impressed if you saw the name tags I stitched into them.' Max shifted the messenger bag to a shoulder.

'You never did?' Stan fixed an astonished gaze on him. 'Stitched them in yourself, did you? Well, our Pearl will never believe that when I tell 'er.'

'And if only I'd known all along the way to impress you was with my sewing.' Prim was pawing at Max's legs, and he reached for her collar to hold her still. 'Not my leadership skills or brilliant landscape designs.'

'Max!' Noelle was rushing across the courtyard trailing Lily and Arlo and clutching a cape falling from her shoulders. 'Aren't you supposed to be going somewhere? Lily mentioned a party.'

'You know I am, Maman.' Max's eyes narrowed as he stared at his mother. 'I'll take these two back and get them changed now.'

Stan was looking at Noelle and Ella saw his cheeky grin had vanished, and apparently with it the power of speech.

'*Bonjour*, Stan.' Noelle gave him a smile and he could only nod as his face became pink. '*Merci beaucoup* for the logs you left in the flat for Ella. She'll be needing more soon, I expect.'

'Be my pleasure,' Stan muttered. He didn't seem to know what to do with his hands and eventually stuffed them into his pockets. 'You needin' more yet, Ms Bourdon?'

'Noelle, Stan, I've told you before.' Noelle even managed to shrug elegantly, and Ella noticed one hand was splashed with paint. 'None of this Ms Bourdon, we are not so formal here, are we? Are we not friends, *ça va*?'

'If you say so.'

'I've got to go.' Max spoke to Ella, removing his hand from Prim's collar and she took off after the children. 'Stan will sort you out if you need anything. Text me a list of the shopping you need for the pizza, I'll bring it back with me. My mother will give you my number. Stan, I'll get the new chainsaw ordered today, I promise.'

'Make sure you do,' Stan muttered as Noelle gathered her cape and fluttered away. 'Cos them trees ain't gonna chop themselves down an' Sandy will be after you if there's not one at church in time for the Christingle service. Sandy's our resident rector an' potter,' Stan explained to Ella. 'You'll see 'er 'ere before long, I shouldn't wonder.'

–

Ella's mum and Dylan had both already messaged this morning, asking for images of her new surroundings, and she thought she might manage to waylay them with a few landscape shots instead. Yesterday had been a long, dreary day spent mostly in the car and her mind was still whirring with the reality of losing her job and finding this new one in little more than a couple of weeks. She needed a run; the outdoor activity balanced her. Very often a walk would become a run, when the only way to let her mind slow was to allow her feet to fly.

And would Halesmere be enough for her, even for now? After her previous job, with its frantic pace and constant buzz, would she be able to lose herself in the landscape here, take the opportunity to run and swim every day if she chose? Or would she regret it, feel as though she'd left Lauren even further behind? Only when Ella was pushing herself, when she could feel her limits and wanted to extend them, did she sense that she was living life hard enough. She needed the feeling of control it gave her, a way to live life twice over. Once for her, and once for Lauren. It was the only way Ella knew how to keep her sister close and Lauren's dream alive.

Ella's kayak was still in the car, and she collected her running trainers from the boot and changed into her kit in the flat. She still hadn't lit the fire and it was chilly inside, gloomy and unfriendly. She'd left her Christmas decorations behind in Brighton; she might buy more to cheer this place up for a few weeks at least. She slipped her earbuds in and locked the door, stretching at the bottom of the steps to warm up.

She followed a stony track away from the buildings, jogging easily and aware that her habits were remaining the same, even though her environment was now so very different. Everything other than the music in her ears was silenced and she felt as though she was quite literally running herself into something new, grinding her old life and career into the rough ground beneath her feet.

Forty minutes later she was heading up a narrow lane alongside a meadow and saw the walls of the house rising out of its garden. She reached the drive and headed back through the arch towards the flat. Time for another dodgy shower.

When she knocked nervously at the door to Noelle's flat later, she was surprised to receive no answer. Her introduction to Noelle's work would have to come another time and Ella couldn't deny she was rather relieved.

–

It was close to three p.m. and going dark when Ella banged her front door shut and returned through the arch to Max's cottage, where a black pickup was sitting on the drive. She'd just had her first proper look around the kitchen in the flat and had known at once she wouldn't be making pizza bases or anything else in there. She knocked, heard Prim bark inside. The door swung open to reveal Max, changed into lounging trousers and a hoodie. His eyes were red behind his glasses, and he covered a yawn with a hand.

'Is everything all right?' He took the glasses off to rub his temples. 'I've got the stuff you need for the pizza; I probably should have fetched it over sooner. Sorry.'

'That's okay. I'm sorry to bother you at home. It is about the pizza actually.'

'What about it?'

'I need somewhere to make it; I can't prepare the dough in the flat.'

'Because?'

'Because the kitchen in the flat is a disgrace and I'm not prepared to use it.' She'd said it now and he could do what he liked with the information. She wondered how far it was to the nearest takeaway. Miles, probably; the food would be stone cold by the time she returned, if she did find her way back here before the children's bedtime. The lanes all looked the same in the dark, edged with trees looming down over stone walls smothered in moss.

'Right. Anything else you'd like to tell me?'

Was she imagining a trace of amusement now? Ella was sure Max wouldn't think it quite so funny if she reported him to environmental health. 'I wouldn't cook for anyone in it, certainly not your small children. There are signs of mice, and I don't want to make Lily and Arlo sick.'

'I don't want you to make them sick, either. I'm not a huge fan of clearing up vomit in the middle of the night.'

She smiled at that, and a pause lengthened as she waited for him to decide. He stepped back against the wall. 'I suppose you'd better come in if you're suggesting what I think you are. You want to use my kitchen instead?'

'Please.' Her quick laugh was apologetic. 'Next time I promise it'll be ready-made bases straight off a supermarket shelf.'

'Next time?'

'Figure of speech,' she added hastily. She didn't want him to think she fancied cosy Saturday nights tucked up in his cottage with him and his children any more than he did. 'You know what I mean.'

'I think I do.' He put the glasses back on. 'I'll make sure to add some to my online order. Go on through, straight to the end. Follow the barking.'

Ella squeezed past Max and a staircase in the narrow hall, pushing open a door, aware of him behind her. Prim bounded over with a big grin, offering a welcome considerably more joyous than Max had. Ella had grown up with lots of pets and she was happy to indulge the lovely young dog.

'Prim, stop it,' he said sharply, pointing at her bed, but she completely ignored him to snuggle up to Ella. 'Usually she can barely drag herself off the underfloor heating, but she obviously likes you.'

'I like her too.' Ella was stroking Prim's head and darting quick glances around the room. This was much better, and she'd be perfectly happy to cook in here.

The cottage opened out into an extended family room, a pair of leather sofas at right angles to a cosy-looking stove already lit, a tall cream dresser against a wall between the sitting area and modern, L-shaped kitchen. She much preferred the clean granite worktops and large Aga to the hob in the flat. An island, with a sink on one side and bar stools on the other, wasn't far away from a table that seated six, a laptop open on it with a glass of beer and a pile of planting books nearby. All the wood was aged oak and she couldn't make out the darkened garden through the bifold doors. Christmas decorations were scattered around the room, a tree smothered in tinsel and baubles and strung with coloured lights glittering near the dresser. She shrugged out of her coat, draping it on the back of a stool.

'We put the decorations up a bit early this year. The kids asked me and there wasn't a reason to say no.' Max had caught her looking. He settled in his chair and touched the laptop, brightening the screen back to life. 'Do you mind sorting yourself out? I was just trying to finish some work before they get home. A friend picked them up from the party and took them back to her place.'

'That's fine.' Ella hadn't exactly thought this through in the urge to leave the flat or imagined she and Max would be alone while she prepared the pizzas. She didn't recognise the classical piano music coming from a speaker but found it pleasant all the same. 'I'll try not to disturb you.'

'You can make as much noise as you like. I'm not easily distracted unless Lily and Arlo start rioting. I mostly work when they're not around so I can be with them when they are.'

'Of course. That makes sense.' Ella didn't know quite what to do with herself in this new kitchen; usually she'd be completely at home in such a place. 'Sorry, maybe it would be better if you could just quickly show me where things are. I don't like to rummage through your private home, it feels a bit too familiar.'

'If you prefer.'

Max opened cupboards, found a frying pan and a chef's knife he assured her was his best. Ella had left her own knives in the flat and it didn't seem worth running back to fetch them now. Tour over, he retreated to the table, and she wouldn't have called it a companionable silence as she added warm water to a well she'd made in the dry ingredients and began to work the dough, kneading it with an experienced hand. She was almost ready to find somewhere for the dough to prove when he stood, holding his empty glass as he crossed to the kitchen.

'Sorry, how rude of me, I should've asked you sooner. My mother would not be impressed with my manners.' His hand was on the door of the American fridge-freezer.

'What can I get you to drink? Glass of wine or a beer? Water? Juice? Coffee?'

'Beer would be perfect, thank you.'

'Is low-alcohol okay? I don't drink very much, living out here with two young children. I prefer being able to drive if I need to.'

'Sure.' Ella had been investigating the Aga and turned to find him right behind her. His hand shot out of the way of her chest and the contents of the glass flew straight down her top. The beer soaked through to her bra, and the short sharp shock of cold liquid on her warm skin made her words a startled gasp. 'Sorry, I didn't realise you were there.'

'Shit, sorry, totally my fault.' Max grabbed a tea towel and flung it at her, snatching at kitchen roll to wipe up the puddle around her feet.

'It's fine.' It wasn't really; the beer was already staining a patch on her yellow top an unglamorous orange. Her bra felt glued to her skin, and she'd probably never get the marks out of the white lace. 'Good thing Lily's not back yet to hear you swear. I think you owe Prim a pound.'

'You're kidding me, right?' He paused wiping and Ella wasn't sure if his outrage was pretend or not until his eyes narrowed as he stared up at her. 'Who's going to tell her?'

'Maybe I will. I'm on her side, you're mean to Prim.'

'Mean! Food twice a day, a snug bed – or on the sofa when my back's turned – and as many treats as she can guzzle, plus all the stuff Arlo sneaks her from the table when he thinks I'm not looking. And I walk her every day.'

'Still mean. You need to love her too, it's obvious she adores you and dogs need love just as much as we do.'

'Go ahead then, tell Lily if you like.' Max finished clearing the puddle away and stood up. 'I already gave her five pounds this morning, and I think I've still got one left to spend.'

He was very close, and Ella's heart somersaulted at the flash of awareness in his gaze. She was overdoing the frantic swiping at her chest, and he backed away hurriedly.

'Sorry about your top.' His eyes were everywhere but on it and he yanked the fridge open. 'I'll get you that drink and try not to throw it over you this time.'

Prim gave a startled bark and leapt to her feet as Lily erupted into the room, skidding to a halt with Arlo, both clutching party bags and bobble hats. 'Ella! Are you making our pizza? Is it ready yet? Daddy didn't tell us you were going to be here.'

'Daddy didn't know. And no, Lily, it's not ready. Ella's not been here very long.' Max left her new drink out of harm's way and casually propped himself against the island.

She had a hand on the Aga's towel rail, her heart still hammering. Insanity, that moment between her and Max, and if she had even a shred of common sense then she'd run right out of that door and leave him to feed his kids whatever the heck he wanted.

'Hi Max, I hope we're not late. I dropped my two at their dad's on the way here.' A woman followed Lily and Arlo into the room, and she too, stopped dead at the sight of Ella.

'Sorry, I didn't realise you had company.'

Chapter Six

'Ashley, this is Ella.' Max offered the woman a smile as she quickly pasted one on her own face and dropped a huge tote on a sofa. 'Ella's our new house manager, Ash, a role dreamed up by my mother and one I had no idea she'd done anything about until last night.'

'How typically cloak and dagger of her.' Ashley came over to offer Ella a hand, and Ella quickly brushed flour from her fingers. Ashley's lustrous brunette hair fell in soft waves around her face, not spoiled even by her having pulled off a beanie. Dark eyes suited her colouring, and she was beautifully dressed in a long skirt and boots below a winter coat. Lily was beside her, and Ashley gently tucked an errant curl behind the little girl's ear.

'Lovely to meet you, Ella. Arlo's been telling me all about this pizza you're making for them. They're very excited, it's so kind of you.'

'Oh, it's…' Ella had been about to say nothing until she caught sight of Arlo's little face, beaming with anticipation.

'Can I see, Ella?' Lily darted to the island and Ella was happy to retreat behind it with her. 'Oh. It doesn't look like pizza yet.'

'That's because we need to leave the dough somewhere warm to let it prove. It's part of the process of making the base from scratch.'

'What's prove?'

'It's when the dough fills with air and rises. Then we knead it again to get it into shape for the sauce and toppings to go on.'

'Please can I help?' Lily dropped her party bag unopened on the island as Arlo settled on a stool and tipped his bag out, scattering crayons and empty wrappers.

'That'd be great.' Ella glanced at Lily's outfit. 'But maybe you should wear an apron, your dress is lovely and I'm sure you or your dad won't want to get it covered in flour or tomato sauce.'

'You're right Ella, he doesn't. Your apron should be in the bottom drawer, Lily.' Max was next to Arlo and Ashley had joined them at the island. Ella was very used to having lots of people around when she cooked but somehow this felt rather intimate and more than a little awkward.

'Okay.' Lily opened a drawer and produced a purple apron, turning round as she slipped it over her head, waiting for Ella to fasten it in place.

'Ashley's an interior designer, Ella, she was a client back in London and persuaded me to sort out her new garden once she'd relocated north. So, it's kind of her fault that we ended up moving here too.'

It occurred to Ella then that perhaps Max wasn't actually single, and she didn't want to be in the way of an evening he and Ashley had planned.

As she showed Lily how to knead the dough, she and Max both snatched at the glass of beer that Lily was about to knock over in her enthusiasm. Ella saw that moment from before again as a smile hovered on his lips, his hand brushing hers.

'Come on, Max, you can't blame it all on me.' Once he'd steadied the glass, Ashley pushed against him, and he grinned as he slid a friendly arm round her shoulders. 'I wasn't to know you'd fall in love with Cumbria and decide to give it a go.'

'Yeah? You should have thought of that before you found the house and insisted on dragging me round it and telling me how amazing you could make it given half a chance and a decent budget.'

'And wasn't I right?' Ashley shrugged. Ella had the impression Ashley didn't need Max to let her know she'd done a great job but would like it all the same.

'You were.' He removed his arm. 'You know I think it's stunning and now we can finally make plans to relaunch it. Ella's a chef, Ash, she's taking some time out to decide what's next in her career and helping us with the holiday business while she does.'

'But that's great.' Ashley turned luminous brown eyes on Max. 'I've been saying for months that you need some support, and the house won't run itself, not if you want great reviews and guests who tell all their friends to book.'

'And Ella's going to be looking after me and Arlo too, Daddy, isn't she?' Lily momentarily paused kneading and splattering flour.

'Well, we still have to see about that, Lily, it's not quite decided. Anyway, how was the party?' Max addressed both his children, but Arlo was too busy loading toy sheep onto a trailer attached to a tractor to reply.

'So much fun, Daddy, but Arlo's had blue ice cream and Herbert.' Lily gave her brother a wary look and Ella casually slid the dough away before Lily could knock it into next week, quickly reshaping it and putting it on a tray.

'Ah.' Max pulled a face. 'Lily always thought that sherbert was called Herbert, Ella, and I'm afraid the name's stuck. So we've got a sugar high to look forward to, then? Marvellous.'

'Actually, I think he's probably over it. My two have been at the same party, Ella.' Ashley's gaze passed over her but warmed up when it reached Max. 'Arlo was racing around our garden for a good hour, so he might be ready to crash sooner rather than later.'

'Thanks, Ashley.' Max gathered up Arlo's party rubbish and dropped it in the bin. 'Tea, bath and bed then.'

'Daddy, that's not fair,' Lily wailed. 'It's Saturday night and we always watch a movie together.'

'When you've not been to a party and are not already tired and grumpy, yes, we do.' Max was trying to prevent a giggling Arlo from climbing up his legs. They tussled for a few moments as Ashley looked on fondly, until Max finally triumphed and sat Arlo firmly back on his stool.

'And when you are tired and grumpy, then the only cure is sleep.' Max shot Lily a look that said he meant it and she pouted. 'So no movie tonight.'

'I already had pizza at the party, Daddy.' Arlo sounded gleeful as Max pushed his stool towards the island.

'You'd better not have too much more then,' he replied dryly, and Ella couldn't resist.

'Vomit in the night,' she suggested casually.

'Quite possibly. And if you're still here then you can help me clear up.' Max flashed her a smile she wasn't expecting.

'No thanks, you're on your own with that one,' she protested. 'None of this was my idea, remember?'

'Chicken.'

Ella remembered the dough and picked up the tray hastily. 'Is there somewhere I can leave this? An airing cupboard would be ideal.'

70

'I'll show you.' In a flash Lily was on the other side of the island. 'It's this way Ella, on the landing near my bedroom.'

'Thanks.' Ella lingered to see if Max would insist on taking it himself so she wouldn't be wandering around his house. 'There's enough for four if Ashley's staying,' she told him.

'Up to you, Ash.' He made it sound as though he wouldn't mind either way. Ashley's laugh was light.

'Thanks Max, but let's leave it for tonight as you already have company for the kids.' She removed a phone from her coat pocket and touched the screen. 'We can talk properly over dinner. I know we said Tuesday but would Thursday work for you instead? Something's come up with James and he wants me to swap nights.'

'That's fine, long as my mother doesn't mind.'

'Shall I book us a table somewhere nice?'

'Sure. Sounds good.' Max had found a cloth and was wiping flour from the worktop.

'Perfect. I think it's your turn to collect me this time.' Ashley put the phone away. 'How did it go with our client this afternoon? I'm sure you smoothed them out and got their expectations back online.'

'I think so. They signed off on the plans anyway.'

'I bet you just wowed them with your Chelsea garden and they fell right at your feet.'

'Don't know about that.' He tried to shrug off her praise. 'They mentioned they'd seen it but didn't follow up as I wasn't practising in the north then.' He glanced at Ella. 'Sorry, it's late to be talking shop now.'

'That's okay.' She handed the tray of dough to Lily. 'We need to take this upstairs and collect it in forty-five

71

minutes. Then we can make the tomato sauce while we're waiting.'

'I never knew making pizza from scratch was so complicated.' Lily sounded awed as she led Ella towards the hall.

'But so worth it, I promise. You'll never want ready-made pizza again.'

'Thanks for that,' she heard Max mutter behind her. 'Pretty sure my freezer's full of the stuff.'

When she and Lily returned, after Ella had agreed to a peep at her pretty pink and white bedroom, Arlo was on the sofa, glued to something on television, the tractor and his sheep nearby. Ashley and Max were still chatting at the island and Ashley turned to Ella as Lily tugged her into the kitchen.

'Lovely to meet you, Ella. Do give me a call if I can help you with the house. It really was a labour of love, wasn't it, Max? Those cabinets you wanted to dump and now look at them.'

'You can hardly blame me,' he protested. Ashley dropped a kiss on Lily's head and did the same with Arlo. Max was following as they left the room. 'They were in a state, and I wasn't to know...'

Their conversation was lost as they disappeared into the hall, and Ella gave Lily a grin as she lined up ingredients with practised efficiency. 'Want to help me with the tomato sauce?'

'Yes please.' Lily was beaming with excitement.

Max returned a few minutes later and to Ella's surprise, he snapped the laptop shut and settled on a stool at the island with the last of his beer.

'Good thing you've kept your apron on,' she told Lily casually, feeling the weight of his gaze watching them. 'Tomato juice can get everywhere.'

'My granny made it for me.' Lily pulled the apron straight so Ella could see the design. 'Do you like the seahorse, Ella?'

'I do, it's so pretty. Noelle is obviously very talented.'

'Oh, it wasn't Mamie.' Lily had undone the apron and was getting the strings in a muddle as she tried to retie it, and Ella was closer than Max to help. 'It was our other granny, our mummy's mummy. She and Grandpa live near the sea, and they're taking us away in the holidays.'

'How brilliant, I bet you'll have a fabulous time. I love being by the sea.' Ella felt a pang for her flat, and the beach where she normally went to swim whatever the weather.

Lily was still chattering on. 'We're going to see them after Christmas and they're taking Arlo and me to stay in a lodge.'

Ella was thinking longingly of her own family scattering for Christmas. Her brother Jamie and his husband were both busy with their careers and the dog shelter they volunteered with. And this time, according to Ella's mum, they were both heading up to the Highlands to be with Nick's parents instead of joining hers in Aberdeen. Ella concealed a sigh; she couldn't blame them for wanting to share their time between their two families. She wondered if her mum would bother making her Christmas puddings this year.

'Can I show you my advent calendar, Ella?' Lily never seemed to stop talking and Ella liked it; it kept the silence humming between her and Max at bay. 'I've put kindness in mine, one for every day until Christmas Eve. Daddy said I could start early as we've already put our decorations up.'

'Kindness? How do you do that? Don't you usually have chocolate in advent calendars?'

'Yes, we've got chocolate calendars as well but Daddy's letting us use Mummy's old advent calendar, from when she was little like us, and I've filled it with kindness. I write one for every day.' Lily was pointing to a beautiful wooden box on the dresser, each tiny drawer decorated with Christmas scenes in differing colours.

'That's a wonderful idea, Lily.' Ella was trying to picture what Christmas might look like for these two little ones, a first spent in Cumbria and far from their old life, the one they'd lived with their mum. 'So what things have you put in the calendar?'

'We made crispy cakes for my teacher last week. And Daddy said at least one kindness should be Arlo and me not arguing for a whole day. He said that would be kind to him, so I'm saving it for later.'

'Wow, a whole day.' Ella caught the flash of Max's smile. 'I could have done with a kindness like that when my brother and I were little.' She and Jamie hadn't fallen out that often but when they had it had been spectacular, with physical fights along with the verbal ones. Then they would make up just as quickly, their argument forgotten.

'And I think another kindness should be Daddy not shouting at Prim for a whole day. What do you think, Ella?'

Her gasp of laughter had already escaped, and she gave Max a guilty look. 'I think the right response to that question, Lily, is to dodge it and say it's nothing to do with me. We should make the tomato sauce now; I don't want to keep you up late.'

'Can you chop really quickly, like proper chefs do?'

'Of course I can.' Ella slid garlic cloves onto a wooden board as Arlo made his way over from the sofa, interested now that something more exciting than kneading dough was taking place. 'Want to see?'

She was laughing seconds later when the garlic was in shreds and the children were staring open-mouthed.

'That's amazing,' Lily breathed, turning to Max. 'Daddy, I want Ella to teach me—'

'Forget it,' he said quickly. 'If you were going to say what I think you were, then if we take out the fact that you using a sharp knife is probably illegal at your age, not to mention highly dangerous, then there are half a dozen other good reasons why it's a very bad idea. Ella will not be teaching you how to chop like she does.'

Lily's pout implied she didn't agree with him. 'Let's get the pan warmed up,' Ella suggested. 'Then when the sauce is simmering, we'll finish off the dough.'

She turned the hob on and added olive oil, then the garlic to the pan, shaking it gently. 'See how the garlic is beginning to colour? That's when we add the basil and tomatoes.'

'What's basil?' Arlo looked confused. 'My friend at school has a cat called Basil.'

'It's this green herb.' Ella picked up a bunch of leaves to show them. 'Doesn't it smell great? I grow it at home on my windowsill in the summer.'

Lily was nodding but Arlo wasn't convinced. 'We tear it up and add it with the tomatoes. You can do that if you like? Then we add seasoning, which is just salt and pepper. When it's about to boil and bubble we sieve it to get the lumpy bits out and simmer it for a few more minutes in the pan. That helps to make a better flavour.'

75

'Then can we eat it?' Arlo looked hopeful and Ella had to smile at his cute and curious little face.

'Nearly, Arlo. Very nearly.'

Once the pizzas were assembled and in the oven, Max got Arlo to help him set the table and Ella realised they'd put out four places.

'You joining us?' There was a slightly forced note in Max's voice as he carried the pizzas across.

Ella was pretty sure he'd rather she didn't but felt obliged to invite her, given the state of the kitchen in the flat and that she'd cooked their dinner. She'd prefer to leave them to it, especially after that moment between her and Max earlier. But she was hungry, and it would be nice to see the children enjoying the meal they'd made together.

'Are you sure?'

'Seems only fair.' He was at the fridge and the decision was made as he passed her another beer.

They sat in a square at the table, Lily and Ella on one side with Max and Arlo facing them. Max sliced up the pizzas and she felt a rush of pleasure at the delight on Arlo's little face as he ate. Lily was taking her time and Prim was at Arlo's side, no doubt hoping for crumbs or better.

'What else did you cook in your restaurant, Ella? I love your pizza.' Lily had a slice halfway to her mouth and her head on one side. She was still wearing her seahorse apron and Ella caught a piece of falling tomato before it hit the floor.

'Thank you, it was fun to make it together. But I didn't work in a restaurant, Lily, at least not in my last job. I cooked for a company who created special parties and events.'

'What kind of parties? Birthday ones?' There was a hopefulness in Lily's voice that had Max jumping in firmly.

'Before you say it, Ella will not be cooking for your birthday, okay?' He'd already finished his first slice of pizza and she was gratified to see him going back for another. 'We still haven't decided what we're going to do.'

'But Daddy, I want a party and it's next month. Everyone in my class is having parties and I want to invite all my new friends.' Lily pouted again. 'It's too far away from home to invite my old ones.'

Ella saw the flash of guilt in Max's expression, certain Lily had played her trump card on purpose. 'What kind of party would you like, Lily?' She hoped he would not mind her asking.

'I don't know yet.' Lily sighed dramatically, giving her father a look that suggested her pleas were falling on deaf ears. 'Daddy says I can invite eight friends as the whole class is too many, but I'm not allowed a sleepover.'

'A sleepover is not practical, Lily, because there's only really me to look after you all.' Max tilted a glass of water at her. 'We can hardly expect your grandmother to crash on the sofa with a bunch of wild seven-year-olds leaping about. And none of the other parents will ever let your friends near us again if I send them all home strung out on sugar and no sleep.'

'I understand, Daddy. Could you give me some party ideas, Ella, please?' Lily elongated the final word into a heartfelt plea and Ella knew she and Max were both being played by this clever little girl.

'I didn't see a lot of the parties I cooked for, Lily.' Arlo held up his plate for more pizza and Ella loved how Max and Arlo were digging into it. The extra cheese had been a success and the sauce was perfect. 'I was always in the kitchen making sure the food was ready exactly on time.'

'I've made a list.' Lily scrambled down to fetch her iPad and dragged her chair closer to Ella's. 'Please will you have a look with me?'

'Lily, we're eating.' There was a warning note in Max's voice. 'This can wait.'

'I don't mind if you don't?' Ella didn't want to challenge his authority too obviously in front of his children. 'I should go as soon as we've finished anyway, so maybe now is a good time?'

'Animals?' Lily wasn't waiting for her father to agree. The screen lit up and she touched it again. 'We could have bugs and stuff or go to the wildlife park but someone in my class already did that and Tilly, my best friend, doesn't like spiders.'

Lily deleted a line from her list. 'I don't want *Frozen*, everyone's done that. Or princesses.'

Two more lines went, and Ella was struck by inspiration, remembering an event she had cooked for last year. 'What about a wonderland party? As your birthday is in December it could work really well, especially for just a few of you.'

'I love that!' Lily jumped up and a frown creased her brow. Max glared as Prim hurriedly left Arlo's side to investigate the source of excitement. 'But what do you do at a wonderland party?'

Ella was rapidly improvising as she tried to remember the details of a party for a millionaire's daughter that had begun at midnight in the garden of a stately home. She wouldn't mention the sleigh though; she was pretty sure Max wouldn't thank her if he had to track one down a real one. 'Hot food as the weather's cold. Maybe hot dogs and s'mores around a campfire, and a scavenger hunt. It would be a lot of fun to search for things like pinecones or fallen leaves of a particular colour. What about hot juice and telling stories, or stargazing? Making a stickman instead of a snowman?'

'That's my party,' Lily shrieked, clambering onto Max's knee and winding her arms round his neck. 'Papa, please, can we do that, like Ella said. Pleeeease? With the s'mores and everything? I can help too; Ella won't have to do all of it.'

'Oh, I don't know, Lily, it sounds complicated and what do I know about a winter wonderland?' Max shot Ella a look and she wasn't sure if his level gaze meant he was pleased with her suggestion or not.

'It'll be fine, Papa, I promise. We won't eat too much sugar and I'll ask Ella really nicely to help us. And I won't ask again for a sleepover.'

'It's not Ella's job to sort out your party, Lily, she has other things to do.' He gently tipped Lily off his knee, but they all knew he was wavering. 'I'd better feed Prim; she must be starving if those sad stares she's giving me are anything to go by.'

'I don't mind helping with the party,' Ella assured Max, happy to see Lily's little face light up and her hands clutched together in glee. 'If you're okay with that?'

'Do I have any choice?' he said dryly as he poured dog biscuits into a bowl and added some meat from a tub in the fridge. 'Looks like you'd better include children's parties on your job description along with the life modelling, Ella.'

'Daddy, what's life modelling?'

Chapter Seven

Ella didn't want to put off leaving once Max had insisted he would do the clearing up, despite her anxiety at the thought of that sad, silent flat waiting. Lily wanted her to stay and talk about the party some more; she was all for planning another meeting of her own and adding it to the calendar on her iPad. At the front door she threw her arms round Ella's waist and clung on for a few seconds. Ella saw Max's impassive gaze above Lily's head as she bent down to hug her back. Arlo was more reticent, offering a shy grin and, encouraged by his dad, a polite thank you for the meal. Ella accepted Max's wry thanks for ruining his children for ever for frozen pizza.

The courtyard was dark and sinister in the frigid air, and she managed not to scream when an owl hooted near the barn. It was far too early for bed and once she'd let herself in she laid the fire, adding sticks to rolled-up newspaper she found in the log basket. The fire barely got going and after an hour Ella gave up and changed for bed, logging into the Wi-Fi with the password Max had given her and scrolling through Dylan's Instagram, half-wishing she was in France with him. Maybe it wasn't too late, perhaps she could get a flight for Christmas? She'd be happy to sleep anywhere if she didn't have to be on her own.

A bang on the front door made her drop the phone and she slithered down the ladder, remembering the dodgy rung just in time, and pulled the door back a fraction. It was far enough to see Max shivering in his hoodie, and she resisted the wild and reckless urge to tug him inside out of the cold.

'I've just got them asleep, and I need to get back.' He waved a baby monitor, speaking hurriedly. 'You can't stay in here, Ella. It's a hovel and that's without seeing it in daylight. I'm sorry it's late, but I thought you should know I don't plan on leaving you in this dump indefinitely.'

'But where will I go?' Her heart began to thump, worry prickling on her skin at the thought of having to leave Halesmere if there was nowhere else for her to live. 'It's fine, it's only for a—'

'No, you can't, I won't let you.' He let out an incredulous laugh. 'My mother, honestly, she just doesn't think.' He was staring into the room behind Ella, and she was taken aback by the sudden intensity in his gaze when it found hers. 'You can move into the house. I'll come back first thing and help you shift your stuff.'

'Max, I can't. It's all ready for guests.' She glanced apprehensively at the wide roof and tall chimneys stretching to the night sky. 'There's no need, really.'

'Ella, this flat isn't fit, and we both know it. I'll speak with the builders and sort it out for you, I promise.'

And he was gone before she could confess, his footsteps echoing as he sprinted back across the cobbles to his children. How could she turn down his offer without admitting the truth? How could she tell him she loathed being alone and the thought of those huge, empty rooms, shadows and solitude in every corner and silence following her around, was worse than the tiny flat and already making her feel afraid?

She was awake until long after midnight, freezing, her senses poised for every squeak and rattle, sure she could hear the mice running through the cupboards in the kitchen. Every breath she took seemed to shatter the stillness until she fell into an uneasy sleep. The light was pouring through the meagre curtains when a knock at the door eventually woke her. She grabbed the Dryrobe she normally used for swimming and had thrown over the bed as an extra layer and set off down the ladder. A second knock rattled like a roar through her sleep-deprived brain.

'Just a sec.' She raised her voice. 'I'm coming.'

The door was flung open, and Ella shrieked as her foot went straight through the broken rung and she landed in a heap at the bottom of the ladder. She let out a howl of pain as her knees made contact with the hard wooden floor and her wild eyes swivelled round to find Max staring at her in horror.

'Are you alright?'

'Fine.' She climbed gingerly to her feet, ignoring the hand he was tentatively offering, horribly aware he'd now had a perfect view of her bottom in pyjamas slipping down the ladder. She hastily wrapped herself in the Dryrobe that had somehow made the descent with her.

'In that case, is it okay to laugh?'

'It is not,' she said through gritted teeth. Her right knee was already throbbing, and her palms were stinging. How had she forgotten to lock the door after he'd left last night? 'Couldn't you have waited? I said I was on my way.'

'I thought you said come in.' Max had already backed out of the flat and was standing closer to the edge of the little platform than Ella believed was safe. 'I'm sorry.'

'Surely you're not here to make me move out so early?' It seemed best to face him as though nothing had happened and she crossed her arms, wincing as she placed some weight on her right leg. She was certain he'd taken in everything he'd seen and was doing his best to pretend he hadn't.

'Early? It's nine thirty. I've been up for three hours already.'

'Lucky you,' she groaned, rubbing a hand across bleary eyes. Another rough night, another late start she wasn't used to having, time wasted she could have spent running or kayaking, or even swimming. Had she really only been here for less than forty-eight hours? It seemed more like forty-eight days after the broken sleep, and right now she felt as though she'd aged every minute of those days as well.

'I've brought you breakfast.' Max held out something wrapped in tinfoil. 'Just a good old bacon butty. Seeing as you've condemned the kitchen as unfit for use.'

'Thanks, that's nice of you.' She caught the smell of the bacon and her stomach growled as she accepted the sandwich gratefully. 'Where's Lily and Arlo?'

'They're having breakfast with my mother. Or rather second breakfast, as we've been up so long. Once we've got you settled in the house, we'll be taking Prim out for a long walk until they moan like mad and demand to return to their screens.'

Ella couldn't help her smile. 'I suppose you need to come in and see what a state this place is. Just in case I was wrong about the mice.'

'I doubt you are wrong.' He closed the door, and she felt her awareness of him leap a notch. If she stepped back any further, she'd fall through the ladder, and she didn't fancy having to ask him to fish her out. 'I saw Stan on my way over and he said he'd found a squirrel in the bedroom.'

'A squirrel? Surely he was joking?' Ella's eyes shot up worriedly, checking for evidence. 'Dead or alive?'

'Oh, very much dead, he thought it had been there a while. He did have a go at the carpet before you came. My mother apparently told him she had a friend coming to stay over the holidays and would he please tidy the place up a bit.'

'That's disgusting.' Ella's feet were bare and her appetite for the bacon butty was diminishing as she thought of what she might already have stepped in. 'Did Noelle actually look inside before she invited me to live here?'

'I doubt it. So that's why I'm moving you out.' Max pointed to Ella's case on the floor. 'What else have you got?'

'I have to go now?'

'Unless you'd rather wait until later?'

'Well, I wouldn't mind eating my breakfast first,' she retorted, waving the butty at him. 'And getting dressed.'

'Of course.' He backed away, a hand on the door.

'I'd offer to make you a drink in the spirit of being hospitable if you wanted to wait, but I'd have to boil the mugs first and I've discovered the kettle doesn't work.'

'Right. I'll come back in fifteen minutes or so.' He dipped his head to step through the door. 'Don't tell Lily I said so, but I probably wouldn't even let Prim sleep in here now I've seen it.'

'Thanks for that. It's good to know I'm below Prim in the pecking order. And you don't even like her.'

'I do like Prim,' he protested, blowing on his hands. 'I like her a lot, especially as she's really good for the kids.'

Ella saw Stan strolling past below and he offered a cheery good morning, happy to hear Max had ordered the new chainsaw. She managed a polite reply, then hurriedly shut the door. Marvellous. Now Stan had seen Max visiting her on a Sunday morning and Ella still in her pyjamas. She curled into an armchair and unwrapped her bacon butty. It was delicious and exactly what she needed, and always her favourite hangover cure. Not that she had a hangover. This made her think of the low-alcohol beer from last night and she glanced at the top she'd worn yesterday, with the orange stain on its chest. It was all the reminder she needed of her and Max staring at one another for those few seconds when he'd flung the beer over her.

Dressed and ready fifteen minutes later, she saw Prim running across the courtyard with Lily and Arlo hot on her heels, Max not far behind.

'Ella!' Lily was bundled up in a hat and scarf with pink wellies, and she halted at the bottom of the steps. 'We've come to help you move out of the flat. Daddy said it's got to be re, re...?' She looked at him questioningly.

'Refitted, Lily, everything's got to come out and be replaced,' he confirmed. 'Wait there, you and your brother aren't to go up, it's not safe. We'll pass you down something you can carry. Those steps need a handrail, that's another thing to go on Pete's list.'

'Pete?' Ella gave her case to Max when he reached the door. She gently dropped the bag with her running trainers in and Arlo caught them. He grinned and she gave him a cheery thumbs-up.

'Pete the Plasterer. That's what they call him, but he's a builder too, a very good one. Ashley put me on to him. I've texted to ask him to put the flat on his list, but he won't get to it before Christmas. Is that all right? They're busy with the old studios in the stables and there's other work he needs to do as well. The barn needs some attention.'

'Okay.' Ella swallowed down her alarm, hoping Max hadn't noticed the flush of anxiety on her face at the thought of weeks alone in the big house. Noelle emerged from the door to his office, swathed in her cape and Cossack hat.

'Oh, Ella, you are moving out already.' Noelle clapped her hands together. '*Parfait*, Max, how very sensible of you to offer Ella the use of the house. It will be so much more comfortable than the flat. I should have thought of that myself.'

Ella glanced at him and spotted the glare he was giving Noelle, who wasn't hanging around for a reply. A red sports car screeched to a halt on the drive through the arch and she waved merrily as she dashed off.

'*Au revoir*, darlings. Maxence, make sure Ella has everything she needs.'

He opened his mouth and Ella was sure he was about to swear until he caught a glimpse of Lily's jubilant expression, no doubt waiting to collect his fine for the dog shelter. 'I never mentioned the house,' he spluttered. 'How does she know where you're going?'

'Lucky guess, I expect.' Ella bit back her smile and grabbed her coat.

It took only one trip between the four of them to carry her few belongings into the house, then the children dumped their load and raced off to explore. Max disappeared upstairs with her case and Prim was made to wait in the porch so she couldn't muddy the new drawing room carpet, looking longingly through the glass.

Certain she was going to feel like a mouse in a mansion, Ella tried to take in her new, generously proportioned home. Doors led off along the hall and a huge atrium allowed light to flood down onto walls painted a warm cream with a suggestion of yellow to lift it. A wide staircase turned twice before it reached the first floor, and she could hear Lily and Arlo charging around somewhere out of sight. Ella was glad of the noise to banish the silence, at least for now, as Max returned to join her.

The space beneath the stairs was filled with books and games, and the overall effect of the house was beautifully stylish and elegant. The paintings were a clever mix of traditional and modern, and furnishings blended period design with contemporary, keeping the effect simple. Lamps stood on occasional tables and a huge fireplace was already laid with logs. A stunning, glossy black grand piano sat in the centre, a matching stool beneath the gleaming keys.

'Wow. And I haven't even seen the other rooms yet.' Ella glanced at him. 'Ashley did all this?'

'Pretty much. The house was very run-down, but we saved everything that didn't need to go in a skip. Some items have been professionally restored and put back. It had already been divided into two when we bought it and made sense to keep it that way. So, two-thirds is for guests, and my mother and I share the rest. You've seen my office, and she has her flat and studio above me.'

'Ashley is very talented; it feels so warm and welcoming.'

Max nodded and the silence seemed to be singing until Ella pointed to the piano. 'Do you play, or did that come with the house as well?'

'No, it's mine. It wouldn't fit in the cottage and it's a shame not to let others play it if I can't.' His gaze found hers and she saw the quick regret in his face. 'Practice is everything and I'm not as good as I was. I keep meaning to buy an upright for home, but I haven't found one yet.'

She sensed the piano was important to him and something he missed; she remembered the classical music he had been listening to last night in the cottage. Ella understood perfectly; she knew what it was to miss something you were good at. She waited to see if he would say any more, and when he did the business-like tone was back, the wistfulness banished.

'Come and see the kitchen. I'm hoping this one meets with your approval.'

'Depends if you've got any mice,' she joked, happy to see him smile as he opened a door and stood aside to let her go first. 'Wow. Again.'

'Wow good or wow bad?'

'I think you know which, Max. This is stunning. Very different to the images I found online.'

'Yes, a new website is another thing on my to-do list, we've taken the old one down now. I think that's something I'm going to transfer to your list.'

'That's fine, I'll look into it this week.'

The holiday business would be her responsibility and Ella wanted to prepare Halesmere for its new future as well as she could for the time she was here. Succeeding was in her nature, and she planned to use all her experience and intuition to make the relaunch the best it could be. Contemporary, white units with dark granite worktops suited the country house vibe and the appliances were excellent-quality and elegant. Walls a shade below the cream in the hall were brightened by light pouring in from two deep sash windows overlooking a garden glittering with frost still clinging to the plants. There was an Aga in palest blue, and Ella was very happy to see a coffee machine matching the one in Max's office.

He propped his hands on one of eight chairs around the breakfast table. 'Will it do?'

'Of course – so much better than that. Doesn't look like you've got any rodent residents in here, so that's a good start.' She felt that shiver of alarm again at the thought of being alone in this big house night after night, rattling through its rooms and waiting anxiously for morning to come.

'I suppose that was my mother's plan all along.'

'What was?' Ella followed him into the hall. The children were making a din upstairs and Max shouted for them to come back down.

'Moving you in here. She knew I wouldn't let you stay in the flat once I'd seen the state of it, and she's been telling me for months it would make a great space for more artists or guests.'

He opened a door and they were in the dining room, painted a rich red that highlighted a wide black fireplace and mahogany table to seat twelve. Max explained that they'd restored the original table even though the house only slept eight in four bedrooms. There was a different view of the garden from here, a large terrace leading to an expanse of lawn surrounded by the overgrown borders Ella had seen from his office yesterday.

A connecting door led them into the drawing room, with French doors opening onto the terrace from the centre of a wide, curving bay window. The fireplace was white with huge church candles on the mantelpiece, a basket of logs and an old-fashioned poker beside the hearth. The curtains were long and floral, and cabinets filled with china stood against walls painted with a shade more lemon than in the hall. Each of the sofas and armchairs in differing colours looked comfortable, decorated with cosy cushions, occasional tables perfect for serving refreshments nearby.

'It's beautiful, Max. I can't think you'll have any difficulty attracting new guests. If you're happy to go ahead, it would make sense to have a professional photographer take images for the website. I'd love to make the best of the rooms and that view.'

'That's fine with me. Stan will probably know someone local, maybe you could have a word with him, or search online if not?'

'Of course. I'm already imagining the house decorated for the holidays with a Christmas tree in the hall, another one in here and guests gathered around the piano, drinking champagne. It would highlight the intimacy and give the impression of being welcomed into someone's home. Perfect for the website until the seasons change and you can add some spring and summer images.'

'That sounds good,' Max said, his gaze somewhere else. 'My mother will never stop gloating about inviting you once she's heard your suggestions.'

'Let's hope you're both happy when you've read my notes,' Ella wondered if he was thinking of how it might feel to spend a first Christmas here without his wife. 'I'd like to talk to you about holding a couple of events in December to generate interest in what you have to offer. I know it's tight for planning but it's a wonderful time to decorate a house, especially one like this.'

'I'm happy to discuss them with you, but I'm not promising anything yet.' Lily and Arlo had returned, their little faces flushed from racing around, and Arlo grabbed Max's leg. 'Hey buddy, ready for our walk?' Max ruffled his son's hair, and the sight brought an unexpected warmth to Ella's heart.

'I'm starving, Daddy, what's for lunch?' Lily seemed hopeful and he grinned as she found his hand to tug it.

'Lunch? You only just had breakfast with Mamie. Walk first, with snacks, and then I'll feed you again.' He removed a bunch of keys from his pocket and passed them to Ella. 'We'll leave you to explore upstairs in peace.' Arlo was pulling him into the hall and Max had to speak over his shoulder. 'See you tomorrow. You know where we are if you need anything.'

'Thank you.' She hoped she wouldn't need anything. She'd already spent far more time with Max and his family since she'd arrived at Halesmere than she'd ever expected.

Chapter Eight

Ella wanted to visit the community shop she'd seen online and the walk from Halesmere along lanes crunchy with fallen leaves was a pleasure. She was relieved that her knee felt fine after her little mishap with the ladder in the flat earlier and she wasn't troubled much by traffic as she marched along. She realised she had forgotten her earbuds – she never usually went anywhere without them – and found herself listening to the things she heard around her instead. Birds calling, the rustle of a breeze through trees, a cyclist flying by with a gust of air and a cheery shout. And silence, still and solemn, something she knew she might have to get used to around here. She passed a couple of houses decorated with early Christmas lights and wished she'd worn a hat; the air was sharp, and frost again tonight seemed certain.

After fifteen minutes she reached a cluster of cottages lining a T-junction; a hamlet really, not even a village. They were a mix of pretty stone and white-painted build-ings, some with planters in place of front gardens. A stream bustled below a row of railings, a hawthorn hedge beside it clinging onto the last of its autumn berries. An older man pruning a tree raised curious eyes and a friendly hand as she passed his cottage, and Ella smiled back.

A pub sat at the head of a hill, a lane snaking off into the distance on either side, and a few hardy walkers were enjoying the winter sun and drinks at tables outside. She saw the shop a few yards further on, and it too had picnic tables outside its wood-framed building. The cyclist she had seen earlier was sitting at one, a coffee and a tempting-looking slice of shortbread at hand, and a bell jangled as she stepped inside the shop. She wasn't sure what she had been expecting but it wasn't the fabulous array of food on display or the choice of gifts, everything from soup flasks to jewellery, candles, books, and handbags. Her stomach rumbled greedily at the smell of fresh bread, despite the bacon butty Max had brought her earlier.

A teenage boy nodded a welcome and left her to browse and Ella took her time, assessing the seasonal vegetables and home-made cakes, as well as the locally produced cheese, dairy, and meat. Handmade chocolates in their own small counter looked delightful, and ideas about Halesmere and this little treasure trove supporting one another were already filling her mind after she noticed small Christmas hampers beautifully presented. She spotted a noticeboard and took a picture of it on her phone. She had no real idea what went on up here, especially in winter, but the local shop was a good place to start finding out.

'Morning. Do you need any help?'

Ella whirled round, clutching her basket already containing pesto, Parmesan, and a candle. The teenage boy had disappeared; the friendly voice belonged to a woman in her sixties behind the counter, a welcoming beam brightening her attractive face, curling grey hair neat and short.

'I was just exploring, there's so much to see.'

'You carry on love, there's no rush.' The woman lifted a huge coffee and walnut cake onto the counter and the sight did nothing good for Ella's hunger pangs. A slice of that would probably do her lunch and dinner rolled into one. Her whole morning was out of whack; normally by now she'd have been for a run, caught up on chores and organised the rest of her time around work, instead of shifting her belongings from one place to another for the second time in three days.

'Now if I had to guess I'd say you're Ella.'

She spun round again, bashing the basket against her sore knee. She'd just dropped in some chocolates and enough ingredients for a couple of simple suppers for the children, and her shopping was getting heavier by the minute. 'Then you'd be right.'

'I'm Pearl, I hear you've met my husband.'

'Of course, Stan.' Ella was glad she was good with names as she thought of the handyman she'd seen earlier. 'But how did you…'

'News travels.' Pearl tapped her nose meaningfully. 'Actually, he was in before for his sausage butty and he told me you'd spent another night in that awful flat. Said he had no idea what Noelle was up to, putting you in there, and that you were a bonny lass with purple hair. How are you settling in?'

'I'm not sure I have yet, I only arrived on Friday.' Ella couldn't resist a smile, even if Stan had made her sound as though she had a lavender rinse instead of expensive highlights in subtle shades of lilac.

'And what do you think of Halesmere? Me and Stan don't live in the grounds, our cottage is just down the road but he's there every day, working or not. He loves that place. Max has got his work cut out, trying to make it pay. Had its share of bookings over the years but folk want more than a decent view and high ceilings these days.'

'I think it's beautiful, I feel very lucky to be living there for now.'

'That's what Stan said when he came up here for a summer job, and he never left.' Pearl winked. 'Just give him as good as you get and you'll be on the right foot, he likes a bit of banter. Now, can I get you a slice of that coffee cake, you've never taken your eyes off it yet. How about a nice Americano to go with it?'

Ella laughed. It felt lovely to be made welcome and she was still hungry. This shop might just prove very hard to resist, especially if they served great coffee. 'You're on, you had me at "slice".'

Pearl chuckled as she carved off a piece of cake that Ella was pretty sure would serve two people, and probably more like four in her previous job. If she was going to be recommending the shop to guests and finding ways to encourage them to buy here rather than rush into town or order everything online, she thought, then she was duty-bound to try everything on offer and make sure it was as delicious as it looked.

'On the house.' Pearl slid a box across and busied herself with the coffee machine.

'That's very kind of you.' Ella picked up a napkin and some fresh olives stuffed with jalapeños. 'Can I have a sourdough please? The malted barley one looks amazing.'

'Course you can.' Pearl left the coffee by the till and started scanning Ella's shopping. 'Now if this is for the house, then you can put it on their account.'

'Account?' Ella picked up some plain brown paper bags and started filling them. 'Do people still have those?'

'Halesmere does, aye, so don't be paying for stuff that's not yours. And if I had to guess again then I'd say you're making tea for little ones, and there's only them two lovely kiddies that I know of up at Halesmere who'd be wanting rainbow pasta.'

Laughter was bubbling on Ella's lips. Clearly Pearl was a mine of information, possibly not all of its hers, and Ella swiftly decided she ought to be careful what she let slip around her and Stan.

'I might be giving them tea a couple of times a week when Max is busy with work. I was a chef before and Arlo was interested – he really likes his food.'

Was a chef. Ella felt a rush of guilt for so easily falling into the past tense. She still hadn't decided that she wasn't going back. She wasn't sure she was brave enough to leave her career for ever; it would be like leaving Lauren behind too.

'Who makes the bread, Pearl?' Ella was hoping to distract her from the subject of the family. 'I'd love to get in touch and find out what else they produce.'

'That's Rowan, she lives down the road and has her bakery on the way into town. No shop though, she sells some online and delivers locally, as well as here.' Pearl was like lightning on the till, and she'd scanned the shopping far quicker than Ella could pack it. 'She's very busy with it all now, gave up her other job to go full-time.'

'I heard this shop is run by the community, is that right?'

'Yes, there's about eight of us that take turns. Other than the pub there's not much here and it makes sense to give local producers somewhere to sell. We get our share of walkers passing through and holidaymakers, and it's not a bad thing if they don't always have to drive into town.'

'Thanks, Pearl. So will I find Rowan's bakery online?'

'You will. Have a look on Facebook or Instagram for Love and Loaves, you can't miss it.'

'And what about the candles? Are they produced locally?' Ella loved the simple clear jars filled with soy wax offering up evocative winter fragrances reminiscent of firesides, woodland walks and cosy evenings indoors.

'Yes, Marta makes them, in what spare time she has. She's a lecturer at the college in town and she lives at the farm who supply our lamb and the sheep's-milk cheese. Instagram, Ella, Hart, and Hearth, same as the name on the jar.'

'Perfect. Thanks.'

Pearl shook her head when Ella offered her debit card, printing the receipt instead and sticking it on a spike. 'On account. Now remember, watch out for my Stan. Keeping him busy keeps him out of mischief. He likes to be doing and he's not as busy as he was since he retired from carpentry.'

'He was a carpenter?' That was more information worth knowing and Ella's ears pricked up.

'Aye, a very good one too, had his own business but packed it in when Halesmere went up for sale as he thought the new owner might turn him out, and now he's a jack of all trades.'

'Thanks for the tip.' Ella thanked Pearl again as she left, jangling the bell on the door, the heavy bags bumping against her legs. She'd have brought the car if she'd realised how well stocked the shop was, and she was still thinking about Stan and the jobs she might give him as she set off back to the house.

—

It was Sunday afternoon and Ella was on the shore of Lake Windermere. This landscape was one of the reasons why moving to Cumbria, even temporarily, had appealed so much. She wasn't the only one wearing a drysuit on such a sharp, cold day. Two people were paddleboarding, one with a dog in a lifejacket on their board. She was also wearing neoprene shoes, a hat, and her gloves; her kayak was inflated and ready to go. Keeping warm was essential in this weather and she was well used to being on the water in winter conditions.

She slid the kayak onto the lake, paddling quickly to stay warm, aware of her surroundings but not slowing to stare. She'd done her research and knew Windermere was home to a group of islands, and today she wanted to explore, take in the shores dotted with boathouses and properties with outstanding views. Further north were the towns of Ambleside and Bowness and she'd need to keep an eye on the ferry near there that crossed the centre of the lake on cables beneath the water.

The icy air was slashing at her face and she loved it, feeling the familiar adrenaline rush as her paddle sliced into the water and arced above her head. She didn't slow down until she neared a large island surrounded by mature trees, through which she glimpsed a large house. Yachts were moored nearby, and she paddled more slowly between them to the far side.

'Nice skills.'

Ella's head whipped sideways to see a man hauling a board down to the shore. He lifted his paddle with a grin. 'I saw you flying along and thought, "now Kev, there's someone who knows what they're doing." And it's only the hardy ones like us who come out in winter.'

'I do love being on the water. And thanks.'

Kev was in a drysuit too, probably mid-forties, and she saw a flash of grey hair as he adjusted his hat to pull a helmet over it. 'You've been kayaking a while?'

'Years.' Close to twenty. Ella realised how quickly and yet sometimes slowly the time since losing Lauren had passed.

'Done any qualifications?' Kev was on the water now and he glided gracefully over to her.

'Some.'

'Like?'

'Level one paddle-sport instructor.' Ella brought her kayak across and let it drift alongside Kev, far enough away not to be blown into him. She'd already noticed the change in the wind as the water in the distance rippled gently, and the breeze was heading their way.

'Music to my ears.' He held up a hand. 'Sorry, I'm being nosy. I work just there.' He pointed to a large house set back from the water in parkland. 'That's Ashfell Outdoor Centre. We run a lot of courses focussed on young people's well-being and development, and I'd love to have a volunteer who can paddle like you do.'

'Sorry, I'm not really here.' She saw his surprise and grinned. 'As in, I'm only working up here for the next three months. Cumbria isn't permanent for me.'

'Well, I'd still love you to come down, see what we do, and maybe you'd be interested in giving us a few hours while you are here.'

'Maybe I will.' And maybe she wouldn't, Ella thought. She had a feeling Halesmere would be keeping her busy and she didn't really see herself making many friends or getting too tied down before she left.

'Okay. You know where we are if you want to get in touch.' Kev tipped his head, and she lifted a hand as he pushed away, heading north.

She increased her speed, knowing she shouldn't get cold, and saw the ferry with a few foot passengers and a couple of cars making the crossing. The shore was busier as she approached the towns and she turned back, gliding smoothly across the water. Sheep were grazing the fields and she spotted a few deer leaping through woodland as she drifted beneath low branches. So very different to the rivers she was more used to; and she was still thinking about Kev's invitation to his centre when she packed up and drove back to Halesmere.

—

Ever since she had lost Lauren and no longer had someone to share a room with, sleep had been elusive for Ella, and she was used to it. Over the years she'd tried most things to help and occasionally something would work for a while, but then she'd be back to square one, half-awake through the hours of night. The change in her routine while she was at Halesmere was going to take some time to settle into.

She cooked a quick supper in the house, moving a few things around in the new kitchen to make it more intuitive for the guests who would come after her. She'd already explored the bedrooms and found that Max had left her case in the master, which had an en suite with a spectacular roll-top bath and rainwater shower.

When she could no longer ignore the need for sleep, she left the lights on downstairs and placed the Bluetooth speaker playing her favourite tracks beside the bed. Every doorknob squeaked when she turned it, floorboards creaked and shifted beneath her feet and the house itself seemed to be sighing gently. Ella got into bed – and leapt straight back out when there was a smack at one of her windows. A cautious peek round the heavy floral curtain revealed a narrow branch tapping against the glass.

She let out a breath and got back in. The bed was perfect, firm yet soft with pillows to match, sheets warm and luxurious against her skin. She read for a while, caught up on social media and messaged Dylan and her brother. But her mind was still buzzing with uncertainty and there was only one way she could try to settle it.

She pulled on a hat and a coat over her pyjamas and crept back down the wide staircase, grateful for the lights she'd left blazing as she tugged trainers on. She unlocked the front door and stepped out into the icy night. The lime trees edging the drive were still, her breath a thin silver cloud blown into the dark. Frost smothered the cars, glittered on shrubs poised in the garden, as she set off along the drive. She didn't know the landscape well enough to leave the grounds at this time of night and she walked quickly, resisting the desire to increase her speed to a run.

Not a thing seemed to be stirring when she reached the empty lane; she felt like the only person awake and watching the world at this hour. She took a few steps down the road, then changed her mind. She really ought to go back to bed; midnight would soon be past, and she couldn't spend the night marching up and down the drive.

She heard Prim before she saw her as she neared the house. The dog was snuffling in the shrubs beside the cottage and a glance revealed Max framed by light from the hall. Ella paused, waiting for him to call Prim and go inside. But neither he nor Prim seemed to be in any hurry and Ella sidled backwards as Prim wandered towards her. She saw the dog freeze, then her tail shot up and she barked once, cautiously, then let out a volley of noise that had Max running after her.

'Prim, shut up, there's nothing there,' he hissed. 'Be quiet, you'll wake the kids up.'

Ella had been looking for a tree or convenient spot where she might hide, but it was too late. Prim had found her and immediately swapped the barking for a madly wagging tail and a desperate wish to put her paws on Ella's shoulders.

'Who's there?' Max called sharply.

'It's me.' She stepped forward, offering a quick smile she wasn't sure Max would see through the dark. 'Sorry, I didn't mean to set Prim off like that.'

'Ella! You had me worried for a minute, Prim's never barked like that before.'

'Just doing her job, aren't you, girl.' Ella stroked the dog leaning against her legs.

'I suppose.' Max was wearing a T shirt over lounging trousers, and he shivered. 'It's pretty late to be out for a stroll. Couldn't sleep?'

'No,' she admitted. 'Walking usually helps.'

'I work rather than walk when I can't sleep.' He wrapped his arms across his body. 'Not so easy for me to leave the house.'

'Of course.' She thought of his children, cosy in their beds. 'But doesn't working too many hours late at night just make you more tired?'

'Yeah.' She saw the gleam of his smile. 'But I've got two excellent alarm clocks who like crashing on my head first thing, so there's not much danger of me sleeping in.'

A gorgeous new image jumped into Ella's mind, one featuring Max being woken with cuddles and love every morning by Lily and Arlo tumbling over him. 'You're not still working?'

'Just finished. I let Prim out last thing before I head up.' Max stamped his feet, blew out a breath. 'It's freezing. You don't fancy a hot drink, do you?'

Not wise, Ella, she told herself. Not wise at all. But exactly what she wanted and quite possibly just what she needed. 'I'd love one. Maybe not coffee though.'

'No problem. I do a mean hot chocolate, and I could throw in a shot of brandy to warm us up.'

'Perfect.' It was, and Prim seemed delighted to be escorting Ella safely into the cottage instead of seeing her back to the silent house.

Chapter Nine

The family room was very different late at night, lit by only the Christmas tree and soft lights in the kitchen; the atmosphere altered without the children's noise and laughter. Ella only remembered she was still in her cosy pyjamas when she took off her coat to curl up on the sofa. Max was busy in the kitchen and it seemed pointless to offer help for so small a task as hot chocolate.

Prim snuggled down with a deep sigh. Her bed had been moved since Ella was here yesterday and was beside a chair; she assumed it was the one Max had been sitting in. However much he pretended to be grumpy about the dog, he obviously liked keeping Prim close. The stove was burning itself out, the embers a flickering glow behind the glass.

'Thank you.' She accepted the large mug he was offering. 'Candy canes and cream? You're spoiling me.'

'Two kids, remember? I have form.' His smile was wry as he found his phone and turned down the classical music quietly playing, then settled on the sofa to her left. 'And it is getting close to Christmas.'

'Well, you're right, you do make a mean hot chocolate.' Ella loved the warmth of the mug in her hands, that first taste. 'This is amazing.'

'Probably the brandy but I'll take that, coming from a chef like you.' Max held up his mug and she did the same. 'Cheers. This is about as racy as my evenings get.'

'What, the luxurious hot chocolate or sitting with a strange woman in your house wearing her pyjamas?' Ella bit her lip. She'd meant it as a joke, but it sounded rather nosy and flirtatious now she'd said it out loud.

'Oh, the hot chocolate for sure. There's never been a woman, strange or otherwise, sitting in this house at this hour before. Unless you're counting my mother.'

'What were you working on?' She glanced at his laptop. A more professional question this time.

'A planting plan for a new client. It's a difficult site, coastal with very poor soil and a lot of prevailing salty wind.'

'I wouldn't know where to start.'

'I very nearly didn't either, it's a lot different to planting London gardens.'

'I saw your show garden. I thought it was beautiful.'

Ella had checked him out online and seen the exquisite and elegant garden he'd designed for the Chelsea Flower Show, apparently wowing the crowds with his work as much as the television coverage he'd had from the clips and comments she'd found on You Tube. He was clearly very knowledgeable, praising the skills of the team who had built his design and enthusiastic about the role the garden would go on to have with the charity who'd sponsored it. She'd read somewhere there had apparently been an offer of more television work and he'd turned it down.

'That's very kind, thank you. It was incredibly hard work with a lot of stress, and every moment was worth it when we finished and could appreciate the final result. And the gold medal, of course. That helped.'

'Who chose Lion for your company's name? I thought it was inspired, it suits you. Something about your colouring.'

'You're not the first to mention it.' His laugh was light as he pushed a self-conscious hand through his messy blond hair. 'Victoria, my wife, suggested it as it's part of my name.'

'Oh?' Ella hoped he would go on.

'Officially I am Maxence William Lion Bourdon Bentley.'

'Wow. That's a mouthful.'

'Yep. Hence Max. And Lily says Lion suits me because I roar too much.'

'Ah.'

'Quite.' His voice on the single word was a monotone. 'Not a ringing endorsement for her father, is it?'

'She was probably just being mischievous. As she is when she's reminding you about swearing.'

'I think you're being kind, Ella. I have to do better.' Max pursed his lips into something that couldn't quite pass for a smile. 'So you googled me?'

'I did.' She didn't see any point in pretending she hadn't.

'That makes two of us. Seeing as the details about you from my mother were so sketchy, I did a little searching of my own.'

'And what did you find out?' Ella's pulse was beginning to hurry as thoughts of the past filled her mind. Images of all she and Lauren had achieved together were fixed in her heart, she had no wish to discover them online too.

'Well, you were certainly a talented swimmer. I found some old pictures from a meet when you swam for your county. But I didn't know about the rowing medals.' Max's eyes were suddenly more serious. 'It's clear you set out to make a success of everything you do, Ella Grant.'

She gulped down a mouthful of hot chocolate, nearly choking on the cream that came with it. Bloody Google, was there nothing private left? Her own Instagram use was scant and mostly confined to her volunteering or recipes, and she shared her history with so few people. Her parents weren't interested in social media and her brother's Instagram was full of dogs.

'It was ages ago,' she replied casually, aware of Max watching her. 'I gave up rowing competitively when I went to university. You must know what that's like. Life suddenly becomes very different, and you're caught up in everything new.'

'Yes.' He paused. 'Forgive me if I'm treading where I shouldn't but did you and your sister always swim together?'

Ella's fingers trembled around her mug and her eyes felt dry, scratchy. So he'd noticed there were no images of her at meets on her own. 'Yes. I gave up after we lost Lauren. I just didn't have the same focus in the pool without her, we were always on the same team.'

'So you switched to rowing instead?'

Ella's shoulders began to loosen their hold around her ears. Rowing was easier to talk of than her years swimming. 'I love being on the water and I've always had lots of energy; my mum used to say it had to go somewhere.'

'What happened to Lauren, Ella?' Max's voice was very soft. 'You know you don't have to tell me if you'd rather not,' he added.

She normally avoided questions like this as though her own life depended on it, but Max was already different. He understood; his own loss wasn't the same, but it was no less profound or hurtful. 'It was meningitis after an infection, it happened very quickly.' Ella tried to even out the shaky note in her voice. 'All these years later I still find it astonishing to remember how suddenly we went from a family of five to four. You sort of know nothing will ever be the same again but it's almost too unreal to actually believe it. I kept thinking Lauren would just walk in one day and I'd laugh, because how could losing her ever have been real?'

Ella shook her head slowly, trying to sort her thoughts into proper order. 'I felt as though I'd lost half of myself, even though we were different in some ways. She was always persuading Mum to let her try new things in the kitchen, she liked how recipes came together to make something exciting. I didn't have a clear picture of what I wanted to do, and when she died it was obvious to me I should be a chef so her dream wouldn't be lost for ever. I was angry for a long time afterwards and rowing, competing, helped.'

'So you push yourself even harder, to make up for what she couldn't do?' Max's voice was very gentle.

'I really want her to know I've tried my best for both of us. And I've done it. Trained, qualified, done the job, got the T-shirt. Lived the life.'

Ella wasn't prepared for the quick touch of his hand on hers when he leaned across, the simple gesture letting her know he understood. That trying to live her sister's life wasn't as foolish as it sounded when she said it out loud, shared the truth with someone other than her family and Dylan. She'd made friends down the years but there weren't any left from before Lauren, only after. Her own friends now, people who knew her as one person and not half of a pair.

'When do you rest, Ella?' Max's hand retreated to his thigh. 'Do you ever do anything just for you?'

She raised a shoulder. 'I run, swim, I have my kayak. I rest when I can. I'm fine. If you're concerned about my taking care of Lily and Arlo, I would never drive or do something silly if I was overtired.'

'This time I was thinking of you. You don't strike me as someone who'd put anyone else in harm's way. Not after everything you've been through.'

Ella wanted to tell Max not to think of her but perhaps she was reading too much into it and he was only being mindful of her as he would any of his other employees. Would she regret this evening when she had to sit opposite him in his office in a few hours? Would she regret sharing hot chocolate in front of a flickering fire with three stockings hanging from the mantelpiece, the Christmas tree blinking beside the dresser? But she couldn't find regret however much she searched for it. It was too late now, wrapped in the dark of night and confessing thoughts to him that she usually only trusted Dylan or her family to keep safe.

'Are you still interviewing me?' She tried to make the atmosphere easier, appreciating Max's quick smile.

'No. That was a formality and the easiest way to learn more about you without resorting to what Google might give up. And an attempt to remind my mother that she's not the one in charge. She doesn't live in England all year round, however much she tries to support us. Not with this climate. She still has a place in France and she's going next week, but she'll be back in time for Christmas.'

'The interview didn't feel like a formality.' Ella wrinkled her nose. 'It felt pretty rigorous, especially after an eight-hour drive and a night in that flat.'

'Yeah, I'm really sorry you spent two nights in there.' Max shook his head. 'Especially when I knew you'd be staying about five minutes after we first met.'

'You're not serious?' A hand hurried to her hair to push it back. 'After that welcome and you trying to sack me before I'd even started the job?'

'Lily would have disowned me if I'd made you leave.' His reply was at odds with the apology for his behaviour in his gaze, and she felt her stomach plunge at his next words. 'I'm beginning to think you're going to be good for us.' His voice was low as he rushed on. 'Good for Halesmere, as my mother said.'

'Right.' Ella swallowed. His eyes had told her something else, had said that he meant more than the house or perhaps even his children. She stared at her drink, not wanting to reveal she believed it too, not yet. This didn't happen to her. She rarely revealed her heart to anyone, but she knew she didn't regret this private, secret time with him. 'I hope working here will be good for me too. I'm looking forward to getting started.'

Max had finished his hot chocolate and put the empty mug on the coffee table. 'And how is the house? You're the first person to stay in it since the renovations. Are you settling in?'

'Of course.'

'But?'

'There isn't one, I'm fine.'

'Sure about that? I just found you on the drive in your pyjamas close to midnight. I'd hazard a guess that you were in bed and didn't want to stay there.' His eyes were fixed on hers and she heard the concern beneath his words. 'What's bothering you, Ella? Will I have to send Prim over every night to make sure you're okay and not roaming the gardens in the dark?'

'You'd do that?' Of course he wouldn't, he was being kind. Or thought she was ridiculous.

'If I was concerned about you. Are you going to tell me?'

Ella was watching Prim. The dog let out a contented sigh as she shuffled into a comfier position. 'I'm not a great sleeper, that's all. I don't really like being alone at night.' She clarified, before he thought she was in the habit of dragging just anyone into her bed: 'I like knowing there's someone else in the building with me. I've always shared.'

She knew it was foolish, and yet not. She'd only ever confessed it to the one boyfriend with whom she'd been in love, a long time ago. When their relationship had ended and he'd told her how pathetic she was, she had never spent the whole night with anyone other than Dylan again.

'Because you shared a room with Lauren?' Max's eyes were laced with sympathy. 'And I've shoved you in that great big house all by yourself. I'm sorry, Ella. That's why you were out walking late.'

'You were being kind and I appreciate it. It's been twenty years; it really is time I learned how to be alone.' She offered him a tremulous smile. 'And your mother did say something about you not letting me stay in the flat for long.'

'She's an interfering bloody nuisance sometimes, she really is.' He raised a hand. 'I know, that's another pound for the dog shelter. And probably unfair of me, given that she moved up here from London to help us out.'

'I wasn't going to remind you about the swearing this time.' Ella liked how he smiled at her gentle tease.

'Then maybe I should make it two pounds.'

Their chocolate finished, she knew this was the moment she should leave. She couldn't deny she was more settled and relaxed in this moment, liking the thought of Max being just across the drive from her. She knew now she could knock on his door if she needed to, could trust him not to mock or send her away. But sitting here as night inched towards day, his children sleeping upstairs, felt easy and right and she didn't want to go. She waited for him to show her politely to the door and confirm their meeting for the morning.

And when he reached a gentle hand down to Prim and closed his eyes, Ella understood he too didn't want her to leave. Maybe he just wanted to chat with a person who wasn't a child or wayward parent, or a client he needed to manage. The thought both thrilled and terrified her as she stared at the hair falling to his brow, just like Arlo's. She wanted to smooth it from Max's face, let her hand linger on the contours of his cheek. Her heart hammering with the realisation, she clenched her fingers together.

'What are you thinking?'

Hastily she dropped her gaze. Had he seen her staring, read the thoughts written on her face? 'Nothing much.'

'Right.' He opened one eye. 'Do you want to know what I was thinking?'

'I don't know. Do I?' She tried to make it a joke.

'I was thinking this weekend is the first time I've begun to see Halesmere as home. That maybe it will turn out all right for the three of us and it wasn't a mistake, coming here.' The seconds lengthened until both eyes were open and Ella saw his bright blue gaze was weighted with the pain of the loss he would always carry, just like her. 'We found out Victoria had cancer when Arlo was three months old and spent the next two years trying to find ways to fight it.'

'Max, I'm so very sorry.' Ella's voice was a whisper, her words almost pointless. A different story, the same ending.

'I know. And thank you.' He was staring straight ahead. Prim nudged his hand, as though reminding him she was still there and offering what comfort she could. 'Victoria was a GP, and she had a good idea about it straight away.' He swallowed. 'It was longer before I could accept it, not that I think I ever did. We didn't get many years or any time in remission. We had a toddler and a new baby and suddenly she was ill. I look back and it's almost as though I'm seeing someone else's life, because what did hospitals and scans and treatment have to do with us just wanting to be a normal family?'

He raised his shoulders, a helpless gesture, not enough to convey the hurt hovering in his eyes. 'And now the three of us are here, supposedly finding more time together as a family. A new beginning, creating new memories while trying to hang on to some of the old ones. The happy ones, not the others.'

'And it's not that simple, is it?' Ella's parents had lived in the same house all her life and she knew she'd have to hide her reluctance if they ever wanted to sell it. Her memories of Lauren were bound up in their old home and she felt closer to her twin there than anywhere else, the too-short life they had shared. 'Halesmere was a lot to take on, Max. I can see why your mother wanted you to have some help.'

'And what will I do with it all, Ella?' He shook his head wearily. 'I thought I could practise here, throw a website together to keep the house occupied and find a use for the studios. But most days it seems enough just to feed Lily and Arlo three times, make sure they've done their homework and check I haven't forgotten something crucial for a client.

'I feel as though I'm failing them, not being the father they deserve, especially after losing their mum.' Max let out a long breath. 'I want them to grow up with a proper sense of my being present in their lives, not someone who works too much and roars at the dog when I'm tired. They'd wanted a puppy for ever and I can hear myself spoiling it for them when I'm frustrated with Prim.

'Other than the kids making friends at school, I haven't got to know many people apart from Stan and Pearl. He chivvies me along and Pearl pops in with a meal for us sometimes, they've really helped. I live in this wonderful environment, and I feel as though it's all passing me by. Like I'm still just a visitor and we'll go home again one day.'

Ella was remembering her excitement when she'd first found the job, the opportunity to explore this exceptional landscape as it reached out to speak straight to her heart. Max didn't know what it was to have the breath of a new adventure blown into his day quite like she did. How could he when he had so much to take care of?

'Sometimes I wonder if we should've stayed in London and just carried on.' His gaze was heavy with indecision. 'But then we take Prim out and I watch Lily and Arlo racing around with her, finding things to show me, and I see the joy she brings them. The space and freedom they have here is so different to what they're used to. We walk to school, which we never did in London, and we bump into people along the way they've already made friends with. Then it feels right, like they really are going to find their way here and they'll be okay.'

'And maybe it's just you that'll still be lost?' Ella's words were a whisper as his gaze clung to hers.

'Maybe. What if I'm really meant to be alone, Ella? Alone was always my default from being a kid. Boarding school, parents travelling, only child until my father met someone else. Victoria changed that for a while and now I have Lily and Arlo to take care of. Alone doesn't hurt as much as a broken heart. I can live with alone as long as they're okay.' Prim sighed as she clambered onto the sofa. Ella could have sworn the dog knew Max needed someone beside him. She snuggled up and nudged his hand until it was gently stroking her head. 'It's like you said before, about Lauren, and the life she'd wanted.'

Ella liked how Max used her sister's name, spoke about her as the real person she'd been, not someone whose existence was measured by the space she'd left in the lives of those who loved her.

'It's not just about what we lose but the lives they should have had too. Every milestone, every moment sometimes with the children, reminds me of what Victoria's missing. Every time they laugh, or Lily tells me off, or I see a glimpse of Victoria's smile in Arlo's. Their eyes, their hair, even, red just like hers was.' His voice caught and he swallowed. 'I wish every single day she could see how amazing they are.'

'Oh, Max.' Ella couldn't help her arm reaching across and lessening the distance between them. She wasn't expecting him to wind his fingers through hers or see the glimmer of tears in his eyes before they separated. 'I'm sorry.'

'She'd be so proud of them, how they're coping, and I know she'd be telling me to go easier on myself. Look at how far we've come, not how far we've still got to go.

This is their life now, one without their mum, and she loved them so much.' He shrugged helplessly. 'One foot in front of the other every day and remembering how to breathe. That's what they say, isn't it?'

'Yes. Keep moving forward. Find the light, avoid the shadows.' Ella's voice was soft, her eyes awash with tears she didn't often cry now. Sometimes it still felt as though she were living without half of her soul, and Max had lost his soulmate too. And Lily and Arlo, living lives made less ordinary because their mum wasn't there to meet them at the school gate and badger them about homework, or bake their favourite cakes, tuck them in at night and tell them she loved them after a bedtime story.

'This is quite the conversation for a Sunday night.' Max offered Ella a smile and her own followed. 'Let's hope we both of us sleep.'

'I should go. It's late and you're probably going to have those two alarm clocks going off early.' She stood up and Prim raised a sleepy head from Max's thigh as though surprised that Ella should want to head outside again. She slipped her coat on, her mind full of all they'd shared, confessed, understood now about the other.

'I'm sorry if you've told me about Lauren when you'd rather not have done.' Max followed Ella to the front door, his arm skimming her face as he reached past her to unlock it.

'It's fine.' And she realised it was. Lauren was half of her heart and Ella brought her to life now with so few people. The icy air wrapped her in its grip as she stepped outside and she shivered. 'I'm sorry about—'

'Don't say it.' Max laid a palm on her cheek, gone the instant she registered its warmth. 'No more loss, no more sorry. Let's both keep moving forward out of the shadows.'

He hesitated. 'Will you be okay, in the house? You can borrow Prim if it helps.'

'That's kind but I think she'd rather be with you.' Ella was still sensing his touch on her skin as she turned away, the memory of it a heat fending off the chill.

Chapter Ten

'So, is there anything you think sets Halesmere apart from other holiday properties in Cumbria?'

It was Monday morning, and Ella and Max were in his office. He'd texted earlier, asking if she'd mind putting the coffee on while he took the children to school. When he'd arrived, she was seated opposite his desk, her laptop open and a notebook to hand. As he settled in his chair and thanked her politely for the drink, she hoped she was projecting more professionalism than she was feeling after their time together last night.

'Can I come back to that after I've had my coffee?'

'If it will help.' She liked the quick smile as he put his glasses on and flipped his own laptop open.

'Did you sleep?' Max was brisk as he picked up his cup.

'Eventually.' Was she imagining the quick glimpse of understanding in his glance? 'Did you?'

'Same.'

Ella hadn't been thinking quite so much about being alone in the big, empty house when she'd returned. Instead she'd fallen asleep remembering his understanding about Lauren, the new life he was trying to make for him and his children. The hot chocolate they'd shared and how his sympathy had warmed her as much as the drink after her short, sharp walk. It was madness to wonder if he'd done the same.

'What was the question again?' He picked up a pencil, put it down to cover a yawn with his hand. 'Sorry. Those alarm clocks did go off pretty early.'

'That's okay. I'm sorry if I kept you up.' Ella was doing it again, picturing the children tumbling into his bed to wake him, and she quickly banished the images from her mind.

'There are hundreds of holiday properties in Cumbria, and I wondered if you think there's anything that might make Halesmere different?'

'Location?'

'Not enough on its own. Spend five minutes online and you'll find lots of cottages with locations just as stunning.' She was starting to enjoy this and took a sip of her coffee, ready for the hit. She'd gone for a run early this morning and felt refreshed, alert from the exertion. Stan had tried to waylay her as she'd returned, and she'd promised to speak to him later. 'Something else?'

'Price?'

Ella pursed her lips. 'Depends. It's a big house and you might not want to be too competitive if you're planning to keep the roof on.'

'Right. Good point. There's only so far the value of two London houses can go.' Max tried again. 'Quality? As in proper mattresses, nice bedding and all that stuff?'

'No, lots of people do that and more. Come on Max, you bought a holiday business, or the potential for one. Didn't you do any research?'

'It's very early for you to be asking me all this,' he grumbled, finishing his coffee in one gulp.

Ella wasn't fooled; she'd seen the smile he was trying to hide behind the cup. 'You haven't read the notes I emailed, have you?'

'Sorry.' He was sheepish now. 'Can I plead two young children and the weekend moving you out of that flat as my excuse?'

'Really? Moving me took you all of three-quarters of an hour, and Lily and Arlo helped.'

'Oh, that's right, they did. Managed to cart a couple of bags across the courtyard, dumped them the minute we were through the door and then took off. I think you'll have to enlighten me.'

Ella touched her laptop, waking it up. 'I know all but one of the artists who were here left when the house was sold. Once the builders have finished with the studios, I think attracting more artists should be a priority. That and sorting out the website so potential guests can start booking for next year.'

'But what difference would more artists make to the house? I can see guests wandering round, maybe buying something, but it's hardly going to be the Tate, is it?' He raised a shoulder. 'And don't tell my mother I said that, either. Her work is still very collectable, and her London gallery is already gearing up for her new exhibition.'

'Is it?' Ella had forgotten about the life-modelling idea and put that worry aside for now; Max probably hadn't been serious about her sitting for his mother. 'And you're right, not everyone who comes to stay will be interested in the studios. But there should definitely be links to the artists' own social media on your website.'

'So what would you say might make Halesmere different?' he asked.

'I'm no expert but I did have a good look around yesterday afternoon. Stan opened the barn for me, it's an amazing space. And as you already have planning permission for change of use, you could hold exhibitions or run courses in there. What if Halesmere could become a hub for creatives to showcase their skills and sell their products? And not just artists but local food producers like Rowan, who's growing her bakery business and already supplies the community shop.'

'Go on.' Max propped his arms on the desk and Ella knew she'd captured his interest.

'Holiday bookings are always going to fluctuate across the seasons but you have the perfect potential to offer the house to those who want to take a course and learn something new, with artists based here year-round. Create short-stay packages, maybe self-catering, catered or luxury, and connect with local guides to take guests hiking or wild swimming. Then there's the possibility of running retreats. The barn would be ideal for yoga or Pilates, maybe wellness or mindfulness, or even a mini festival. You could offer special packages and experiences for Christmas and New Year. Imagine the house decorated for the holidays and those images on your social media.'

Max leaned back, eyes wide behind his glasses. 'Wow. I think you've blown my mind. I hadn't thought of even half of this.'

'It depends on what you want to offer, of course, and who would run it for you,' Ella added quickly. 'I'm conscious of your own practice and if you just want to book the house out for guests without offering anything else, then that's fine.'

'I'd need to think about it and hear more, but I like your ideas, Ella. I'm impressed.'

'I'm pleased you're pleased.' She felt a gratifying warmth stealing across her skin. 'I was hoping for a "that's interesting", so I'll definitely take a "wow."'

'And so you should. Have you seriously come up with all of this since Friday?'

'Not all of it. And seeing the house and courtyard in person has helped. But don't forget I've sat in loads of event planning meetings and I know people adore something different. Especially if they find some special touches they aren't expecting, like that first meal in the fridge, fresh fruit, chilled wine, a bedtime book for children, a handwritten welcome note letting them know what's on in the area, a discount if they rebook within a certain time. Once you have artists in the studios,' she went on, 'you could make sure you use their products in the house and offer one as a gift to take home, maybe a candle or a few chocolates. You could provide personal recommendations for restaurants and pubs, why you like them, and create packages for special anniversaries and romantic proposals.'

'I should've asked for help with that one. I just asked Victoria to marry me after we'd had our first scan with Lily. We were still in the hospital car park.'

'That's romantic in its own way.' Ella felt a rush of sadness at the picture Max painted of proposing to the mother of his first child, elated by the new life they'd created and the future they wanted to share as a family. 'But I'd probably leave out the car park thing for guests who might want to propose here.'

'Agreed.' She saw him blink away the reminder of Victoria. 'Is there anything else?'

'The pub up the road, the White Hart. Do you know most of its reviews are five star, and that food and service, along with value, consistently score highly?'

'I didn't.'

'It's a twenty-minute walk along a lovely lane, shorter if you take the footpath, and that's a huge advantage to

Halesmere. You should point guests in their direction, particularly with the range of craft beers they brew themselves. I checked if they sell them online and they do, but not in any other pubs or restaurants. So I'd be giving guests a free sample and making sure they know where to enjoy them alongside a meal within walking distance.'

'Have you been to the pub already?' Max's gaze on Ella's was surprised. 'You really have had a busy weekend.'

'I haven't yet, but those hours when I can't sleep are useful for something.' She dragged her eyes from his. 'And the community shop is a mine of information, there's so much going on.'

'Is there?' Max looked blank. 'Think I've only been in about twice.'

'Then that ought to change,' she told him briskly. 'You should shop there, at least for some things. And they'll deliver within a few miles. They're really switched on to how to reach people and make themselves relevant in an online world. The shop is packed full of local suppliers, and we should approach them to see how we can offer support and vice versa. I've got a meeting with the local baker and a woman who makes candles later.'

Ella had googled Rowan, the young baker Pearl had told her about, and discovered a burgeoning business and a growing reputation. Rowan's Instagram was full of gorgeous images of delicious-looking bread, and Ella had seen the appeal at once. She'd emailed Rowan to introduce herself and they'd set up a meeting at the bakery, hoping Rowan would supply Halesmere. Ella couldn't imagine many people would turn down a fresh sourdough loaf sitting in their kitchen when they arrived for a holiday or weekend of tramping the fells. She'd also arranged to meet up with Marta, who made the candles, near the college where she taught.

'Did you know that Halesmere has an account with the shop?'

'No. But as we don't shop there, nobody will have been using it.'

'Ah.'

'Let me guess. You're already using the account I didn't know we had and have no idea how to pay?'

'So, not so slow this morning then, hey?' That came out more flirtatiously than Ella had meant but she couldn't regret the low chuckle it elicited from Max. 'And you really should shop there. I know you won't get everything but it's so important to support local producers and you might be surprised by what's on offer.'

'I'll definitely try it.' He leaned forward, pressing his hands into a steeple. 'If I asked how you think we might encourage more artists to Halesmere, would you have an answer? And local producers too?'

'Of course.' Ella was two steps ahead of him. 'Have you ever been to a supper club?'

—

'Hey, Stan the man! You busy?'

Ella saw him grin as he climbed out of the red pickup parked beside his workshop. 'Never 'eard that one before,' he called as she caught up with him.

'I could do with borrowing you for a bit.'

'I thought things were lookin' up since you got 'ere, young Ella.' His eyes lit up and she knew she had his interest. 'What do you want me for?'

'Pearl was telling me about you being a brilliant carpenter. How do you fancy making some new doors for the barn? Those old ones are very nearly past it and we could do with the space being weatherproof as soon as possible.'

'Could we?' Stan unlocked the door of his workshop. The donkey jacket was back on, and he'd added a thick woolly hat in bright green for good measure. 'You comin' in for a brew so you can tell me what it's all about?'

'I'd love a brew, thanks.' Ella noticed a large box sitting open on the floor. 'So you got your chainsaw then?'

'Aye.' He gave the box a loving glance. 'I've got some Christmas trees to cut down. What's this about new barn doors?'

'They need a proper job, Stan. Someone like you who knows what he's doing.'

'Do they? Well, you've come to the right bloke then. Tea or coffee? Or Bovril?'

'Tea please.' She settled on a stool, glad of the stove that was quietly burning and throwing out welcome heat. She'd had enough coffee for now and tea would make a pleasant change. 'I've never tried Bovril.'

'It's either that or the tea.' Stan was rinsing out mugs in a tiny sink and Ella resisted the urge to shudder; the mugs looked like they'd never seen a dishwasher or boiling water. 'I 'aven't got any coffee.'

'Then why did you ask me if I wanted it?'

'It's good manners to offer me visitors a choice, so Pearl keeps tellin' me. An' it stops the boss 'angin' around an' checkin' up on me if I 'aven't got coffee for 'im to drink. Max doesn't like Bovril. Can't think why not.'

Stan's grin was merry as Ella accepted a mug of tea and a home-made mince pie he produced out of a tin. The pie was outstanding, with perfect shortcrust pastry, and she told him so. 'It even makes up for offering me coffee you haven't got.'

'I'll tell Pearl, she'll be 'appy to 'ear it.' He dropped into a worn armchair. Every scrap of space was neatly arranged, and there was a tidy workbench, a piece of wood clamped in a vice with a hand plane nearby and shavings on the floor. 'So what's with the barn, then? Why do we suddenly need new doors?'

'We're having an Artisan Christmas Open Day.' Ella sipped her tea. It was just how she liked it, dark and strong, and she couldn't help wondering if Stan always brewed tea that way. She was smiling at the thought of his disgust if she asked him for milky and pale instead.

'An' what's 'appenin' on this open day?'

'I'll come back to you on that if I may. But how do you fancy joining me at the pub for dinner and a team meeting one night? I thought it might be nice to get everyone together there and go through some plans.'

'An' who's on this team then?'

'Are you always this suspicious, Stan?' Ella spotted a range of small, hand-carved animals on a shelf. They were beautiful, delicate and lifelike. 'Did you make those? They're lovely.'

'Aye, when I 'ave a few minutes spare.'

'Are you coming to the pub or not?'

'Who's payin'?'

'Me, of course. I wouldn't expect Max to without asking him first.'

'Aye, I'll come. Anyone else you want me to fetch?'

'Anyone you think might be interested in helping Halesmere support local arts and food producers.'

'An' who would I know who does that?'

She gave him a smile and put her mug down. 'Because you know everyone, Stan, and I think you might just be Halesmere's secret weapon.'

'Am I?' His chin rose a fraction at her praise. 'Aye, well, Pearl always said I was dangerous.' He winked. 'If you know what I mean.'

'I get the picture very clearly.' Ella winked back and saw him grin. 'Let's talk about those barn doors – and the big window frame at the back is rotting too.'

'I can't be too long.' Stan checked a wooden clock on the wall. 'Noelle needs me for me sittin'.'

'You what?' Ella nearly choked on her last mouthful of mince pie and a few crumbs hit the sawdust on the floor. 'Did I hear you right?'

'Can't say, Ella, you'll just 'ave to wait an' see. Noelle says she's puttin' me in 'er exhibition. I'm keepin' me 'at on.' He pulled a face, head on one side. 'It's not a five-minute job, you know, them doors.'

'I do.' Ella had almost recovered from the idea of Stan sitting for Noelle and quickly explained her ideas. He was enthusiastic, telling her he didn't really have enough to do and was afraid of being forced to retire, or 'slung on the slag 'eap', as he preferred to call it. They parted a few minutes later and Ella headed back to the house. She had work to do and for that she needed Wi-Fi.

–

Rowan was younger than Ella expected when they met in her unit on the tiny industrial estate on the edge of town, probably mid-twenties, with short brunette hair and warm hazel eyes. She was very happy to show Ella around her bakery and interested to hear of her career and what had brought her to Halesmere. She wasn't familiar with the house and accepted an invitation to the supper Ella was planning next month, and they promised to keep in touch.

Ella carried on into town and found the coffee shop where she and Marta had arranged to meet to discuss the candles Ella had found in the community shop. The cafe, just up the road from the college where Marta taught, was all pale wood and Scandi in style with Christmas decorations to match, not the cosy country tearoom Ella had been expecting. She recognised Marta from her social media, sitting at a table at the back, and headed over.

'Hi, I'm Ella.' She offered a hand and Marta took it, standing to greet her with a grin.

'Ella, hi, come and join me. Marta.' Marta pushed a laptop and a glass of water out of the way. 'I haven't ordered yet. I can recommend the Florentines if you'd like a treat.'

'That sounds perfect, I'd love one.' Ella still felt a little tired after the late night with Max, and she thought the sugar might help. She took a notebook from her bag. 'Thank you for agreeing to see me.'

'A pleasure. My candles have become a bit of an obsession, so it's lovely to chat to someone who's happy to listen.' Marta's rich dark hair suited her colouring, and her eyes were a velvety brown above full lips. She had an attractive and expressive face, and Ella already sensed they were going to get on.

'Pearl said you make them alongside your career at the college?'

'Yes, I teach art and design. Full-time, so evenings and weekends are often spent pouring.' Marta beamed at the waitress who'd come over, and she and Ella both ordered

Florentines with flat whites. 'One of those hobbies that quickly became a passion. I gave some to friends and before I knew it, I was getting requests that turned into orders and now I have a website.'

'How brilliant. I've seen the website and I'm following you on Instagram. Your social media is gorgeous, and the candles are so elegant and simple. I'm already part way down my first, I light it whenever I'm in the house.'

'Thank you, Ella, I'm so happy you're enjoying it. Which one did you choose?'

'Autumn. It's lovely, it reminds me of being outdoors crunching through leaves and the scent of berries.'

Marta clapped her hands together. 'Then you have the meaning exactly. I was trying to capture the warmth of amber with the scent of moss I find everywhere here.' She wrinkled her nose. 'So many stone walls, so many ancient woodlands.'

Their coffees arrived and Ella picked up her delicate Florentine, already detecting the aroma of dark chocolate and ginger. 'I read on your website that you're inspired by the Cumbrian landscape?'

'Yes, so very different to San Sebastián, where I grew up.' Marta wiped a trace of coffee from her lips. 'I see you wondering how I ended up living in the damp English Lake District instead of the Spanish sunshine.'

'I was. I'm sorry, I don't mean to be nosy.'

'It is fine, Ella. I do not think I would be pouring candles if I were still at home in Spain, there is much more warmth and light there.' The waitress came to check if there was anything else they needed, and Marta assured her they were fine. 'I had a pen pal who lived here, and I came to visit him when I was seventeen. I fell in love.'

'With your pen pal?'

'No, firstly with Cumbria and then with his cousin Luke.' Marta's face was lively with amusement. 'My pen pal was very nice, and we still see one another occasionally. But his cousin, now he was very different!' She raised her hands. 'And we are still together after all these years and somehow, I have become the partner of a shepherd who works crazy hours and loves his dogs at least as much as me. A romantic tale, yes?'

'Definitely.'

'I think so too.' She pulled a face. 'A bit less romantic in the middle of a freezing night in March when I am lambing a sheep.'

'I bet you don't put that in your candles.'

Marta roared, throwing back her head, dark hair tumbling over her shoulders. 'No, Ella, I do not. It is a smell all of its own and one that I do not want in the house, hence my obsession with candles.' She held out an arm. 'I have small hands and Luke does not. Small hands can be helpful for lambing.'

'I had no idea.' Ella had little experience of farm animals, just the pets they'd had at home.

'Sorry, I am changing the subject.' Marta checked her phone. 'I will have to get back to college soon. Pearl told me about your role at Halesmere, Ella. How might I be of interest and help you?'

'You know that Max is relaunching the holiday business in the New Year?'

'Yes, we have met him. Luke's brother has a landscaping company and he is working with Max now. Our farm is only a couple of miles from Halesmere. I think you will be good for the holiday business, Ella, I can tell that already through your enthusiasm.'

'I hope so, otherwise I won't be there long.' She was sharply reminded she wasn't meant to be long at Halesmere anyway. 'I've suggested to Max that having new artists based around the courtyard could be a great way to bring the house and studios together by offering retreats and courses. There's a huge barn just sitting empty, and I'd love to offer guests an opportunity to shop local and fill the house with little touches they can take home.'

'Like my candles?'

'Exactly. I know the chocolates in the community shop are produced nearby and the craft beer at the pub is brewed on site. To give you some context, I used to be a chef.' Ella took a breath. There it was again. *Used to be.* 'A chef for an events company, and it's often something different, something intangible that sets a venue apart. Location perhaps, the landscape, hiking – the house has all of those, but I'd like to offer guests more. A more personal experience, something that feels tailored to Halesmere. I'm already learning what an incredible food and arts culture there is here, and I think we could be a part of that.'

'That sounds wonderful, Ella. So why not come and see me at home? I will show you my candles and we can talk about how I can help.' Marta scribbled something on a card she'd produced from her bag. 'In the meantime, would you do something for me?'

'Of course.'

'Please email my colleague Leah, who is the course leader at the catering school at the college. They regularly bring in guest chefs to teach the students and I think she would leap at the chance to work with you.'

Chapter Eleven

'Ella! I need you!'

The following morning, Ella, on her way to find Stan, saw Noelle emerging from the house looking worryingly determined.

'Now is a good time to see my studio, *non*?' She was enveloped in a fringed tartan cape today, her hair captured inside a turban. Ella spotted Stan heading off in his pickup down the drive and her heart sank. She'd missed him and now Noelle wanted to drag Ella up to her studio and make her do heaven knows what once she'd got her inside.

'Actually Noelle, I'm really busy, if you don't mind. I don't want Max to think I'm skiving.'

'What is this skiving?' Noelle frowned. 'Maxence, he does not have the monopoly on your time, Ella. It was my idea to bring you here and there are occasions when I may need you as well. Like now.'

'I've got a meeting with someone about the open day in a bit.' In a couple of hours actually, but Noelle didn't need to know that.

She planted slim hands mostly free of paint on her hips. 'What has Max been saying to you about me?'

'Max?' Ella would really prefer it if her senses didn't leap into high alert whenever his name was mentioned. Reminders of their conversation on Sunday evening still slipped into her mind at the most awkward of times. Like now, facing his mother and catching a resemblance of his eyes in hers, flashing with impatience. 'Oh er, not much. He just mentioned your exhibition and how busy you are painting. I'd hate to hold you up.'

'Ella, you look like a frightened rabbit whenever I speak of my studio.' Noelle slapped her thigh and chuckled. 'Has Max told you that I want you to sit for me and that I like to paint nudes?'

'Something like that.' Ella felt about ten years old as her face flushed. Noelle would think she was a very gauche young woman who'd never had her share of excitements. Actually, maybe some of that was true. And sitting for Noelle would certainly be up there on Ella's very short list of trying something daring and new.

'Silly boy, he just does it to annoy me. Ella, *oui*, I would love to paint you. *Non*, it does not have to be nude.' Noelle winked. 'Not unless you would like that?'

'Better not.' Ella's pulse began to settle. 'I might be able to manage the sitting bit but I'm not sure I like the idea of anyone seeing it afterwards.'

'*Assez juste*. Then we will improvise. I have some beautiful couture gowns from my days modelling, and I am certain I will find one to suit you. Does that sound better? Would you sit for me in a gown?'

'I think I would, yes.' Ella knew nothing about couture, but this plan of Noelle's sounded as though it could be fun. 'You were a model?'

'*Oui*, until I fell pregnant with Max and then those days were over. So, we will leave the studio for today as you are so very busy with your new job but come and have some tea with me tomorrow morning, and I will show the gowns to you then.'

'That sounds lovely.'

'You are collecting the children this afternoon and giving them tea, *non*?'

'I am.' Max had caught up with Ella yesterday after she'd returned from town and asked her if she would do today as a trial run. Her new DBS hadn't arrived yet, but she'd emailed him a copy of her previous one, which was less than three years old.

'Thank you, Ella.' Noelle suddenly looked stricken. 'I must make more time with them, but it is difficult, to stop working at three p.m. when I am painting. I cannot always recapture that moment in quite the same way when I return, and I am sometimes too tired to paint in the evenings and the light is terrible here in winter. I will do Thursday this week as usual and then I will be away. I must be ready for the exhibition and then I can step back.'

And Noelle was gone as suddenly as she'd arrived, her cape billowing in the damp breeze as she disappeared to her flat and the door clattered behind her.

Ella returned to the house and began looking up the other local suppliers she'd found in the community shop. Max had agreed to her hosting a supper next month and she planned to invite some producers and create a delicious menu to highlight their work. She also googled the local catering college and discovered it had an excellent reputation for teaching young people with a passion for hospitality, and that students were often snapped up by local businesses straight after graduating.

That gave her an idea and she emailed the course leader, Leah, offering her services as a guest chef as Marta had suggested. She hoped that if she made this contact she might be able to ask some students to help at the supper, both with front of house and cooking. She also found an agency further north who specialised in private staff and made some notes; she was thinking of a third, luxury package for potential retreat guests and a butler might be a nice touch.

She felt decidedly conspicuous as she walked down to the primary school later. Encouraged by Noelle, whom Ella had spotted enticing Stan upstairs to sit for her again, she'd collected Prim from the cottage and brought her along. Prim was delighted to be out, always ready to go faster, and as Ella had her trainers on she began to run with Prim following at her side. It was fun, if she didn't count the hairy moment when they had to dodge a van after Prim spotted a squirrel racing up a tree, and they were soon at the little school a mile from the house. Ella hung around at the back of the crowd gathered outside the playground, conscious of curiosity from the other adults. One or two came over to make a fuss of Prim, who happily lapped it all up. The church was next door to the school, and it sat square in the middle of the dark churchyard.

'Ella!'

She heard Lily's shout and searched among the bustle of children spilling from the building. Lily ran from the playground and Arlo joined them moments later, each trailing lunch bags and reading bags as well as hats and scarves they didn't want to wear.

'Hey you two, how was your day?' Ella wasn't expecting the armfuls of stuff flung her way. She gathered it all together as the children bent down to cuddle Prim, who was predictably thrilled to see them.

'Good but we had to do PE inside cos it was raining, and then it was wet play at lunchtime and the teacher put *Frozen* on.' Lily pulled a disgusted face. 'It's SO boring and I hope I never have to watch it again.'

'Right.' Ella had never seen it. Without nieces or nephews, she had little experience of recent or current family movies. 'And how about you, Arlo. Was your day fun?'

He nodded, and she wanted to smooth back the hair flopping to his brows. His eyes were tired, and he looked a little worried. 'Are you making tea for us?' he asked hopefully. 'Mamie said you would be.'

'I am. How does pasta and roasted vegetables sound?'

'Good,' Arlo confirmed.

Lily took Prim's lead and once Ella had checked for non-existent traffic, they set off. The afternoon was already going dark, brightened only by lights from the occasional house or vehicle along the lane. Max had texted Ella to say he'd be home around six, and she planned to leave him and the children to enjoy their evening.

'Will Daddy be home before I have to go to bed, Ella?'

'I hope so. I know he doesn't want to be late and miss you.' She looked at Arlo. 'He had to meet a client at their house who couldn't see him until this afternoon. And I'll be staying with you until then as your grandmother's painting.' She thought it better not to mention Noelle was probably painting Stan; it might produce more questions than she knew how to answer from this inquisitive pair.

They strolled along, with Lily and Prim exploring verges smothered in soggy leaves and damp grass. It wasn't long before Ella felt Arlo's cold little hand inside hers. She'd wanted to hold it but hadn't dared try for fear of treading where he might not want her. She squeezed his fingers to let him know she liked it and saw his shy smile. She'd noticed some of the other children wandering off hand in hand with their mums and had gulped back the rush of emotion at the sharp reminder of Lily and Arlo being unable to do the same.

Once back at the cottage there was a minor battle over how much stuff the children were allowed to dump in the hall, and Ella got them to put away their bags before they went off to shut up the chickens. The birds were already inside their wooden shed and Lily informed her that Stan often helped to feed them when Max wasn't around. Back at the cottage, Lily fed Prim, and Ella soon had the vegetables roasting nicely in the oven while she prepared the pasta for cooking. Arlo was doing homework at the island and Lily joined him, and Ella gave them a bowl of snacks to keep them going until tea.

The stove was laid with logs and she lit it, switching on the fairy lights strung across the dresser, and the Christmas tree lights, making the family room feel snug and warm. Lily had soon finished her homework, and put a playlist of Christmas songs on her iPad and showed Ella a few of her best dance moves, managing to persuade Ella to join in. She was trying her best to copy Lily's choreography to a song being performed at the school nativity next month – it seemed to involve a lot of arm movements and a fair bit of hopping – and they were all laughing when Max burst through the door from the hall and stopped dead, his messenger bag hitting the floor.

Ella's eyes shot over to his and she froze at the shock she read in them. The music was still going, and she hadn't heard the bang of the front door announcing his arrival over the din. Lily, Arlo and Prim all raced over, and he hurriedly dropped down to hug them as Prim tried to clamber onto his knee. Ella went to the oven to check on the vegetables and get the pasta going. She hovered beside the hob as she heard him asking the children about their day and if their rehearsal for the nativity had gone well.

'Really well, Daddy, I was just practising "Rockin' around the Christmas Tree" with Ella.' Lily grabbed his hand, tugging him over to the kitchen. 'Watch us, Daddy, please. Ella was really good.'

'Oh, I can't, Lily, I'm sorry.' Ella tried to soften her refusal with a smile, not certain Max would appreciate her dancing with his daughter. 'The vegetables are nearly ready, and I can't leave the pasta boiling on its own with you guys nearby.'

'I'll watch it.' He shrugged out of his coat and joined her on the other side of the island, sending her pulse leaping a level at the flare of awareness in his eyes, red-rimmed with tiredness. 'You looked like you needed the practice when I came in.'

'Hey, that's not fair,' Ella protested. His arm brushed hers as he glanced at the pasta. Even through the aroma of the vegetables and herbs roasting in the oven, she caught traces of the cologne he wore, reminding her of something warm and woody with a suggestion of vanilla.

Max scooped out a bit of penne from the pan and tasted it. 'Not quite there, chef. You go ahead with Lily; I don't think even I can burn this.'

'Yes! Come on, Ella.' Lily needed no further encouragement and Ella had little choice other than to line up. Lily insisted on doing the routine twice and although Ella had got it pretty quickly the first time round, her movements felt awkward and less natural with Max watching, leaning on the Aga with folded arms.

'What do you think, Daddy?' Lily went to her iPad to turn down the music.

'Brilliant, Lily, I think you'll smash it at the nativity. You were fantastic.' He gave the pasta a prod.

'But what about Ella? Wasn't she good too?'

Ella was hovering at one end of the island, watching Arlo. He'd finished his bit of homework and was using a tractor to load bales into a trailer. She pushed a couple of bales towards him, and he dropped one and tried again.

'Well, let's just say she's a great chef, Lily, hey? That pizza the other night was amazing. Dance moves, not so much.'

'Thanks a lot.' Ella heard Lily's gasp of laughter and saw her give Max an astonished look. 'I bet your dad's moves are rubbish, Lily.'

'They are not. I do a mean salsa and my waltz is pretty good too.'

Was he flirting with her? His lowered voice and suddenly lazy smile certainly felt that way. Ella felt a warmth stealing through her, couldn't resist her retort. 'Then be my guest, Mr Strictly, give it your best. Let's see what you've got. I'll watch the pasta.'

It was ready when she checked, and she turned it off. Lily found the track on the playlist again and Arlo even put down his tractor to watch. Max had seen them perform the routine twice already and apparently didn't need another reminder of the choreography. Ella's laughter was a mix of happy and sad as she watched him and Lily, and he was as good as he'd said.

When the routine ended, with Max and Lily on their knees, arms in the air and fingers twinkling like stars, Ella could only applaud and hope he hadn't noticed the emotion she was trying to hold back. It had been a long time since she'd had such simple fun and she couldn't let any of them think it was going to last. She'd signed up to a couple of agencies as a backup before arriving at Halesmere and one had already got in touch with the possibility of an interview, which she'd put off for now.

'So, Lily, who's the winner?' Max stood and lifted Lily back onto her feet. 'Your dad, who bought you a puppy and has a hotline to Santa and his elves, or Ella, who's only got pizza to recommend her?'

'You're shameless, using Prim to get Lily to choose you,' Ella protested. 'That's definitely below the belt.'

'I don't know, Daddy.' Lily was considering it seriously, despite Max's attempt to sway her. 'You were both really good, but I think you were more in time.'

'So I've won then?' He tickled her, and she giggled, trying not very hard to escape. 'It's a ten from you?'

'Nine,' Lily squealed. 'I'm giving Ella a nine too.'

'What?' Max was outraged as Ella busied herself draining the pasta and tossed it with the vegetables. 'You just said I was better.'

'Yes, but Ella tried really hard, and you've seen it before.' Lily flung her arms in the air. 'Dance-off! Then I'll choose a winner.'

'No, Lily, really.' Ella was half-horrified, half-ready to accept the challenge of dancing with Max. 'Your tea's ready.'

'I think Ella's just conceded.' He gave Lily a wink. 'So that means I win.'

It had been a long time since Ella had fought her way to the front in a competition and she felt all her instincts kicking right back in. Ridiculous, for something so insignificant, but she wasn't about to give up. 'I do not concede.' She slid the pasta bowls into the warming oven. 'We've got two minutes tops before the food dries up.'

She fixed a look on Max, let him read the challenge, her decision. 'Let's go.'

When Lily started the music Ella gave it everything, knowing he was trying his best to beat her, and when they ended on their knees, fingers twinkling like stars again, she was laughing as much as he was. Lily declared that Ella was the winner as he had apparently missed a move at a crucial moment, and he accepted defeat with good grace, giving Ella a high-five to acknowledge her success. He set the table while she brought the food across.

'You're not eating with us?' He pushed Arlo's chair closer to the table as Lily sat down. Ella had brought over three pasta bowls, but she saw now that Max had set four places.

'No, I only did enough for the three of you.' She was backing away. 'I thought you'd prefer not having to cook something for yourself once you'd got home.'

'What about you?' He tucked a napkin over Arlo's school polo shirt, smoothed his hair with a gentle hand. 'When are you going to eat?'

'Later.'

'Right. Because that makes sense, does it? Cooking for us and not including you? You'd really rather eat alone?'

That was Max's trump card, and she knew he understood she couldn't say yes and be truthful as well. 'Please, Ella, sit down. I'll bring another bowl.'

'There isn't that much. Really, it's fine, you guys have it.'

'We'll share.' He tipped half of his food into the fourth bowl. 'There's some garlic bread in the freezer, I'll stick it in the oven.'

So here they were again, the four of them at his table and sharing a meal. None of this had been in Ella's plan when she'd arrived at Halesmere. Not walking home from school hand in hand with Arlo or dancing with Lily, and then against Max as though Ella's life depended on it. She didn't want it to feel like home quite as much as it did, didn't want to hear the merry playlist Lily had forgotten to turn off or see the Christmas tree flickering as he thanked her for the meal and told her how much he appreciated it after a long day at work. The children were weary and starting to squabble and Max put the television on as he quickly cleared up.

'I have to go.' Ella collected her coat and Prim raised a hopeful head. 'I'll walk you again another day,' she told the dog quietly, and Prim seemed to understand, head going to rest on her paws, huge eyes still staring.

'But Ella, you said you were staying until I go to bed.' Arlo's voice was a wail and he spun round to glare at her. 'You can't go yet, we're watching *In the Night Garden* and I want you to stay.'

'I'm sorry, Arlo.' She hated disappointing him. 'I meant that I would stay until your dad got home and I've already been here much longer than that. You need some time with your dad before bed.'

'That's not fair.' Arlo stuck out his bottom lip. 'I want you to read me my tractor story.'

'Hey buddy, I've got a better idea.' Max held out a hand and the little boy looked hopeful. 'Why don't we all walk Ella back to the house? Then you can say goodnight to her, and we'll make sure she's safely home, okay?'

She had to drop her head so Max wouldn't see the rush of surprise and pleasure on her face. He might only be suggesting it to appease Arlo and have Ella leave without causing a scene. But then again, he might be offering because he knew she didn't want to have to let herself into the big, dark house on her own. She blinked the emotion away, and a quick glance at Max was enough to know it was the latter as she read the understanding in his expression.

It took a few minutes to bundle the children back into coats, then they raced across the gravel to the house with Prim, excited by this new evening adventure. Ella opened the door and Max reached for the switch, chasing the darkness away and replacing it with welcome light.

'Don't disappear you two, we won't be long. It's bedtime,' he warned the children as they took off upstairs.

'Well done, I think you managed to avert Arlo from having a proper strop.' She wondered if Max would notice the note of cheerfulness she forced into her words. She didn't want them to go, but she couldn't let him realise that for even a moment.

'He's tired, needs his bed.' Prim nudged his hand and he stroked her head, his gaze steady on Ella's, all traces of the fun they'd shared earlier gone.

'Me too,' she joked. 'It's been a busy day.'

'Thank you for collecting them from school. Was everything okay?'

'Fine, I enjoyed it and Prim certainly did too.'

Prim whined, plonking a paw on Max's feet and staring up at him, as though asking why they were still standing around in the hall instead of settling somewhere more comfortable and preferably in front of a fire.

'So you'd be okay to do it again three days next week? I always pick them on Mondays and Fridays unless something urgent comes up and I can't.'

'Of course. It's partly why I'm here and I'm happy to help.' Ella tilted her head, trying to identify what Lily and

Arlo were doing from the noise they were making. 'I think they're bouncing on the beds.'

'Oi you two!' Max roared up the stairs. 'No bouncing, you'll ruin the mattress. Come on, we're going.'

'Was that your best lion impression?' Ella saw his grin.

'I've been known to do better.' He ran a self-conscious hand through his blond hair. 'Thank you, for everything tonight.'

'My pleasure. I had fun; I think they did too.'

'They definitely did, I could see that the moment I came through the door.' The children were still shrieking, but Max ignored them to fix his gaze on hers. 'It felt like home when I saw you all. Felt like family, laughing together.'

There was a yell from upstairs and Ella pulled herself free from the surprise hovering in his eyes. She hadn't needed words to show him she'd sensed it too, had loved being with them, and sharing that time made it even harder to face being alone in this house until morning. But she needed to be rational and not allow a false hope to replace good sense. His children couldn't be hurt again, and she had no wish for a casual fling with someone whose heart was still sore when her own life was so uncertain.

Lily had reached the bottom stair. She was crying, holding out a hand as she ran to Max. He scooped her up as Arlo thundered after her, protesting that it wasn't his fault she'd fallen over, and Max gave Ella a long look as she closed the door behind them.

Chapter Twelve

The next morning, Ella had to knock three times on Noelle's door above Max's office before she opened it.

'Ella *chérie*, how lovely. What brings you here?' One hand was covered in charcoal, and she tilted her head. 'Maxence is behaving himself, *oui*?'

'You invited me to come and see your studio. Yesterday, when we spoke in the courtyard. We arranged it for this morning.' If Noelle was busy, then at least Ella could get some work done. She had plenty to do; the college had replied to her email and requested a meeting. There were a couple more food producers she wanted to visit, too, and last night she'd started planning the supper menu, wide awake, thoughts of Max and that look in his eyes as he'd left with the children still lingering.

'Are you sure?' Noelle raised elegant brows. 'I remember we spoke about you seeing the studio, but I don't recall inviting you this morning.'

'It's fine.' Ella didn't want to unnerve her. 'You were going to show me your collection of gowns, but we can do it some other time, especially if you're painting.'

'*Non, non*, come in.' Noelle caught Ella's elbow and drew her forward. 'I am sorry, *chérie*, when I am painting things sometimes get forgotten. I will show you, as you said.'

Ella followed Noelle along a short corridor, and they emerged into her studio. Like Max's office, it faced south, lit by deep sash windows allowing in what winter light there was. It was as haphazardly arranged as Ella had expected, with white walls, splashes of green foliage plonked in vases, and some colour from winter flowers. Canvases were stacked all around the room and she was slightly alarmed to see an easel holding an unfinished nude of a man. She almost didn't dare look in case she'd found Stan posing in all his glory. Thankfully, though, it was someone she didn't recognise. He was standing, his back to the artist, one elegant leg poised behind the other, a hand on his hip, long hair swept back to skim his shoulders.

'You'll join me, *oui*?' Noelle was adding hot water to porcelain cups containing herbal tea bags. She looked up and caught Ella staring at the painting. Noelle brought the cups across and passed one to her. 'Of course, it's not finished yet, but it will be in my exhibition. What do you think?'

'It's beautiful, Noelle.' And it was. She had captured the grace and elegance of the man's form that made it feel very real; Ella almost expected him to move, stretch weary limbs.

'Now these are what I wanted to show you.' Noelle took Ella's cup, seeming not to notice that she hadn't had even a mouthful yet, and set it down on a small table. She led Ella to a corner of the studio where a rail of clothes stood beside a screen.

'I know nothing about couture but these are exquisite.' She wanted to run a hand along the sumptuous fabrics enticing her to touch them but didn't dare, afraid of leaving a mark or snagging a loose thread.

'They are wonderful, are they not? I modelled for a few different designers and occasionally managed to buy a piece or was given it.' Noelle lifted a hanger from the rail, a swish of fabric that she shook out and held up. 'Now this is the one for you, *chérie*.'

'It's stunning.' Ella had never really been one for dressing up, preferring to be thrashing through a pool or racing on a river, but this rose-patterned ivory chiffon gown was certainly tempting.

'I think it will fit you perfectly.' Noelle pointed to the screen. 'Try it on.'

'Oh no, thank you. I might mark it or something, and it would be such a shame to spoil it.'

'Nonsense.' Noelle handed the gown across, and Ella took it reluctantly. 'They were made for showing off, not sitting on a rail gathering dust. Try it, then let me see.'

She stepped behind the screen and hung the gown carefully, then took off her jumper and jeans. Her bra was going to be in the way, so she removed it as well. She stepped into the gown and slid the straps up over her bare shoulders. The chiffon felt exquisite against her skin, almost a caress, a softness she was completely unused to. It was backless and almost sheer, only the roses stitched into the bodice and flowing through the skirt protecting her modesty as she admired herself from every angle in a full-length triple mirror. She looked taller, even barefoot, and so elegant. She loved how the fabric clung to her body, outlining the femininity of her figure.

'May I see?'

Ella stepped out, holding the gown carefully in one hand. It was a little long without shoes and she didn't want it to trail or snag on the floor.

'Perfect,' Noelle pronounced with a flourish, taking Ella by the shoulders and turning her full circle. 'Now *chérie*, please will you sit for me and wear this gown? I want you for my exhibition too.'

'Me?' She hoped her quick laugh had covered her astonishment. 'I wouldn't know what to do.'

'You need do nothing, other than stand for a little while just as I say. There is something about your face, the story in your eyes that you do not wish to tell me. Maybe I can draw it out of you, capture it on my canvas.'

'Don't I need shoes?' Ella felt her resolve to refuse weakening in her desire not to remove the gown just yet. She raised a shoulder, popped a hip and tilted her head. Her laugh was self-conscious, aware of Noelle watching.

'*Non*, I like you barefoot, just as you are. As though you are about to run to someone, and shoes would be in the way. Perhaps you will carry them, we will decide later. I must make a start as soon as possible.' Noelle was eyeing her critically and Ella had the sense that she was already assessing the dimensions of her body and how to pose her. Ella wondered if she ought to have worn more make-up than just her usual mascara and lip gloss, or done something more elegant with her hair, but Noelle assured her that she looked perfect and far more natural without anything else on her face.

'I really should be working.' But Ella was wavering, hoping this first time might not take too long. 'I have meetings this afternoon and then—'

'Leave Maxence to me.' Noelle's eyes seemed to be gleaming, and Ella wasn't sure Noelle would let her escape now. 'There is nothing for him to object to – and if he tries, send him to me. *Oui?*'

'Mmm.' Ella had no intention of doing anything of the sort. She couldn't pack her new boss off to his mother for a scolding if he found out she wasn't around to do her job. She'd just have to sneak back to work and hope he hadn't noticed.

'Take off your watch, *chérie*, it is in the way.'

She did as Noelle asked, a hand ready to sweep her hair from her face. She was about to ask again if oughtn't to be wearing shoes to keep the gown from trailing on the floor.

'Don't move.' Noelle's shriek made her jump, and her watch dropped to the floor with a clunk. 'That expression, hold it, Ella, please. Let me work, don't say a word, just think exactly what you were thinking in that moment.'

'I was—'

'*Non!* Do nothing, say nothing. Just stand, exactly as you are. I must draw.'

Ella didn't dare say another word as Noelle's hand flew across her easel. She soon discovered that standing still and trying to maintain whatever expression she hadn't realised she was wearing was very difficult. It wasn't long before her muscles started to ache and the arm supporting the hand near her face was grumbling.

'I don't think I can stay like this for much longer, Noelle, I'm sorry.'

'*Oui*, Ella, you should move now. You are not used to this, and you will be tired very quickly.'

'May I see?' Relieved, she stretched protesting muscles, lifting the dress to point each foot and unwind her aching legs.

'*Non*. This is rough, my first opportunity to read the shape of your body, capture your form.' Noelle met her protest with a shrug. 'Later, when you will hopefully recognise yourself. That is enough for today, I can build on what I have begun.'

Her concentration was still fixed on the easel, a hand moving across it again. 'Max tells me he is impressed with your ideas for Halesmere, Ella.'

'That's nice.' She felt a warm tingle of pleasure. She'd known it for herself, but it was lovely to hear it from Noelle too.

'Of course, his mind is full of the children and his practice. It is no surprise the holiday business is not a priority to him.' Noelle stuck her head round the easel to nod thoughtfully. 'And that is where you come in, lovely, clever Ella.'

'Oh?' She was lingering. She knew she ought to be out of this gown and back in her jeans looking for Stan to talk about the open day, but Noelle seemed happy to chat now as she sketched.

'I knew you were right for us the moment we spoke. Energy, ideas, support, that is what he needs after all that has happened.'

'I was so sorry to hear about his wife. Such an awful thing for you all, especially with the children being so young.'

'It was.' Noelle shook her head as though banishing a memory she no longer wanted. 'And I encouraged him to move so far away from London and you always wonder, don't you? If you have done the right thing? I was not always present in his life, *chérie*, and I regret it. You don't at the time, of course, other than guilt when you are busy. It took a while, to find our way back together.'

Ella was staring through the window, thinking of last night, Max and the children, how easy it had been to be with them, the fun they'd had dancing. 'I imagine it must.'

'Boarding school did not suit him, and he hated it.' Noelle's expression was anguished as she caught Ella's eye. 'I should not have left him there, but his father and I were travelling, and we could see no other way at the time. Today things are different, and he does not want to be the same father that he had.

'Not that he sees his father very often, you understand; he lives in Brazil with his other partner and their children. He is a photographer, and he must live in the light. He hated the weather in England, and we were always moving. We both thought that Max would find stability at school. Stability yes, but not enough love from his family, and in time he loved only his music.'

Noelle frowned, glancing from the easel to Ella and back again, even though Ella was no longer holding the pose. 'He plays so beautifully. Has he played for you yet?' She carried on before Ella could reply. 'You must ask him to play for you if he has not done so. It held him back, of course.'

'What did?'

Noelle flushed, a redness creeping over her cheeks. 'His lack of confidence. He didn't make friends easily; he was always a very self-contained boy. He could have been good enough to play professionally had he found a way to overcome his nerves. But he hides it well. He laughs off what he does not want to hear or let people see. Victoria helped him for a time but of course she is gone and can do no more.'

Noelle's sigh was stricken. 'And now he has placed the piano where he cannot easily reach it. He cannot leave the children at night, and he assures me he does not want to play when I tell him I will stay with them. Sometimes I wish he would sell it; I think it only reminds him of what he used to do. He doesn't seek joy in his life, Ella. He lives for his children.'

Ella's heart was reaching for Max again, thinking of their conversation late on Sunday night when they'd talked of love and loss, always easier in the darkened hours before dawn. She, too, understood how to be alone in a crowd and wear a mask that she didn't often let slip. She understood how shattering loss could hold a person back and make their lives less. She knew how caution, fear and uncertainty brought an ability to assess the risk of future hurt and whether the risk might outweigh the gain. How could she not understand, when she'd reduced her own life to the one she thought her sister might have lived? And Max too, a life lived for his children and not himself.

'It was my fault, Ella, I know that I failed him. And now I can only try to be the grandmother his children deserve and offer them all my love and support.' Noelle's anguished gaze found Ella's. 'For as long as I can.'

Silence enveloped them as Noelle continued to sketch. Ella slipped behind the screen, carefully stepped out of the dress and hung it up, dislodging the rail. It faltered before tottering into a tangle of material and the gowns slid to the wooden, paint-spattered floor. Horrified, she gathered the gowns one by one, hanging them back up and scanning for signs of damage. Relieved once they were all in place, she pulled her jeans back on, searching for her bra, which had disappeared in the melee. She jumped as she heard the studio door being flung back and hurried footsteps clattering into the room.

'Maman? Have you seen Ella? I need a word and Stan said he saw her coming up here.'

Aghast, she clutched her arms across her chest. Stan was another one who saw far too much; he seemed to know everyone's movements. Ella spotted her jumper and grabbed it as though it were a lifebelt, yanking it over her head. It was better than nothing right now; she wasn't entirely certain that Noelle wouldn't direct Max straight to her hiding place behind the screen.

'I see.' Ella heard Max let out a breath. 'You're sketching her.'

'Ella is here, Max, of course she is.' Noelle sounded astonished that he should be surprised. 'And you know better than to burst in when my door is closed. She is sitting for me, and I had to make a beginning.'

'A start, Maman.'

'Whatever. She is behind the screen, changing.' A pause. '*Belle, non?*'

'It's not beautiful yet, it's only the suggestion of a person. How do you expect me to tell?'

'Yes, but you would already recognise Ella, would you not? The shape, her form? I had to draw her exactly as I saw her in that moment.'

'I suppose.' He sounded resigned. Ella's toes were curling at the thought of him staring at the sketches. 'Are you quite finished with her for today? May I borrow her?'

'For today, *oui*. Ella?'

'Yes?' She was still clutching her arms over her chest.

'Max is here for you, *chérie*, our time is gone. Are you dressed?'

Did Noelle really have to raise her voice quite so much, Ella thought crossly, she was only ten feet away. 'Yes, just coming.'

She strolled out from behind the screen, wearing a confident smile and fifty per cent of her underwear. She'd make an excuse to race back to the house and find another bra, this minute. Right now. Eyes firmly fixed on Max's impassive face, she opened her mouth, but he was quicker.

'We'd better run, the builders are about to disappear to collect something they need first thing in the morning. There are some decisions to make about the studio below the flat and I'd like your advice. Good to go?'

Would he mind if she said no? Ah well, grin and hopefully not bare it, she thought wildly. 'Sure.'

Noelle bid them a distracted goodbye, already returning to her sketches as they left the studio. The two builders and their apprentice were waiting as Ella crossed the cobbles with Max. He introduced her and explained the builders had been on site for months, working on the renovations on the house after they'd extended his cottage before they moved on to the studios.

She hadn't seen inside the old dairy below the flat before now. It was empty, covered in cobwebs, with stone walls that must once have been white but which were now a faded, muddy grey. Just one window at the back let in what bit of light it could and a view of an orchard. The room was a decent size, though, and she knew it would be useful for something once repainted.

'What do you think?' Max ducked his head to get through the door. 'What would you do with it?'

'It might depend on your long-term plans for the flat.' He wasn't any closer than he had been last night and still she felt his proximity like a touch on her skin. 'But I'm guessing you don't have any plans yet?'

'No but I'm open to your suggestions.'

'What do you think about having an artist in residence?'

His eyes narrowed as he offered her a wry grin. 'I've already got one of those, thanks very much. And she's quite enough trouble to be going on with.'

'I wasn't thinking of your mother.' Ella was conscious of the builders hovering outside, waiting to get on with their work. 'What about offering the dairy and the flat as a working and living space for someone in the arts? Maybe a writer, photographer or a musician?' She threw that last one in on purpose. 'You decide together how long they stay, maybe as part of a collaboration with other Cumbrian arts organisations, or something further afield. Perhaps it could be for young creatives just starting out and needing a base while they build their reputations and a body of work.'

A glance at the four men and Ella knew she'd got at least Max considering it. The other three looked decidedly more doubtful and one, scratching his bald head, she could practically see wondering what artists and residencies had to do with their work on site. He perked up, though, when she mentioned the flat, back on familiar ground.

'So, the flat could be designed for more than just very temporary living,' she went on. 'Functional, absolutely, but don't skimp on things like the kitchen worktops if it's going to be someone's home for weeks or months. The best appliances the budget can afford, with a proper freezer, not just a shelf in the fridge. Obviously, an excellent coffee machine.'

'Obviously.' Max smiled and it was easy for Ella to return it. 'Anything else?'

'Much better storage.' She was thinking about her two nights up there. 'There's room to build a wardrobe under the eaves. If it's going to be more than a holiday rental then it would be good to make it a home from home, a place to be inspired.'

She was rushing ahead, catching sight of Pete the Plasterer. He was probably adding another zero to the budget, judging by the way a hand moved from his head to rub his chin thoughtfully.

'What do you think?' Max was addressing Pete. 'When could you have it ready?'

Pete sucked in a breath, adding a shrug for good measure. 'Hard to say,' he eventually replied. 'I'd need my lad to take a look upstairs for that wardrobe and he's tied up on another job.'

'Stan could do it.' Ella hoped Pete wouldn't mind her side-lining his lad before he'd even assessed the work required. 'When he's made the barn doors and new window, of course.'

'Do you think the barn will be ready in time for the open day?'

'Can I let you know after we've been to the pub?' Ella told Max and saw Pete grin.

'Is that the team meeting I've heard about?' he asked.

'Stan mentioned it, did he?' Ella was glad Stan had spread her idea around; it had saved her a job.

'Aye. Said the more the merrier.'

'What team meeting?' Max was perplexed and she resisted the urge to laugh. He looked exactly like Arlo, the way his lips had pursed into a line and a frown creased his brow.

'I've suggested we get together in the pub to chat through our plans up to Christmas and how best to arrange the work that needs doing.'

'And when were you going to invite me to this team meeting?'

'Maybe I wasn't.' She hadn't meant for that to sound as flirtatious as it did. Pete was still grinning.

'And don't you lot have homes to go to?' There was a wry curve to Max's lips as he addressed Pete.

'Aye, but we've all got to eat sometime, and I like the sound of team meetings in the pub. Could be the new future and if you're paying, then all well and good.'

'Paying? Ella's not even invited me.' Max glanced at her. 'So am I? Invited?'

'What about Lily and Arlo?' She'd love Max to come but she didn't want to add any more pressure to his schedule. 'It's not that I don't want them there, but they'd probably get bored pretty quickly.'

'I'll ask Maman to babysit. She owes me for stealing you away.'

'It was only an hour or so.' Ella was discovering how much she liked teasing him. 'Are you sure you want to?'

'I am. I'd quite like to hear more about all these plans you're making. You certainly don't let the grass grow underneath your feet.' Max ducked his head beneath the door frame and Ella followed him out of the dairy.

'I'll sort out a date. It would make sense to meet around five thirty, if that works?' She addressed Max and then the builders. 'I know it's early, but it saves anyone going home if they're already on site.'

'I'll definitely be there if I can.' Max fastened his coat against the cold.

'Ella, *chérie*,' Noelle's voice was a roar. It took Ella a second to locate it; coming from Noelle's flat on the top floor through an open window overlooking the courtyard. 'You forgot your bra!'

She was merrily dangling the stray underwear in one hand. Ella's cheeks flushed to match the hot-pink lace as she saw the faces of at least two of the men and the young apprentice transfixed at the sight of her bra, suspended in the air. She'd meant to wear something more practical and rather less skimpy this morning, but it had been the first one she'd found in her half-unpacked case, and she hadn't imagined – rather foolishly as it had turned out – that she'd be removing it again before bedtime.

Own it, Ella, she thought grimly. She laughed and it was only a trifle forced. 'Thanks Noelle. Keep it for me, will you, it's part of a set. I'll pop back later.'

Chapter Thirteen

Ella felt as though the days were flying by now that December had arrived, and Christmas was on its way. There was much to keep her busy as she took over supervising the builders' work, researched retreats for the house, wrote content for the new website, met potential suppliers and invited them to the supper she was planning. She'd finally turned down the agency interview but had agreed to another one early in the New Year after the recruiter followed up two emails with a call. Another Michelin-starred restaurant, this time opening on the Norfolk coast. Ella knew it could be a great job, and she would need work after her time at Halesmere was over. But the future lay ahead, blurred, uncertain, and she was enjoying the present too much to commit to something more than a possibility right now.

She and Max had fallen into having coffee together each morning after he'd walked the children to school, if he didn't need to be elsewhere. She liked it, looked forward to that time with him and sensed he did too. He'd show her the gardens he was designing and was enthusiastic and supportive about the plans she was making. Their conversations gradually eased into the more personal and she was enjoying a naturally developing friendship, discovering they shared similar values and a sense of fun she thought they'd both missed.

If Ella wasn't in his office when he returned from school, he'd send her a coffee emoji accompanied by a grinning one to remind her. One morning when she couldn't make it, she'd sent an emoji sticking out its tongue straight back. The row of laughing ones that had followed from Max was worth the moment of realisation that she probably shouldn't be pulling cheeky faces at her boss.

Sometimes Noelle would join them, but she wouldn't stay long if Ella and Max were busy; she'd disappear with a wave and a promise to see them another time. Ella ran down to school with Prim three afternoons a week to collect Lily and Arlo, and she loved taking care of them, despite the bickering over whose turn it was to hold Prim's lead on the way back and Arlo's reluctance to do his homework while she cooked their evening meal. Occasionally Max made it back in time for the school run when it was Ella's turn, and he'd catch her up, taking the children by surprise and making them squeal with delight when he swung them into big hugs, and she was the only one who had to hide her pleasure when he arrived home from work.

She'd given up trying to evade his insistence that she eat with them on the nights she cooked for the family. Sometimes Lily and Arlo would persuade her to stay long enough to read them a bedtime story as well, and once or twice Max had been asleep when she came back downstairs. She'd let herself out of the cottage and return to the house, despite longing to linger instead and watch him wake.

Stan often brought her mugs of tea, and she was amused when he produced a sachet of instant coffee one day and said he'd make her one specially the next time she popped into his workshop. He was keen to help with Lily's birthday party on Saturday and was taking his duties as campfire supervisor very seriously. Ella liked hearing Stan muttering or Pete whistling as they wandered past her base near Max's office or stuck their heads round the door to ask how she was getting on and if there was anything she needed. Stan had also introduced her to Sandy, the ceramist and rector of the church next to the school.

Today was Wednesday and the first team meeting and dinner at the pub was set for five thirty. Before she collected Lily and Arlo from school, Ella had a Zoom with Kev, the paddleboarder she'd met on the lake during her first weekend at Halesmere. Afterwards she'd googled the centre where he worked and discovered Kev was the learning and development team leader, responsible for delivering the residential programmes. She'd emailed him and they'd arranged to chat through the requirements for volunteering.

Kev was no-nonsense, direct and empathetic, and Ella really liked him. After she'd run him through her previous experience, he was more keen than ever to have her join. There were several roles he felt she would fulfil with ease, and they agreed to meet after Christmas, although she reminded him her plans were flexible and she was very likely to move on in the spring. But she couldn't deny the pull of the outdoors and the excitement at the thought of sharing her skills once again.

After talking to Kev, and fitting in a visit to a local vegetable grower, Ella left her car at Halesmere, fetched Prim, and ran down to school to collect Lily and Arlo. They were excited to see her and even more so when she promised them a surprise at home, all three laughing as they tried their best to make her reveal it and she refused.

Back at the cottage they hung up their belongings and fed the chickens. Dylan had left Ella a voicemail and she sent a quick message, promising to catch up properly online soon.

She'd already made a vegetarian cottage pie and left it on timer in the oven so she could help the children put together the pieces of a gingerbread camper van she'd picked up in town. She'd thought of them the moment she'd seen it, and it was only when Noelle arrived, so Max could join the meeting at the pub, and Lily was decorating one side of the van with sweets and icing and Arlo the other, that Ella wondered if Noelle or Max would mind her finding festive family things for the children to do. She had a few ideas up her sleeve for next week as well, the final week of term.

Arlo asked Noelle for help sticking the van together, and then Ella served their meal. It smelled amazing, with creamy mash over vegetables, sweet potato and cheddar, and Noelle was happy to eat with them. Ella left the three of them tucking in – and heard Noelle confirming to Lily and Arlo that both sides of the camper van were equally good and would be even more delicious to eat if they finished their tea – and smiled as she went off in search of Stan, who'd promised her a lift.

The pub was exactly as Ella had hoped, comfortable and welcoming with three rooms leading from the central bar, each one smaller than the last, all painted the same cosy shade of red. Wooden tables and chairs were scattered in between comfy-looking settles against the walls. There were a mixture of landscape and portrait paintings on the walls, and the fire was roaring, throwing out heat she was grateful for. The smell of food being carried to the tables was making her hungry and festive music was a pleasant backdrop to the chatter. Garlands were strung across the walls and a Christmas tree blazed brightly in a cosy corner.

'What you drinkin', young Ella?' Stan propped a foot on the rail beneath the bar. Judging by the way people greeted him with either a grin or a raised hand, or a reminder about darts on Friday night, he seemed to know just about everyone.

'I'll have a pint please, Stan. This one.' She pointed to the pub's own beer on draught. 'Ask them to start a tab for me, please.'

Stan introduced her to the landlord, Phil, who'd taken the pub over six years ago, and she promptly invited him to the supper at Halesmere next week. Surprised, he accepted, subject to staff coverage, and she ordered enough bottles of beer for the night with some to spare. He told her about the previous occupants of the house and how it had been two flats and then a holiday home. Not all the people who'd lived there had been well known around the community and he liked her idea of the house becoming a base for artists and retreats. Ella explained she believed having an excellent pub within walking distance was part of the house's appeal and he was quick to agree.

Pete the Plasterer rolled up with his shy apprentice and Phil suggested that Ella take the whole of the smallest room for her group, and she thanked him. She loved the idea of holding regular team meetings here and she was sure Phil would too. She dragged the tables together while Stan fetched their drinks. Pearl arrived with her knitting needles and wool, and Ella was admiring the beautifully patterned bouclé scarf in shades of ivory, cerulean, violet and olive that Pearl was making as a Christmas gift for her daughter-in-law when Max appeared and headed to the bar. Ella went over.

'You've made good time. Are the children still settled with your mum?'

'I hope so, I haven't been back to check.' There was amusement in his eyes, and she was sure her own smile was revealing her pleasure that he was here. 'What's this about camper vans made from gingerbread? Lily sent me a photo because she said they were going to eat it and it would be a shame if I didn't have the chance to see it before it was gone and apparently it was all your idea.'

'Not eating it all in one go,' Ella protested, feigning horror but trying not to laugh. 'I said they ought to make it last, so I'm refusing any responsibility for the consequences.'

'Thanks. You might feel a bit more responsible if I'm banging on your door in the middle of the night to clear up the vomit.'

She was about to tell Max he'd have to drag her out of bed first, then hastily decided against it. Instead she pointed to where the others were gathered. 'We're in there, Phil said we could have the room to ourselves.'

'Phil?'

'The landlord.' Ella tipped her head to one side. 'Please tell me this isn't your first visit to the pub, Max.'

'All right then, I won't.'

'But it's on your doorstep. Haven't you even had Sunday lunch here or treated Stan to a quick fish and chips?'

Max held up his hands. 'I know, it's really bad of me. We usually end up at a farm or animal park when I take the kids out, so may I plead two young children and a lot to do?'

'You may but it might be good for you to come here sometimes, even just for lunch. It would help Halesmere if you spent more time and money locally, and personal recommendations are always better.'

'And how does treating Stan come into that?' Max looked amused as Phil came over and Ella introduced them. They chatted about the pub and the house, and Max ordered another round of drinks for their table, switching the tab to his card instead. 'You're not paying for dinner, Ella,' he said firmly. 'They're my staff and my builders.'

'Yes, but they're helping me, and they've been great. And as for treating Stan, it wouldn't do you any harm now and again. He's a gem.'

'Is that right?' Their drinks had arrived, and she was nearer. She picked up the tray. 'Not sure I'd go as far as calling him a gem.'

'You do know he's sitting for your mother?' Ella was weaving through the tables with the tray, Max following her.

'Don't tell me, it's not something I want imprinted on my mind. What goes on in that studio stays in that studio as far as I'm concerned. I try to keep well out of it.'

She reached their table and put the tray down. Stan greeted Max cheerfully and he pulled out a seat, accepting the builders' taunts about finally getting him in the pub to pay for a round of drinks. Sandy the rector and ceramicist had arrived along with a very attractive young man with short dark hair. Ella went over to say hello and Sandy introduced him as her son Marcus, whom she'd brought along as he was a web designer; they had thought Ella might find his work of interest. Sandy couldn't stay too long, she explained; their church hall was out of action due to boiler failure and they were holding a parish council in another room of the pub later.

Ella shook Marcus's hand and they chatted while Phil sorted out drinks for the new arrivals. She learned from Marcus that he was based in Carlisle but, like everyone, it seemed, worked remotely for clients all over the country. He promised to email her the link to his business and she invited him to Halesmere to see the house and studios the next day. Time was of the essence, and he'd said he might have the capacity to take on the work soon. She introduced everyone as menus were passed around and Stan wasn't the only one going for an early Christmas dinner; Pete's shy young apprentice decided to join him.

'Sorry I'm late, I hope I haven't kept you waiting.'

Ella hadn't expected to see Ashley, who was hovering at their table, and Max quickly stood up. 'Of course not. Glad you could make it.' She took his place and Ella shuffled along, leaving room for Max between them. He passed Ashley a menu. 'We've only just ordered. What would you like to drink?'

'Oh, a glass of Shiraz please.' Ashley slid out of her coat, saying hello to everyone and asking the builders about their workload. Sandy introduced her to Marcus and Ella didn't miss how the younger man's eyes lit up. She wondered if she should have worn something a little more sophisticated than striped tights with winter boots and a short wool skirt. The waiter returned to take Ashley's order and Max brought her glass of wine and settled on his new seat on Ella's left.

She opened her laptop and scanned through her notes. There was a sense of anticipation in the air as they waited for her to outline the reason for gathering them together.

'Thank you all for coming.' Standing seemed to make more sense and she pushed her chair back. There was a flutter in her stomach, reminding her of the days when she'd been competing, had relished the shiver of anxiety, had used it to push herself and drive away the doubts. She'd never been afraid of a challenge, and if they could all work together to pull off her ideas, then Ella hoped to leave in the spring knowing she had set something in place upon which Halesmere could flourish.

'Couldn't resist a free meal on the boss,' Pete the Plasterer chirped up. 'This gonna be a regular thing then?'

'What, team meetings or free meals?' she quipped, looking at Max to test his reaction. It could get expensive, and she didn't want to presume, or blow his budget.

'Not promising every week, Pete.' Max glanced around the group. 'But it might be nice to do it again after Christmas for anyone who wants to join us.'

'I'm in.' Stan's first pint was gone and he clattered the empty glass to the table. Pearl, next to him, was busy knitting the scarf and Ella was astonished by how quickly the long needles clicked together as the garment grew. Pearl wasn't working from a pattern, Ella saw, and her gaze could roam around the room without her needing to constantly watch her hands.

'Thank you for giving up your time, free dinner notwithstanding. I really appreciate it.' Ella grinned at Pete, and he gave her a wink. 'I'd love to run you through Halesmere's potential for the future and how we might work together to create exceptional experiences for guests.'

She sensed the silence becoming more thoughtful as she began with the idea of running the house as a retreat alongside artists and creatives who would be based in the studios. She spoke of the possibility of having an artist living in the flat and of using the barn for locals and visitors alike, offering craft mornings, exhibitions and maybe even church events, as their hall was currently unfit for use. Sandy gave her a surprised and appreciative beam, and Pearl was nodding as she knitted.

'I know time's tight to host an event before Christmas and there's a lot to do if we're going to be ready for local artists and creatives to exhibit in the barn. Hopefully we'll get some interested in basing themselves at Halesmere and I'd like the studios to be ready to move into in January.'

'January?' Pete let out a low whistle. ''Ave you seen the state of them, Ella?'

'I have.' She gave him a grin that said she wasn't going to be dissuaded. 'And it's not more much now than elbow grease, a skip and some paint, Pete, and I really need your help. The basics are there, and I think people will come to the open day. I know there are plenty of events taking place around the county but there aren't many near us, and if we work together, I know we can pull it off.

'Obviously word of mouth is really important, and meeting here is a start. I've mentioned the open day to Phil, the landlord, and he's very happy to let visitors know and put posters up, share it on social media. And of course, social media will be a big part of what we're doing and how we'll let people know what's happening.'

'I wouldn't mind doing the social media, Ella.' Pearl glanced up from the scarf. 'I do it for the shop anyway and it would make sense for the two to work together.'

'It absolutely would, Pearl. Thank you, I think that's a brilliant suggestion. Your posts are fantastic and there's already a lot of engagement.' Ella was beaming. It was all coming together and her excitement was beginning to bubble. It had been a long time since she'd felt so enthused by her work. 'Let's chat this week if you're free. As many refreshments as possible for the open day should come from the producers who supply the shop, and you know them better than me.'

'What sort of refreshments are we talkin' about, Ella?' Stan looked hopeful, a hand on his stomach.

'Decent coffee and no Bovril for a start,' she quipped and saw him grin. 'Mulled wine and mince pies, of course. I'm still thinking of others.' She glanced at Pete. 'You're right about it being tight to be ready, Pete, and much as I'd like to offer lots more, we can't go mad. There isn't the time.'

Ella quickly moved on to the idea of encouraging guests to buy local by showcasing the variety of producers on their doorstep, including those who already supplied the community shop. The possibilities were almost endless, she told them; and she'd already approached the chocolate maker to discuss creating a flavour exclusive to Halesmere inspired by a damson cocktail.

'I was thinking we could have a page on the new website called Loving the Lakes, featuring all the producers working with us. This would enable guests to see what's available and order everything all in one place rather than having to approach each one individually.' She looked at Marcus, who was listening and making notes on his laptop. 'I know it's not all about the national park and Cumbria extends beyond the park's boundaries, but the name will resonate with people, and they'll know exactly where we are in the UK without having to look it up.'

Their meals had arrived, and Ella thanked everyone for listening and sat down. The food was hearty and homely, as good as the reviews had promised. She was starving, and glad to fall on it. She knew she had hit the team with lots of information and allowed her enthusiasm to run away with her.

Ashley was talking to Max, their heads bent together. He leaned back, turning to Ella.

'Did you want to ask Ash about decorating the house for Christmas, Ella? You mentioned something about it.'

'I did, yes.' She put her cutlery down. Their waiter had returned and another round of drinks was ordered. Then Ella leaned towards Ashley, trying not to loom over Max. 'We've invited a group of local producers to supper at the house next Wednesday and I'd love to have it decorated so we can take some images for the website. I've booked a photographer.'

'Have you?' Max's glass paused halfway to his mouth.

'Yes, sorry, I thought I'd told you. She's local to Cumbria, studied at the college and set up her own business after a few years travelling.'

'That sounds great. You really are finding your way around.'

'It's my job,' she reminded him, not lingering on the suggestion of approval in his gaze. Ashley was waiting and Ella returned to their conversation. 'I appreciate you're busy with your own clients, Ashley, so if you haven't got time I do understand. But Max thought you'd do it brilliantly.'

'I think I can squeeze it in, Ella.' Ashley flashed Max a smile before picking up her phone. 'Let me check my calendar. I'd need to move a couple of things around and make sure I've got cover for the girls after school, but I'd love to see the house all set for the holidays, like a real home.' She placed a hand on his arm. 'Ready for if you do ever decide to live in it.'

'No plans for that, it's too big for the three of us, and I like the idea of retreats. And we need the business if we're going to be able to stay.' His eyes flickered over Ella before returning to Ashley. 'But thank you, we appreciate it. And you'll join us for supper?'

The pause seemed to be lengthening. Ella was thinking of how easily Max had used the terms 'we' and 'us' in that final sentence and how much she liked it.

'I'd love to.' Ashley's hand moved from his arm to squeeze his fingers. 'Anything to support you and the kids, Max. You know that.'

'That's very generous. And thank you.' He squeezed back until a cough required the use of his hand to cover his mouth.

'I was hoping you'd give me the name of your hair-stylist, please, Ashley? Yours is gorgeous and I'd love to find someone who knows what they're doing with colour.' Ella bit her lip; she really hadn't meant to sound as though she were rudely pointing out Ashley's hair wasn't naturally that exact shade of chestnut with a suggestion of cinnamon.

'Of course. If you give me your number, I'll message you with their details,' Ashley said. 'But they are absolutely rammed between now and Christmas. I could have a word about fitting you in, but I'm not sure they'd be able to.'

'That's okay, I think I can last until the New Year. Thanks for that.'

'My pleasure.'

Ella reeled off her number, watching as Ashley added it to her contacts.

'Why don't I pop in tomorrow morning straight from school, Ella, and you can talk me through your ideas for decorating?' Ashley looked at Max. 'You should join us, we need to get your input too.'

'Can't, sorry, seeing a potential client at nine thirty.' He gave Ella a grin. 'Forgot to tell you that so I won't be there for our coffee. Don't break my machine again.'

'Hey, that was once, and I didn't break it.' She resisted the urge to laugh at the tease in his eyes, noticing Ashley looking stiffly ahead. 'If you'd refilled it like you said you would then it wouldn't have run out of beans in the first place.'

Chapter Fourteen

They were a merry bunch and people began throwing out questions for Ella as their meals gradually disappeared. A few people changed seats, and she ended up next to Marcus with Sandy on her other side, learning more about his business as he ran her through a few brief ideas he'd already had for the website. Nearly everyone had dessert, glad to indulge in luxurious winter treats, and local sticky toffee pudding with warm caramel sauce and thick double cream proved the favourite. Sandy had to leave to join the parish council meeting in the next room and Marcus also left, along with Pete and his apprentice. Max settled the bill and Ella made sure she'd thanked everyone for coming and listening to her ideas.

'You ready, Ella?' Stan, nearby, nodded at the door. 'Pearl's got the car an' we're 'eadin' back now.'

'I'm going to walk, Stan, I could do with the exercise. But thanks for the offer.' She hadn't managed a run again today, other than the quick one to school. She really needed to sort her mornings out, find some sort of proper routine before she started work.

'You sure?' Stan sounded doubtful and he gave Max a look.

'Of course, it's not even twenty minutes, less if I run.' Ella saw Stan taking in her boots. They were not designed for running on slippy roads; she'd be walking, unless she fancied Christmas in plaster with a broken ankle.

'Max, would you mind dropping me home please?' Ashley appeared at his side and he helped her into a coat. 'The girls are staying with James tonight.'

'I'm sorry, I can't.' Max put his own coat on, wrapped a scarf round his neck. 'I walked down, the pickup's at home. And I've had a couple of drinks.'

'Oh.' Undeterred, Ashley whipped out her phone. 'Then I'll call us a taxi, we can have another drink while we're waiting.'

'Actually, I thought I'd head back with Ella if you don't mind. It would be a good opportunity to talk about decorating the house as I'm out tomorrow. But we'll wait until your taxi arrives.'

'There's no need to do that, Max, not if you're ready to leave.' Ashley's laugh was warmer than the glint in her eye. 'I'm a big girl, I can wait here by myself.'

'No need for that either, love,' Stan piped up. 'You can come with us, it's only ten minutes down the road from ours.'

'No, really, I'll wait for the…'

'Makes sense, Ash, save you waiting. I've heard taxis round here can take a while.' Ashley's face revealed her disappointment that her plans had gone awry, but eventually she nodded. He bent to kiss her cheek and she murmured something into his ear that clearly wasn't meant for everybody.

'See you in the morning, Ella. And I'll see you at dinner tomorrow, Max,' she called, following Stan and Pearl out of the pub.

Max turned to Ella. 'Ready?'

'Yep.'

She thanked Phil again as they passed the bar and he told her he was looking forward to supper and he'd deliver the beer she'd ordered to Halesmere on the day. Outside it was perishing and the cloudless night sky was glittering with thousands of stars blinking through the inky blackness. The outline of the woodland was ghostly and silent, and everything seemed suspended in the frigid air. Ice had formed over puddles, creating slippery patches Ella didn't notice until she slithered on one, straight into Max.

'Sorry.' She grabbed his arm, and he clutched her shoulders, keeping her upright. 'Maybe walking home wasn't such a bright idea.'

'I'm glad you wanted to.' She saw his breath glisten in the dark, the quick gleam of a smile. 'I don't get many chances to walk without the kids, and I like it.' He tucked her hand through his arm. 'Don't let go, you might slip again.'

'Thanks. Maybe next time it'll be my turn to save you from falling.' She felt the solidity of his arm beneath her hand, the cool scrape of his coat against her bare fingers. 'So do you have any thoughts on how you'd like the house to be decorated?'

'Actually, that was just a ruse to get you alone.'

'I'm sorry?' Ella clutched his arm as surprise raced into her voice. She didn't need the ice to make her feel unsteady this time.

'Sorry, that came out a bit wrong,' Max replied hastily. 'I just wondered what you're planning to do for Christmas, and I didn't want to ask in front of everyone else. You mentioned your family is going away and you'd probably stay here.'

The reminder of Christmas Day and spending it without those she loved had Ella holding in a sigh. 'I'll probably take the kayak out and enjoy the peace and quiet. I've been pretty busy, so it'll be nice to have some time to myself.'

'Why do I get the feeling that's not quite true? It's obvious you love your family to bits; I can't imagine you want to be alone if you're apart from them.'

'Are you suggesting what I think you are?'

She felt Max shrug. 'Why not? The offer's there. You don't have to spend the day knee-deep in plastic and boxes building kids' stuff, you can just join us for lunch if that's all you want to do.'

'Max, I...' She hesitated. And then where would she be? And his children? What might they think of Ella joining them for Christmas when she would be leaving in a couple of months?

'I've already invited Stan and Pearl as their daughters can't get up on the day. One's a nurse and the other's in Germany with a partner in the military.' Max halted and turned to face her. 'I know what it's like when Christmas becomes something you need to get through, Ella. This will be our first at Halesmere and I've been thinking it might be good to make it open house, invite those around us. Those quiet family days we had with Victoria are gone and I want to create something new, something to see us down the years here.'

'That's a lovely idea.' Ella recognised the rush of emotion in his words, the desire to begin a new tradition and find a way to fit it around the old ones. 'So is this the bit when you tell me you need a chef to help cook the lunch?'

They were strolling again, and he tucked his arm through hers. 'Ice, remember? I need you to hang onto me. Of course I'm not expecting you to work. Obviously my talents in the kitchen don't come close to yours, but Stan's apparently a dab hand with a roast and Pearl's promised the best stuffing I've ever tasted. You can just join us, Ella. You don't have to do anything.'

'What, and be waited on hand and foot all day? I'm in.' She liked his quiet chuckle, gone when he skidded on a frozen puddle, and she grabbed his arm. 'You were right. You did need me to help you.'

'Maybe more than you know.' His voice was very low, and her heart bumped in shock as their arms straightened and the back of his hand brushed against hers. Her fingers seemed to have a mind of their own and one hooked around his, waited a beat. She could see the entrance to the drive up ahead, they were going to run out of road very soon. Her pulse was hurrying, and it turned into a roar when his warm fingers slipped between hers to hold them.

'Thank you for all you're doing for Lily's party. She's so excited. Stan wouldn't let me in his workshop this morning. Said it was top-secret and he was trying something on.'

'He wouldn't let me in either. I've got a funny feeling he's planning to dress up.' If they weren't holding hands then Ella might've believed their relationship was back to discussing practicalities and parties, not this simple connection that felt more intimate than holding hands had ever done before. 'And it's a pleasure to help her, Max. I'm glad she's happy.'

'She definitely is. Pearl's got a friend who makes cakes, so that's sorted at least. Before you came along, I was just planning to invite a few of her friends over and hope none of them broke something important or threw up before I sent them home again. Now Lily's marching round the cottage consulting her iPad and asking me if I've remembered to order the stockings for the party bags and exactly how many chocolate biscuits do I think we'll need for the s'mores. You've got quite a bit to answer for, Ella Grant.'

'Is that right?' They were approaching his cottage and the security light came on, driving away the dark and illuminating their faces. 'Sounds like Lily's a perfect party planner in the making. It's all about the detail.'

'Either that or a dog trainer. She's always on YouTube watching training videos and telling me exactly where I'm going wrong with Prim.' They drifted to a halt outside the front door of the house. 'You were brilliant tonight, Ella. Everyone loved your enthusiasm for Halesmere, and you've got them totally on board.'

'Hardly brilliant, Max. It was just a few ideas, and I can't see any of them through without their help. I shouldn't get too carried away.'

'Is that a metaphor for the fact that we're still holding hands?' He shook their arms gently. 'I think we're both in danger of breaking the "don't get involved at work" rule.'

'It's not too late to reinstate it.' She slipped her hand free, saw him watching.

'If that's what you want.'

'Was that a rhetorical question?' Ella's heart was hammering as she hovered between what she wanted and what was wise. 'I don't think either of us need any more complications, Max. Especially not you.'

'I know you're right, at least in theory.' He shoved his hands into his pockets and his smile was rueful. 'I was going to ask if you wanted me to come in, just to switch the lights on.'

'Better not. I am getting used to it. I hope you're planning to find room for a roll-top bath in the flat. This house is spoiling me.'

'Hardly, but I'm glad you're enjoying it. You don't seem like someone who allows herself too many indulgences.'

'Work has always been enough.' Ella shrugged, trying to bring her thoughts back to the flat and not the reminder of living her sister's dream. 'I think there's room for a rainforest shower head in there at least.'

'I was going to suggest I have a word with Pete but maybe you should instead. He seems to have taken to making himself scarce whenever I show up. Think he's been taking lessons from Stan.'

Ella unlocked the door, Max behind her. Noelle was still at his cottage with the children, and they couldn't keep her waiting all evening. 'I'm planning to have a working lunch on Friday and I wondered if you'd like to join me?' Ella said. 'Strictly business. I know you're out tomorrow.'

'I am. On site all day then dinner with Ashley to talk about a client. My mother's having the kids once they've eaten with you. And lunch sounds good. Do you have somewhere in mind?'

'I do, it's a bit different and I'm certain you won't have been before. I'll book a table for noon if that suits you?'

'Let me check.' Max found his phone and it was only a moment until he nodded. 'That's fine. It's in my calendar now, so it's a date. A working one,' he finished quickly, and Ella smiled. She'd loved the feel of their hands wrapped in one another's, the press of their arms, as they'd walked home together. But they were right to reinstate their rule before anything else changed and a bit of light flirting led them along a path neither was able to keep treading. He lifted a hand as though he was thinking of running a finger down her cheek, but seemed to change his mind, his arm falling away. 'See you Friday.'

—

The following morning Ashley was friendly and enthusiastic as she took Ella on a tour of all she and Max had done to restore the house to its former glory, and over coffee in the kitchen they agreed on a theme for the Christmas decorations. Ashley seemed in no hurry as she spoke of knowing Max back in London, how much in love he and Victoria had been and how he still needed time to come to terms with his family's loss.

Ashley was interested in hearing about Ella's career, and she confessed she'd turned down another approach just this morning. She really hoped she wouldn't regret revealing why after Ashley managed to elicit from her that the executive head chef who'd got in touch was her former boss and her dodgy ex to boot. Ella had no desire to work with him again, even after Ashley's casual suggestion that Ella might want to take more time to think it over as the job sounded perfect.

Ella had promised to help Pete and his team of two in the studios and after Ashley left, they worked flat out for the rest of the day. The builders had already finished a couple of the spaces and Sandy was due to move her ceramics into one of them after Christmas. Each of the five studios was a good size, but the last one at the far end of the courtyard was larger than the others and Stan told her it used to be a forge. Evidence of the blacksmiths' presence still lingered in the tools and bits of broken nails from the horseshoes they found.

Pearl popped in to show Ella her ideas about social media, bringing everyone a very welcome lunch. They crammed into Stan's workshop, where he brewed up and lit the stove. Ella gave Pearl her approval to go live on social media and sent her some images she'd taken of the work they were doing to prepare for the open day. Pearl knew as well as Ella that creating interest early was vital.

By the time she finished for the day she was filthy, but happy, especially when Pearl messaged to say they'd already filled three tables in the barn and two of the artists were interested in viewing the studios as potential places to work.

Marta had messaged as well, inviting Ella to supper on Friday night. Marta and her gorgeous candles were a big part of the atmosphere Ella hoped to create in the house and she'd already ordered a dozen for the supper next week. She saw a school mum she recognised dropping off the children outside the cottage about five thirty. They disappeared through the arch towards Noelle's flat, trailing their belongings as ever. Just before six Ella locked up the last studio, ready for a shower. Stan, in his pickup, stuck an arm through the window as he headed off down the drive. She waved back as she headed to the front door of the house, and then jerked to a halt as she heard Noelle shouting behind her.

'Help me, Ella, please, I don't know where Lily and Arlo have gone.' Noelle's voice was high-pitched and frantic with worry, and she was without a coat, shivering in the harsh winter air. 'Help me, please.'

'Of course I will.' A sharp stab of alarm was already prickling Ella's skin as Noelle clutched at her arm. 'Are you saying they're not in your flat?'

'*Oui, oui*. I was working and I told them to amuse themselves for half an hour and then we would eat. But they've run away, I don't know where.' Noelle's mouth opened again, then closed, as though she was grasping for meaning beyond her reach. 'What will I do if they are gone? Where could they be? They do not usually wander. Max will be frantic and it's all my fault. What if they have gone to the tarn or run along the lane alone, in the dark? Oh *non, non*, what will I do?'

'Noelle, try and stay calm, okay.' Ella thought of the glimpse she'd had of the children only half an hour ago. 'They'll be here somewhere; I don't think they'd go down to the tarn on their own. Go and check your flat in case they're hiding, playing a game. Is Max's office locked? Can they get in there?'

'I do not know.' Noelle suddenly looked frail and much older in the glare of the security light as her terrified gaze rested on Ella's, her usual confidence in tatters.

'Then check the door on your way past. I'll start in the courtyard.'

'Should I call Max?'

'No, not for a few minutes. I think we should look first. I don't want to worry him if they're hiding under your bed. What about the cottage?'

'It is locked, they do not have keys. They cannot get in.'

'Right. And the house is locked as well, so I can't see them being in there.' The spike of anxiety was now lodged in Ella's stomach, and she felt for car keys and phone in her coat pocket. If she didn't find them in the next five minutes, she'd call Stan; he knew the place backwards and would be here in a shot to help. She raced off through the arch without waiting for Noelle and tried the studios first. She didn't find the children in there and hadn't expected to; she'd seen Pete locking them before Lily and Arlo had returned. She checked the one she'd been working in and again there was no sign.

The barn was a possibility, and she dragged the heavy doors apart, using the torch on her phone to search as the electricity was still disconnected, calling the children without trying to panic them, telling them their tea was ready. That at least, she was certain, would bring Arlo from any hiding place he'd lodged himself in. Please let them be safe, she prayed, please let them be here. How would Max go on if one of them was lost, hurt, worse? Ella was just wondering about fetching Prim to see if the intuitive and clever dog could lead her to the children, when—

'Ella! Help, please. Ella!'

At Lily's terrified scream, she flew out of the barn into the courtyard. The little girl was teetering at the top of the steps to the flat, the yellow front door lying open behind her.

'Lily, get back from the edge,' Ella roared. 'I'm coming to get you right now.'

'It's Arlo,' Lily screamed again, backing away from the drop and pointing inside the flat. 'He's hurt his arm and he's crying.'

Ella's relief at finding them was laced with a new worry as she raced up the steps and caught Lily, hurrying her back into the darkened room. Ella's pulse was roaring in her ears as she hit the light switch, and an icy dart shot into her heart as she saw Arlo lying on the floor beneath the remains of the broken ladder. He was clutching his left arm as tears streaked his face beneath eyes wild and frightened. He was pale and she let Lily go to him and followed. Ella touched his forehead with a gentle hand. It was cold and she knew he was in shock.

'Hey, you, what have you been up to?' She gave him a smile, keeping her voice very calm, and was mightily relieved to see his own tremulous one as she looked him over for signs of bleeding or obvious trauma beyond the way he was holding his arm and the long scratch on one side of his face. 'Don't tell me you were trying to drive your tractor in here.'

'We were playing hide-and-seek. I wanted to go upstairs and the ladder broke.'

'I can see that.' Ella yanked off her coat and covered Arlo, pulling the splintered rungs away from him as she did so. Something caught her hand and she winced at the flash of pain and saw blood but focused back on him. He was trembling and she was certain it wasn't just because of the cold. 'Where does it hurt, Arlo?'

'My arm.'

'Where else?'

'Just my arm. I feel sick.'

'That's because you've had a nasty fall and it surprised you. I'm going to leave you for a second to bring the table across, okay. We need to lift your legs and I promise I'll be careful. If they hurt at all I'll stop.'

Lily helped and they soon had Arlo's legs raised to help increase blood supply to his vital organs. Ella loosened the polo shirt he wore under his coat and he wanted to sit up.

'Not yet, sweetheart.' She fumbled for her phone as she heard Noelle calling outside, her panic and fear even greater than before. 'Lily, go to the door and absolutely no further and shout Mamie, okay. Tell her we're here and to call an ambulance.'

Ella stroked Arlo's forehead as she waited for a response. Noelle's frightened cries continued as Lily came back in a few minutes later, her voice a worried whisper. 'Mamie says the ambulance will take a long time. I don't think she knows what to do, Ella. She was busy when we got home, and we thought we'd explore for a bit.'

Lily edged backwards until she was on Ella's other side and Ella snuggled her too, feeling the dampness of the little girl's tears as Lily wound her arms round her neck. Ella wasn't expecting the sudden blast of love and tenderness that rushed into her heart. She pressed a kiss against Lily's forehead. 'I've got you both, I promise. I'll look after you.'

'Are we in trouble?'

'No, my love, you're not.' Ella was thinking rapidly and still trying to process the rush of emotions filling her senses. She could see Arlo's colour was already improving. 'We just need to get Arlo to hospital so they can check him over. I think his arm might need some help and he can probably get up now.'

'I feel sick,' he said again, and proved it when he shifted his legs and vomited all over Ella's coat. She helped him stand and he stared at her with wide eyes swimming with tears, clutching his arm. 'It hurts.'

'That's disgusting.' Lily sounded horrified and Ella knew some of her relief had returned now that an adult was taking charge of her troublesome brother.

'Okay Lily, we know.' Ella cleaned Arlo up as best as she could and took off her jumper, pulling it very carefully over his head and wrapping it round him. 'I need to get you downstairs, Arlo; I don't think we should wait for the ambulance.'

Ella made Lily go down the steps on her bottom to where Noelle was waiting, crying as she pulled her granddaughter close. Then Ella helped Arlo walk to the door and sat down, sliding him cautiously onto her knee. 'We're

185

going down the same way as Lily, okay. I won't touch your arm.'

The stone was freezing beneath Ella's legs, and she was hugely relieved when they made it safely to the bottom. Arlo was crying silent tears and she thought how incredibly brave he was being. She was pretty sure his arm was broken, and he must be in a great deal of pain. One glance at Noelle's stricken face and Ella knew she would be little help. She felt for her car keys again, trying not to shiver in her T-shirt.

'I'll drive, Noelle. You need to sit in the back and support Arlo.'

Chapter Fifteen

Ella drove through the December night along unfamiliar roads as quickly as she could, very grateful to see the lights of town popping up after half an hour. All the way Noelle had been chattering nervously to the children, and Ella also heard her leave a voicemail for Max in anxious and hurried French. She didn't understand everything Noelle had said but she could hear how frightened she was from her tone.

Once they got to A&E, they were quickly through triage and into a cubicle. Arlo had been given pain relief and was perking up now, excited about this new adventure and all the attention he was receiving. Ella was ready to cry gulping tears of relief when the young doctor examined him and everything except for his arm checked out normally. An X-ray was soon arranged; the doctor was as sure as she could be without further examination that Arlo's arm was broken.

'Oh *non*, *non*, this is all my fault! Will he be all right?' Noelle wailed, her hand clutching Arlo's foot. The doctor was quick to reassure her that Arlo would be fine and hopefully surgery on his arm would not be required. Going over what had happened and why was not for now. Ella knew that would come later, and was a conversation Max needed to have with his mother.

Arlo's right hand was gripping Ella's and when she tried to slip hers free so the nurse could lift him into a wheelchair for the trip to X-ray, he clung on even tighter, his eyes pleading with her not to let him go. She didn't, gently smoothing the hair flopping on his face as he was settled into the chair. His temperature was normal now and the doctor was satisfied he wasn't hypothermic.

Lily wouldn't let go of Ella's other hand and she persuaded Noelle to wait in A&E in case Max arrived while they were gone. Ella felt the old terror of hospitals returning in the adrenaline still not quite dispersed from her limbs and the dull glare of lights, the strange stillness in the stricken faces she saw as they marched along corridors to the X-ray department. She wished her mind hadn't taken her all the way back to that day when Lauren had been rushed from home and into hospital, remembering how quickly her apparently fit and healthy twin had faded as her body succumbed to the illness that had ravaged her so suddenly.

Ella felt the hurt hovering, threatening her outward calm, her concern for Arlo bound up with the relief that she'd got him safely here and the nurses and doctors would take care of him. That she'd bring him home again and see him tucked up in his own bed, a new day waiting and not the end she had feared in those first frightening moments when she'd seen him flat out on the floor beneath the broken ladder.

Her hand had stopped bleeding and she thanked the nurse who gave her a wipe to clean it. She was still covered in dirt from working in the studios, her hair felt grimy and dull, and she had blood on her T-shirt. They had to wait for Arlo's X-ray results and she sank onto a chair beside him. Lily scrambled onto her lap and Ella began to tremble again as the warmth of the little girl's body snuggled into hers. She saw the fright still apparent in Lily's face and slid an arm round her shoulders.

'It's okay,' Ella whispered against the top of her head. 'Arlo will be fine, and we'll all be home again soon. Once they know more about his arm, they'll be able to do something to help it mend.'

'Will Daddy be cross with me for letting Arlo get hurt?' Lily's voice was a murmur against Ella's chest and her heart clenched.

'Of course he won't. Sometimes these things happen.' She gently brushed Lily's curls from her face. 'My brother fell out of a tree once after we'd had a row. And another time he crashed his bike and broke a tooth and had to go to the dentist to get it fixed, like us being here with Arlo to get his arm fixed. But my mum and dad weren't cross with us, and your dad won't blame you either.'

'You have a brother? What's his name?' Lily's voice was sleepy. 'Do you have any sisters?'

Ella swallowed back the truth; that was for another time. 'My brother's called Jamie. We used to fight when we were little, like you and Arlo, but we love each other really, and he's always there when I need him.'

'I want to be there for Arlo too when I grow up, like you and your brother, Ella.' Lily raised her head to fix a serious gaze on Ella. 'My mummy would want me to look after him because she's not here. And Daddy too.'

'Of course she would.' Ella hugged Lily tightly, pressing her lips against her forehead. 'But you're still very young and it's the adults' job to take care of you both.'

'Until I'm grown up?'

'Yes, until you're grown up – and good luck with bossing Arlo around then.' Ella felt Lily smile. 'I think he'll try and do a bit of bossing of his own. He loves you, Lily, just like your daddy does. And your daddy won't be cross with you, I promise. He'll just want to know you're both safe and well because he loves you so much.'

The results were back, and Arlo was delighted to have a confirmed diagnosis of a break above his wrist. He was excited by all the drama and happy to be on his way to the fracture room as a nurse wheeled him along, cracking jokes and making him laugh. The sound of something so ordinary made Ella almost giddy with relief.

Lily snuggled on her lap once again as they settled in the new room. Both children were fascinated by the plaster technician when he explained what he was going to do and asked Arlo to choose his favourite colour for his special cast.

Lily was standing on Arlo's right side with Ella, staring at his arm as the technician worked carefully. She heard footsteps thundering down the corridor a few seconds before Max tore into the room with Ashley. His eyes raked Ella's and she couldn't miss the worry and relief in them as his gaze shot over to Arlo. She quickly backed up so Max could reach him, Lily's hand still clamped in hers.

'Hey buddy, what have you been doing?' Max threw the technician a grateful glance as he ruffled his son's hair and kissed the top of his head, trying not to get in the way. 'This is a lot of excitement for a Thursday evening.'

'I've broken my arm, Daddy, and I'm getting a special cast to make it better. Look!'

Ella felt a smile hovering at the triumph in Arlo's voice. She was starting to shiver now her adrenaline had finally fled and Max was here to take care of his children. The room was warm yet she felt cold, achy almost, and a pressure was increasing in her temples.

'Is that right?' There was a suggestion of amusement from Max, and he let out a weary sigh.

'We were playing in the flat and the ladder broke when Arlo tried to climb it, Daddy, I'm sorry. Mamie was busy and we wanted to explore.'

Lily's voice was an anxious whisper and Max spun round. He held out his arms and Lily let Ella go to dart into them. He pulled her tightly against him, lifting her up, and Ella had a crazy wish to join them.

'It's all right, Lily. It was an accident and not your fault. There's nothing for you to worry about. I've seen Mamie and she told me what happened.' Max's eyes found Ella's above Lily's head and she could guess at his own worry still unabated, the questions, the recriminations over how this had happened, the guilt that he hadn't been there to look after the children himself. 'The flat is definitely off-limits for playing though. It's not safe.'

'I should probably go back now,' Ella said, eyeing the single chair at Arlo's side. There were four adults here, including Noelle waiting in A&E, and she didn't want to be in the way. 'I could take Lily home if you like. Maybe she'd like a hot drink and something to eat before bed.' She wasn't sure Lily would want to leave Max or Arlo yet, but it was worth a try. It was late for the children and they'd both be shattered tomorrow, after such drama.

Ella wasn't expecting the grateful look Max gave her or the way Lily immediately held out her arms. He transferred her across and his hands brushed Ella's bare skin.

'You're cold,' he muttered, his eyes sharp on hers. 'Where's your coat?'

'Arlo was sick on Ella's coat, Daddy, and she gave him her jumper too.' Lily yawned, snuggling her head into

Ella's shoulder. 'Please will you stay and read me a story when we get home?'

'Of course I will. I'll stay until your daddy and Arlo get back.'

'Take this.' Max shrugged out of his coat and draped it around Ella, tucking it over Lily too as best he could. 'You can't go outside in just a T-shirt, it's freezing.'

Ella was trembling again and his warmth still lingering in the fabric made her feel as though he'd hugged her too, had wrapped his arms round his daughter safe in Ella's hold.

'I'll see you at home, we'll be back as soon as we can.' He dropped a kiss on Lily's head, bringing his face close to Ella's. She felt his hair brushing her forehead, the second when his cheek bumped hers. She gave Arlo a cheery grin and made him promise to show her his cast later, and said goodbye to Ashley.

Lily fell asleep on the way home and Ella carried her into the cottage. Prim was barking and she realised they'd forgotten the poor dog in all the drama with Arlo. She quickly let Prim into the garden and settled Lily on the sofa with a cosy blanket and a book, then fed Prim and rustled up the promised hot chocolate. It didn't take long to make cheese and tomato on toast as well, and Lily demolished two slices to Ella's one. Lily was less keen on the idea of going to bed without seeing Arlo, but after a story Ella tucked her in and she was asleep in moments. She switched on the nightlight Lily wanted and returned downstairs to wait.

The family room felt subdued with only Ella and Prim in it, and she was grateful for the dog's company as Prim rested her head on Ella for a cuddle. She switched on the television, staring at the screen without really seeing it.

Anything to take her mind off the frantic dash to hospital and her memories of Lauren leaving home that hideous night.

Prim heard the front door open before Ella did and offered a solitary bark, her tail thumping as she recognised the footsteps approaching down the hall. Ella hurried over and almost bumped into Max carrying Arlo as they reached the door at the same time.

'How is he?' Arlo was asleep, his arm encased in his bright red cast. Max's smile was as relieved as the resignation in his eyes.

'He's fine, they've given him some more pain relief so I'm going to get him changed and into bed.'

'Can I help?'

Max, at the bottom of the stairs, turned. 'I don't think so but thanks.' He hesitated. 'I'd love a coffee when he's settled. Decaf though.'

'Wouldn't you prefer some peace and quiet?'

'Not unless you would?'

He waited long enough to see Ella shake her head. He was back in twenty minutes and pointed to the television still on. 'Would you mind? I'd much rather listen to music than that.'

'Of course not.'

'Is classical okay? I find it relaxes me the most.'

'That's fine.' She brought their coffee over. The room felt weighted with expectancy without the children's usual chatter and squabbles to lighten this new atmosphere. 'Is Arlo all right?'

Max was busy on his phone and the sound of the television was soon replaced by a piano concerto Ella didn't recognise. 'Crashed. I thought it might take a while to settle him, but I just about managed to get him out of the

193

bathroom and into pyjamas with a pillow underneath his arm before he was gone.'

'That's good, he'll need the rest.'

'Mmm.' Max leaned back and closed his eyes. 'Not the only one.'

'Have you eaten?' Ella was curled on the sofa near his and wrapped Lily's blanket around her; too tired to go back to the house and find another layer. 'Sorry, I'd forgotten. You had dinner with Ashley.'

'Actually, I didn't. We'd only got as far as ordering when I got Maman's message.'

'I could make you some cheese on toast?' Ella threw the blanket aside and was off the sofa in one movement. 'Lily and I had some earlier, it won't take—'

'Ella?' Max caught her hand and she halted, staring at his fingers around hers. 'It's fine. I'm not really hungry and it's certainly not your job to feed me.'

'No, you're right.' She laughed, a light, brittle sound, as their hands separated, and she returned to the sofa and the blanket. 'It's your kitchen, you can make what you like in it. Sorry.'

'And don't apologise either, I know you were being kind. I appreciate it.'

'Okay. Thanks.'

'That's your thing, isn't it?' His voice dropped, and Ella was glad of the blanket and Prim coming over to distract her, as though the blanket could shield her from his gaze, suddenly piercing. 'Taking care of people,' he went on. 'Encouraging them, helping them grow. You haven't been here long and already Stan's strutting around like he's ten feet tall because you've taken the time to recognise his skill and find him more to do. You've made connections at the village shop, got the landlord of the local pub offering

194

me a discount on his craft beer and suggesting we build a meal at the pub into our retreat packages. My mother's persuaded you into one of her gowns to sit for a portrait and Pearl's giving away tables for the Christmas open day faster than I can keep up with her messages telling me so. And then tonight, taking care of my children and my mother the way you did.'

'Anyone would have done the same.' Ella hesitated, thinking of Noelle's distress earlier. 'How is she?'

'Frightened. Apologetic and frantic, and we both know there's a difficult conversation to be had. She's not really cut out for taking care of them, however much she tries.' He sighed, running a hand across his face. 'She told me how calm you were and how you looked after them all.' He paused. 'She also told me I'd be crazy to let you go.'

The colour drained from Ella's face and the hand stroking Prim's head trembled as the soothing piano notes from the speaker drifted around them. 'I'm not really here, Max,' she told him quietly. 'And it's probably time to let you get some rest.'

'Back to an empty house you don't want to be alone in?'

'That's not fair. I don't have any choice while I'm here.' She gently lifted Prim's head and threw the blanket off.

'I'm sorry, I shouldn't have said that.'

His gaze was unflinching, and Ella saw the sudden truth written on his face. He didn't want her to leave either.

She jumped to her feet and was at the door before him, shivering in her T-shirt the moment she pulled it open. The icy air reached in, wrapping her in its grip, the heat in his gaze moments ago no longer enough to keep away the cold.

'Thank you for everything you did tonight.'

She wanted to tell him it was fine, but the words caught on a sob that clutched at her throat. She saw again in her mind the ambulance arriving to take Lauren away, her dad staying behind to look after her and Jamie while her mum, white-faced and still, clutched Lauren's hand as she was rushed outside. Ella had never been able to forget the long hours waiting for news, praying for improvement, hoping for the best and fearing the worst as time moved on and her family's world ground to a shocking and horrifying halt.

It hadn't been the same tonight, with Arlo, but her fear, the fright, the possibility of a future for Max and Lily without him were the same in those first terrifying moments when she'd found him slumped on the floor of the flat. Ella's shivering worsened into tremors reverberating through her body and she couldn't make her feet move towards the house. Didn't want to leave Max and the understanding she saw in his gaze. He reached out, swiftly pulling her against him. She hated that grief had found her once again, even as she clung to him and her tears dampened his shirt.

'Ella, it's all right, I've got you.' His lips were against her hair and gradually her sobs subsided as they held one another. 'I can't make it okay but I'm here. I've got you.'

She knew what would happen the moment she tipped her head back and saw his eyes, urgent on hers. She felt the push and pull of what they were about to do, and her stomach fell away as longing slammed into her. Her breath was already catching as they waited, almost daring the other to act first. Then his mouth landed on hers and she wanted nothing more than to give herself up to the kiss his eyes had been promising for days. His hand was in her hair, the other hard on her back as they kissed with frantic longing. It was a fierce, life-affirming, consuming kiss that had her pushing him back inside until he was against the wall, their lips refusing to relinquish one another.

His wide shoulders were firm beneath her hands, and she slid them down to his chest. She was dazed, dizzy, lost in the passion they'd unleashed as his hands ran down her arms, thumbs skimming her breasts until they edged beneath her T-shirt to rest on the bare skin at her waist. Max dragged his mouth from hers, their eyes heavy with desire, lips crushed, breath snagging as it left her body, limbs trembling and unsteady.

'I've been wanting to do this since that night I found you on the drive,' he muttered hoarsely. 'I hate the thought of you being alone when I want you beside me.'

'Please don't say something you'll regret in the morning.' His heart was thudding beneath Ella's hand, and she held back a gasp as she felt him tracing a pattern on her skin beneath the T-shirt. She ought to step away but instead she lifted her hands to his face. Felt the scratch of his stubble against her palms as she saw the wonder, the glimmer of tears hovering. 'We're both tired and stressed after what happened, Max. It was just a mad moment. And now...'

'And now, what?' His gaze was loaded with a surprising certainty, and he blinked back the brightness from before. 'I don't regret anything I've said or done, Ella. But maybe you do?'

'You know I don't.' She couldn't offer words that differed from the reply to his question her body had already given him. Her pulse was still soaring, and she let her hands fall to rest lightly on his shoulders. She wanted more, longing to unfasten the buttons on his shirt so she could uncover the reality of what she'd been imagining for weeks. Her fingers went to his chest, the first two buttons already undone, and he dragged in a breath. His hand covered hers, sliding it to the next button, but she stilled, his skin hot against hers already blazing.

'We can't do this.' Her voice was a muttered whisper, an attempt at reason full of regret. 'It would change everything and working together would be so much worse when it ends. I don't want some casual fling I have to hide from everyone else, most especially your children.'

'Neither do I, Ella. And it's complicated, I get it. They can't be hurt again.' Max sighed as he lifted her hand, slowly kissing her fingers one by one, and she attempted a smile.

'Can you please not do that either, not unless you plan on closing the door and telling Prim to go away.'

'What?' His glance fell to see Prim, waiting expectantly next to Ella. 'I didn't even know she was there.'

'That's because it's not your foot she's standing on.'

'Actually, it's because I was thinking about the incredible woman in front of me and whom I very much wish didn't have to leave.'

Prim was wagging her tail and whining softly. 'Bugger off,' he hissed, and Ella stifled a laugh when the dog tilted her head to one side, as though asking him to repeat the instruction. 'You really are a bloody nuisance sometimes,' Max muttered as he stepped aside, and Prim followed him happily into the family room. He closed the door firmly and Ella straightened her T-shirt.

'I think that's my cue to go.'

'I suppose it is. I wish you didn't have to.' His was smiling as his hands covered hers.

'I know. But I do. Are we still doing that working lunch tomorrow?'

'Better not, if you don't mind. I've promised Arlo I'll stay with him, so it's tractors and telly all day.'

'Sounds perfect.' She blinked at the new tenderness in Max's expression, unprepared for the suggestion of regret that still lingered. 'I can change the booking; we can do it another time.'

'The lunch? Or something else?' There was mischief there now too and she smiled. Maybe she would regret this in the morning when day replaced night and light sent away dark. Maybe tomorrow would bring with it all the reasons why their fooling around was so unwise. But all she could think was how much she liked being with him, as she stepped into the night, his hand holding hers until she reluctantly tugged it free and turned away.

Chapter Sixteen

Ella left the house just before first light for a run, feeling as though she had woken in a whole new world. Surely she wasn't imagining that the festive lights Stan had hung from his workshop were glittering more brightly or his whistle sounded especially cheery? Or was it merely false hope, a feeling not to be given voice despite the incredible kiss she and Max had shared last night? She knew they had both been overwrought and anxious. Arlo's accident and her and Max's separate, urgent flights to hospital had seen to that.

She checked her watch. She needed to get back if she was going to catch the children before Lily left for school. And Max. Ella wanted to see him too, to find his eyes in the new day and learn what was in them now. Would it be regret, dismissal, a quick laugh to shrug off all they'd shared? Or something different, a realisation that he too, wanted to cling to the intimacy of those final moments in his house and find a way to move forward? There wasn't time for a shower, and she knocked at the cottage door still in her running kit, warm, with her breath slowing, hair tucked into a baseball cap. The door swung back, and her anxiety dissolved the moment she saw a grin lighting up Max's face. He made a grab for Prim as she darted outside to greet Ella.

'Come back here, you little monster.'

'Little!' Ella gasped, trying to curb Prim's exuberance as she bounced with joy. 'She's nearly as big as me when she does that.' She pushed at the paws trying to reach her shoulders and Prim finally backed off, sitting down firmly on the gravel and staring intently at Ella.

'Looks like I'm not the only one who's happy to see you,' Max said dryly. 'I really do have to take her to training again after Christmas.'

'Yes, you should. I just came to see how the patient's doing.'

'That's thoughtful of you. He's still asleep, otherwise I think he'd love to see you too. He's very proud of his cast.' Max pulled the door back and Prim sidled in first. It was starting to rain, and she shook herself with great enthusiasm. 'He woke early for more Calpol and was away again straight after.'

Prim wandered off and Ella saw Lily at the island eating breakfast in her uniform. 'Can I help? I could stay with Arlo while you take Lily to school.'

'Thanks, that would be great. I wasn't looking forward to having to wake him and get him in the car so I can run her down. Quicker than walking today.' He paused, a flash of something darker crossing his face. 'I didn't want to disturb my mother or have her getting upset again in front of Lily.'

'I understand. How is she?'

'Okay, but she's still shaken. She called earlier.' Max checked over his shoulder to make sure Lily wasn't listening. 'Apparently she was painting and hadn't expected them to leave the flat. Didn't hear them go until it was too late, and then she couldn't find them.'

'I hope she's okay, I'll drop in later. She wouldn't have wanted any harm to come to them, not for the world.'

'I know. But how can I rely on her to care for them if I'm wondering the whole time if she's got distracted? Anyway…'

Ella touched his arm as she squeezed past on her way to see Lily.

'Ella?'

'Yes?' She paused.

'How are you, after last night?' There was hesitancy in his lowered voice, and she saw his glance dart over her shoulder again to his daughter.

'I'm fine. What about you?'

'Still no regrets, if that's what you mean. Even after four hours' sleep.'

'I guess that makes two of us then. And I managed five.' She liked the quick pleasure on his face, his hand reaching out to squeeze hers.

Lily was having toast and Max made some for Ella too, before he scooped up a protesting daughter to drive her to school. It was Lily's party tomorrow and Ella had plenty for her and Stan to do. She was at the door waving Lily off when Stan appeared, concerned about Arlo and the drama that had taken place after he'd left last night.

'Made 'im this,' he said gruffly, passing Ella a little wooden figure. It was a beautifully carved tractor in miniature, and she turned it over, admiring his craftsmanship and the cleverly executed wheels and cab.

'Oh Stan, it's beautiful. Arlo's going to love it. Thank you, Max will be thrilled.'

'Let's 'ope so,' Stan said, blowing on his hands. The donkey jacket was on, along with a bright yellow bobble hat; Ella was sure she recognised Pearl's handiwork. 'Come on then, young Ella, if we're gonna find them trees,' Stan went on. 'Can't stand around 'ere all day, not if you want me to lay a trail an' build a campfire for tomorrow. An' then there's them barn doors an' a new window to finish. I'm gonna be askin' the boss for a Christmas bonus with all this work you've given me. I can feel an 'oliday comin' on.'

'I can't leave yet; I'm staying with Arlo. I'll come with you as soon as Max gets back.' Ella thought privately that a Christmas bonus wasn't a bad idea and resolved to have a word with Max herself. 'How about Secret Santa, shall we do that?'

'What, when we all spend a fiver an' give each other mugs?'

'Same principle, but let's see if we can't be a bit more creative with the gifts. Shall I organise it?'

'Aye, long as I don't get our Pearl. I 'ave enough problems tryin' to buy her presents without findin' another. I reckon she's tryin' to trip me up in knittin' needles, she 'as that many.' Stan stamped his feet. 'I'll be in me workshop when you're ready.'

'Won't be long, I promise.' Ella indicated her running kit. 'No time for me to have a shower and change first?'

'Nope. We've got a party to sort an' trees to fetch. Them kids deserve a good time an' there's gonna be a Christmas tree in the courtyard if it takes me all night to get it up.' He coughed awkwardly. 'If you'll pardon the expression.'

'Never even occurred to me.' She saw his grin and returned it, then closed the door before Prim could take off after him.

After the excursion with Stan to find trees, Ella was lying in the roll-top bath in her en suite and admiring Pearl's social media posts for the Christmas open day. Although the shower in the house was a revelation after the sorry little drip in the flat, she loved a good soak and had decided she could spare twenty minutes of her working day. She and Stan had found five Christmas trees in the far reaches of the woodland that belonged to Halesmere and he'd cut down the first one and dropped it off at the church on their way back. It was apparently a tradition for the house to supply the church with a tree and Sandy was delighted with their choice.

When she stepped out of the bath and wrapped herself in a huge, fluffy towel, she felt refreshed and ready to tackle more preparations for Lily's party. She had left her bedroom door open, and she padded across the new carpet to close it. Her hand stilled on the doorknob as she heard music rising from the hall beneath. She walked slowly across the landing, drawn by the sound and peeped over the banister.

Max was sitting at the grand piano, playing with something she could only believe was an exquisite joy and ease. Goosebumps rose on her body, and she felt the hairs on her arms standing up as she listened. Something in the melody seemed familiar but she couldn't have named it. She watched, captivated, as his body followed the lightness and skill of his hands, needing no sheet music to remind him of the notes. He might have been playing from his soul straight to her heart; she was holding in tears, smiling through the emotion she'd rarely found in classical music before now. The house was still and yet felt suddenly alive with beauty and life, and she wanted this moment to never end as the music filled her senses.

'Ella!'

She jumped, clutching her towel and trying to hold on to those few, intimate memories of Max playing. The music abruptly ended and through the open door to the drawing room she saw Arlo on a sofa. Max sprang up and backed away from the piano.

'Come and see my cast, it's red.' Arlo was squirming excitedly, and Max glanced from him to Ella on the landing.

'I'm so sorry, I didn't know you were here,' he said quickly. 'I thought you were still out with Stan. I would never have come in if I'd known.'

'It's fine, please don't apologise. Stan needed me in a hurry. And it is your house.'

'But yours for now, and you deserve some privacy at least.' Max avoided her gaze as he pushed the stool in under the piano. 'We'll leave you in peace.'

'You don't have to. I'm on my way out again, so stay if you like.' She was lingering, wanting to let him know how she felt. 'Your playing was beautiful. It made me want to cry but in a good way.'

'I'm glad you liked it. But I'm out of practice for a piece like that, I'm sure Rachmaninov wouldn't thank me for nearly murdering it.' Max's smile seemed shy, almost self-conscious as he shrugged a shoulder. 'I always played for the kids at night when they couldn't settle. Arlo was fractious and his arm was hurting, and he asked me to bring him over so I could play. He fell asleep and I couldn't resist carrying on.'

'I wish you hadn't stopped.' Ella's own smile was wistful too.

'You might not be saying that if I had carried on.'

'I think I would.' She was still holding the towel in place, and she saw his glance flick over her, felt the jump in her pulse. 'I'd better get changed, I want to see Arlo's cast and Stan will be hunting me down if I'm not hiding stuff in the garden in the next fifteen minutes.'

–

Later Ella ran down to school with Prim to meet Lily, who came out laden with the usual bags and belongings, plus cards and gifts for Arlo. Several adults came over to ask how he was, and a few said they'd see Ella tomorrow at Lily's party. She was giddy with excitement and Ella told her very firmly that she was not allowed in the garden or the courtyard until it was time for the party. Back at the cottage, Arlo was happier to see his gifts than his sister and once she had gone to change out of her uniform, Max pointed to the kitchen island.

'Look at this. Pearl's dropped in some shopping in case I can't get away and she brought my mother a bottle of wine to cheer her up. Sandy from the church called and read Arlo his favourite story, and Pete's wife has sent vegetable lasagne and chocolate cake, so I don't have to cook tonight. And now all this from school. Everyone's been amazing.'

'So not as invisible as you think then, hey.' Prim was hovering, waiting for a meal, and Ella went to the kitchen to feed her. 'People do know you're here, Max. You are part of the community, even if you don't realise it.'

'I haven't given much back though, have I?' His eyes were glistening, and he shook his head.

'You have time to change that, to make Halesmere a proper home for you all.' Ella put Prim's bowl down, smiling as the dog dived in. 'How is your mum? I did call earlier but she must have been working.'

'Okay.' He let out a long breath. 'She was thinking about cancelling her trip to France, but I've said she should still go. With you here, Ella...' He caught her hand for a second. 'I know you'll look after Lily and Arlo if we need you.'

Ella knew if she and Max had been alone, she would have gone to him, slid her arms round him. But Arlo was on the sofa, and she couldn't show Max what it meant that he trusted her to take care of his children. 'Any time.'

'I know. And thank you.'

–

By three p.m. on Saturday the light was already fading, and the task of keeping tabs on the children was made harder by Stan's inventiveness in hiding items for the scavenger hunt. Ella had also elicited his help in stringing fairy lights around the garden, and he'd managed to fix a huge Christmas tree in the courtyard. It looked magical, shimmering with coloured lights, candy canes strung on the lowest branches as part of the winter wonderland hunt.

The campfire was burning nicely, and Stan was wearing his favourite, festive fancy dress costume. Not Santa Claus, as she'd wondered aloud yesterday when he'd refused, smirking, to tell her. He'd turned up dressed as a rather rotund elf and the children adored it, especially when he got them all reciting that the best way to spread Christmas cheer was to sing aloud for all to hear.

'This party is going to go down as legend, Ella.' Ashley was wrapped up in a chunky scarf with a matching hat, stamping her feet as they stood together. Snow was forecast and the air was frigid. 'Max loved your suggestions and it's clearly a huge hit with the kids.'

'Thanks Ashley.' Ella had seen her helping little ones with the scavenger hunt. The children were gathered at a safe distance around the fire now as hot dogs and warm juice were handed out. 'I'm glad it's not actually my job to organise children's parties. The pressure is relentless.'

'For sure, we'll all be ready to crash later. Whenever my two have a sleepover, I can't wait to hand them all back again the next morning.'

'I can imagine.'

'How are the plans coming along for supper next week?' Ashley had to raise her voice over the din. 'I'll be with you all day on Wednesday to decorate.'

'Really good, thanks, everything's on track. And thank you for helping, I can't wait to see the house all set for Christmas.'

'Is your photographer coming?'

'Yes, I think the festive images will be a lovely way to showcase the house online until we have other events later.'

'You're planning to stay, then? At Halesmere?' Ashley waved to one of her girls, who was brandishing a plate of goodies.

'Until my contract is up anyway.' Thoughts of the kiss Ella had shared with Max were still in her mind, along with the realisation that she was coming to feel at home in this place and she liked his company – more than that. 'I'm looking at creating another event in the New Year, possibly a short retreat. Once the website is live, we need to keep the content relevant.'

'Of course. And there's that job you mentioned, the one with your old boss. You must give it serious thought, Ella, despite what happened between you. Max was telling me how talented you are, and he knows he can't keep you babysitting Lily and Arlo indefinitely. He's very mindful of your role here being temporary and he wouldn't want you to pass up a great opportunity for him. Or Halesmere.'

Max was approaching with Arlo and Ella was relieved to change the subject, thinking about what else Max might have told Ashley about her and if she'd imagined the suggestion of steel in Ashley's voice. The little boy's broken arm was bound up in its sling inside an old coat of his dad's, fastened to keep the cold away.

'I think this one's had too many s'mores, it's time to get him away from the sugar.' Max gave both women a grin and Ella saw his gaze through the firelight lingering on hers until he glanced at Arlo. 'I hope I'm still going to get that lie-in you've promised me tomorrow, buddy. I'd really appreciate sleeping past six a.m. on a Sunday for once.'

One of Ashley's girls was shrieking, and she gave Max an apologetic look as she marched over to deal with the problem. He dropped his head towards Ella. 'Keep your eye on the gate,' he said, and she saw the flash of his smile. 'I might have gone a bit overboard on the winter wonderland theme.'

'What have you done?'

'Listen.'

Ella tried. 'I can't hear anything other than excited kids and a crackling fire.'

'Sure about that?' Max put a hand on her shoulder, turning her to face the wide entrance into the garden.

'Bells?'

'Yep.' His voice rose as he called to the children. 'Look everyone, I think we have visitors.'

They spun round just as two inky-black horses pulling a carriage trotted onto the wide gravel path, the carriage and their harnesses lit by hundreds of shimmering fairy lights with softly jingling bells. Ella was aware of gasps as the kids scrambled to their feet to see that Stan had driven his pickup right up to the gate to light the horses' path to the party.

'Oh, Max.' She was enthralled. 'You've made their day and Lily will be so thrilled. No one's going to forget this party in a hurry.'

'Thanks to you.' He seemed to be very close as he dropped the words in Ella's ear, lifting Arlo into his arms so he could see better.

'Me?' She wanted to feel Max's words skimming her skin again. 'I hardly did a thing, Stan's done most of the work.'

'Yes, you did,' Max said simply. 'You took Lily seriously when she asked you for help, and then created all this for her.'

'It was—'

'Don't say nothing.' His eyes were fixed on hers in the firelight, brightening his face through the shadows. 'It's everything to Lily, and happiness has been in short supply these past two years. And seeing them happy makes me happy.'

'Oh Ella, thank you, thank you!' Lily had reached them, and she threw her arms round Ella. 'This is just the best party ever, I'll never forget it!'

'Your dad did this, Lily, not me. The horses were his idea.' Ella bent down to hug Lily back, but she was already gone, flinging herself on Max.

'Thank you, Papa, I love you.' Then Lily was racing to join the others and stare in wonder at the horses snorting gently through the frigid air. Someone screamed in nervous excitement when one stamped a large hoof, jingling the bells. Ella and Max followed with an awed Arlo.

'Daddy, come on!' Lily grabbed Max's hand, dragging him towards the carriage. 'It's big enough for us all to ride together.'

She insisted that Ella join them and sit by Max, Arlo excited and secure on his lap, with Ashley opposite them. The children were nearly demented with glee as the horses walked forward and the carriage rolled gently after them along the drive. They were off, the fairy lights shimmering through the darkness as the bells jangled merrily.

Stan followed with the pickup and the horses circled at the bottom of the drive, snorting and blowing silvered breath into the air as they returned to the house. Ashley got out first to record the family, and Ella, inside the carriage until it was their turn to climb down. Arlo didn't want to get out at all and took a bit of persuading from Max as tears threatened.

Everyone was watching as the horses returned to the lorry parked at the end of the drive. The fairy lights went out and the black horses seemed to vanish in the shadows, making the children gasp as though they'd just witnessed a magic trick. Then tiny Christmas stockings filled with goodies were handed out by Noelle and parents gathered up overexcited little ones still gushing about the horses. Max thanked everyone until it was just the four of them left, plus Ashley and her two girls. Stan, still in his merry elf costume, drove past in the pickup, tooting his horn and waving a green arm through the open window.

'Christmas bonus for Stan, I think. Dressing as an elf is above and beyond his regular duties.' Max put Arlo down, holding on to his good hand. 'Time for a chill, buddy. You need a rest.'

'How about that takeaway we talked about?' Ashley smiled at Max. 'The kids could do with a quiet couple of hours before bed and I'm famished. We could put a movie on for them.'

'Sounds good.' Max found his keys in his pocket. 'Ella, you're welcome to join us,' he said casually.

'That's really nice but you guys go on ahead. I'm ready to crash too, don't think I could last long enough to eat a takeaway.' She had met Marta at her farm last night and had a lovely long evening that had seen her back at Halesmere much later than she'd expected. Marta had shown her the tiny room where she poured her candles and crafted her creations, already planning next spring's range and wax melts for summer. She was very interested in a studio and had taken a table at the open day.

'Sure?'

'Absolutely.' Ella bent down. 'Lily, I hope you and your friends have had the best time – and don't forget to give your dad a lie-in tomorrow, okay?'

'Okay, Ella,' Lily assured her with a serious expression. 'Thank you for arranging my party, it was amazing.'

'My pleasure.' Lily's arms around Ella were slight as they hugged. Then she shared a gentle high-five with Arlo on his good hand. 'See you at work, Max.' She dropped that in to try and suggest a professional distance she knew they were moving beyond. 'Bye Ashley, hope you enjoy the rest of your weekend.'

'You too, Ella, I'll see you Wednesday. I'm looking forward to trying your special menu. Ready, Max? We'd better order before it gets too late.' Ella watched Ashley walk into the cottage and shrug out of her coat, draping it on the newel post at the foot of the stairs.

Lily was tugging on Max's hand as they followed. 'Daddy, is Stan one of Santa's special elves?'

'I don't think so, Lily. I think Santa would need him to spend more time at the North Pole rather than here. But he is a very good elf, I was impressed.'

Ella watched them leave, already regretting refusing Max's invitation to join them. But with Ashley there, her sharp attention always on him, Ella knew it would be very difficult to pretend she wasn't coming to care for him and the children so much.

Chapter Seventeen

Ella had eventually fallen asleep after midnight and was still dreaming about horses galloping through the gardens when something crash-landed on her bed. She jerked up from her pillows with a scream to see Lily sitting on the end with a smile.

'Lily! How did you get in here?' Ella's pulse was thudding as she sank back, thankful she hadn't knocked her off the bed in shock. She checked warily for signs of Prim or anyone else coming to join them. The lights were blazing on the landing as usual, and it was still dark outside. Her eyes narrowed as she gave Lily a mock glare. 'Your dad's not with you, is he?'

'He's still asleep, so's Arlo. I found Daddy's keys.' Lily was looking decidedly pleased with herself. 'I'm sorry I woke you up.'

'That's okay.' Ella stifled a yawn. 'But I don't think your dad would be very happy you've left the cottage on your own and come over here.'

'But it's his treat on our kindness calendar and he's having a lie-in. I want to take him breakfast in bed, but I don't know how to make it. I'm not allowed to use the kettle or his coffee machine.'

'Ah.' Ella smiled, despite the rude awakening. 'So you need some help with breakfast and thought you'd ask me.'

'Is that okay?' Lily tilted her head, looking hopeful.

'Depends.' Ella grinned. She was enjoying teasing her. 'What time is it?'

'Half past six, I checked my iPad.'

'Lily!' Ella pulled a pillow over her face. 'What about my lie-in too?'

'You don't need one as much as Daddy does.'

'Is that right? And how do you know I don't need a lie-in?'

'Because me and Arlo aren't there to wake you up in the mornings.' Lily was triumphant. 'You can get up whenever you like.'

'Well, right now I'm not sure I want to get up at all.' Ella was half-sighing, half-smiling behind her pillow. 'Oh, go on then, it's only sleep. Hopefully I can have some more tonight. Wait on the landing and don't touch anything that might make a noise.'

Lily scampered from Ella's room, and she dressed quickly. She hadn't been expecting to see the family today and certainly not at this hour, but she liked the anticipation of bumping into Max so soon. Outside Lily insisted that they creep into the cottage as silently as possible in case they woke him or Arlo. Prim almost gave them away when she barked a couple of times and thumped her tail.

Lily couldn't decide what Max might like best, so after a check of the fridge and cupboards Ella suggested bacon, scrambled eggs, sourdough toast, coffee and juice. There was much giggling and whispering from Lily, who was helping and hindering in equal measure. When it was ready Ella carried the tray upstairs, insisting firmly to Lily that she was not staying to eat with them. She would simply deliver breakfast to Max and then she was off. Back to bed, if she had any say in it. Running could wait for later.

When their little party reached his room Lily charged inside yelling 'surprise' as though she was a marauding elephant, and Ella stifled a laugh. There was little chance of Max sleeping through that commotion and he shot up in bed just as she had, blinking rapidly and running a bewildered hand over his face. She was already realising that she had not thought this through. Why wasn't he wearing a T-shirt to bed in December? When he spotted Ella he grabbed one, pulling it over his head. That helped, she thought; the glimpse of muscular, golden chest at this hour of the day was far too distracting.

'We've given you a lie-in and brought you breakfast in bed to say thank you for my party. It was the kindness for today on our advent calendar, Daddy. I've already eaten the chocolate one.' Lily clambered across and plonked herself next to him. 'Ella helped me.'

'So I see. And why did you badger Ella to help you with breakfast on a Sunday morning? She's not supposed to be working.' He glanced across. She liked his grin and returned it with a smile of her own.

'I woke her up.' Lily sounded very proud of herself as Max lifted a hand to sweep back the hair falling to his brow.

'Is that right?' There was a stern note among his sleepy amusement. 'So you let yourself out of the house, went alone into the other one and got Ella out of bed to make my breakfast? Wow. Sorry, Ella. But top marks for initiative, Lily and don't do it again. And where's your brother?'

'Still asleep, I checked. We've left him some bacon.'

'What time is it?' Max leaned over to pick up his phone. 'It's not even seven thirty yet. This is not a proper lie-in, certainly not for Ella, you terror.' Lily snuggled into him, and Max kissed her head. 'But thank you for the thought.' His eyes flickered over to Ella. 'It's very nice of you.'

'Here's your breakfast.' She didn't really want to stand at the threshold of his room debating lie-ins and wayward children much longer. Either he was coming to get the tray or she'd have to carry it over, and it didn't look like he was getting out from under that duvet any time soon. She crossed the room to the bed, choosing the side furthest away from him, and set the tray down. 'Here you go.'

'Thank you. That looks amazing.'

'Ella, we're going for a walk with Prim later. Would you like to come with us?' Lily's beautiful brown eyes, beneath red curls made wilder by sleep, seemed to be pleading. 'Daddy said I shouldn't bother you as it's the weekend, but we're going round the tarn, and I'd really like you to tell me about swimming.'

'Why not?' Max was looking at her in a way that would have had Ella joining him in bed if they were alone. 'Then we could try out Sunday lunch at the pub to improve my shop local, eat local ethos, like you suggested.'

'I should really go for a run.' But Ella was wavering and she wanted nothing more than to spend the morning with Max and his children. 'What time were you thinking?'

'Eleven?'

'Okay.' She could catch up with a few chores and her mum before then. She still needed to have a long-overdue call with Dylan; he wanted to know if she was coming for a visit and kept sending gorgeous images of Chamonix to tempt her. She'd sent him a few of Halesmere and their messages were bickering ones over who had the best views.

'Yes!' Lily clapped little hands together. 'Maybe next time you could take me in your kayak, Ella. It looks really cool and I have my own wetsuit, Daddy bought us them in the summer.'

'That sounds like a plan, Lily. We should probably wait until Arlo's arm is out of plaster and you can both have a go.'

'See you later, then.' Max slid the tray onto his lap. 'You'll know when we're ready, you'll hear the din.'

—

Ella was locking up the house when Lily and Prim erupted from the cottage to join her, Max following.

'Pearl's called, brought them some treats and offered to let Arlo stay with her while we walk Prim,' he explained as he met Ella halfway across the drive. 'I thought it was a good idea, and he's already got his tractor book out.' He looked at Lily laughing, and Prim bouncing around her. 'But these two are ready for some fresh air.'

Ella found the pace very different to her usual exercise as they walked through the garden and Max opened a narrow wooden gate into the meadow leading to the tarn. She had run round here before and liked it, enjoyed the challenging and changing ground beneath her feet. Lily was content to rush on ahead with Prim and Ella saw the water glistening in the cold air, the dark ridges of the fells cutting into the sky. The tarn was much smaller than Windermere, and she thought it would be a nice spot to let Lily have a first go in her kayak.

'You're thinking about the water, aren't you?' Max said.

'Was it that obvious?'

'You had that look on your face again.'

'What look?'

'The concentrating-fiercely one, like you were assessing the conditions and how cold it might be. Are you still planning to swim here?'

'Maybe not over winter, it is pretty cold.' They were strolling and she liked how their arms brushed together, the quick feel of his hand against hers. 'Do you swim here?'

'No, we stick to paddling. If I could get away first thing then I probably would try it. In summer, obviously – I'm not as hardcore as you, Ella Grant, before you suggest watching the children and making me do it.'

'Well, the offer's there,' she joked, bumping against him on purpose. 'Maybe you could do a dip for charity, one of those GoFundMe things. A crazy stunt on New Year's Day or something.'

'I will if you will.'

'Oh?' Ella heard the idle note in his voice and her competitive instincts kicked right back in. 'Don't say things like that if you don't mean them.'

'Why wouldn't I mean it?' Max turned so he was facing her, walking backwards with a grin. Lily and Prim were investigating the edge of the woodland at the side of the meadow and paying them no attention. 'I don't imagine you'd shirk a challenge, Ella.'

'You're actually serious?' She was shaking her head. 'So, we're what, both going to swim in the tarn on New Year's Day? Like a race?'

'Not a race, I'm not that crazy. You'd beat me hands down.'

'Watch out, you're—' Too late; Ella saw him back straight into a patch of soft, wet ground that had dirt flying up and splattering his jeans. 'Going to step in that mud if you're not careful,' she finished.

'Thanks for that.' He grabbed her arm, pulling her until they were both in the puddle and she felt it squelching over her walking boots. She was against him, and his hands went to her shoulders, pretending to steady her.

'That wasn't very nice,' she protested. 'Now my feet are wet as well.'

'Sorry.' He didn't sound it and Ella saw Lily running with Prim, the big white dog bounding joyfully at her side. 'They're getting ahead of us. Looks like we're not the only ones with dirty feet.'

Max dropped his arms, glancing ruefully at his own muddy jeans, and resumed his place beside Ella. 'I haven't had a minute alone with you since Thursday night,' he told her softly. 'I've missed you.'

'Oh?' She liked his lowered voice, felt the kick in her pulse as she remembered seeing him in bed earlier. 'Did you want one then?'

'At least one and probably two.'

'And what would we do in two minutes?'

'Is that another challenge?' He raised a brow and she laughed.

'Maybe. I'm not putting that on GoFundMe.'

Lily was merrily waving a branch and Max called to her, 'Don't throw it for Prim, Lily, sticks aren't good for her.'

They'd walked round the far end of the tarn and were steadily making their way back towards the house sitting in the overgrown garden.

'Thanks for offering to take Lily out in your kayak, she'll love it. And I know you'll look after her.'

'My pleasure. I would do it sooner, but I don't want to start a riot if Arlo can't join in.'

'Very wise. I think he might not mind about the actual kayaking, but he would object to being left out, if only to make sure his sister isn't going on adventures without him.'

Lily and Prim had reached the gate at the top of the meadow and were waiting for Ella and Max. Ella was enjoying their moments together, the cold, sharp air on her face, the glint of the low winter sun brightening the day. They caught Lily up and she grabbed Ella's hand impatiently. 'Come and see what we've found. I think it's a hole for rabbits, Prim didn't want to leave it alone.'

'Aren't you ready for lunch? I'm hungry.' Ella was happy to let herself be towed along beside Lily. 'Someone woke me up very early. I always used to be starving after a swim or a run, my mum used to say she could never fill us up.'

'You and your brother, Ella?'

Lily hadn't missed Ella's slip-up and she swallowed. She really didn't want to draw Lily back towards her family and her loss, so she settled for something more casual.

'Oh, just whoever had come to training with me. My brother didn't swim, at least not competitively. My mum took it in turns with a friend's mum and we all used to travel together.'

'Why don't you swim in competitions any more?'

'I don't have time to train properly,' Ella replied lightly. 'And you need to do a huge amount of training if you're going to be good at competing.'

'Are you too busy with work? That's what Daddy says whenever he tells us we can't do something.' Lily was staring up at Ella. 'Please will you teach me to swim? We've had swimming lessons before, but they were boring, and I don't think you would be boring. And when it's summer can we play in the tarn, Ella? Daddy says it's not safe in winter.'

'Watch this space, Lily,' Max replied easily. 'I think I might have just challenged Ella to swim in the tarn with me to raise money for charity.'

'In winter,' Lily breathed, looking admiringly from Ella to Max. 'Are you raising money for the dog shelter, Daddy? Does that mean you're giving up swearing?'

'Probably not,' Max said, diving down to swing Lily off her feet, and she squealed. 'But I'll definitely give it a try.'

Stan was working in the barn when Ella, changed for lunch, went to find Noelle to say goodbye before she flew to France. She was anxious about leaving Max and the children. She hugged Ella, telling her how thankful she was that Ella was here and making her promise to call if she had any concerns. Ella assured her they would be fine, and she would keep a close eye on the children. It was part of her job after all, no matter how much she was coming to feel for the family. Once Noelle had left, Arlo was ready for a change of scenery as well and Max drove them to the pub.

Phil the landlord was happy to see them, and Max took the children off to a table while Ella brought them drinks and found menus. The pub was busy with walkers as well as locals, and she made a mental note to remind future guests to book in advance if they wanted to be sure of a table. Another link to add to their website. The Zoom on Friday with Marcus about the website had gone well and she had some provisional ideas to go over with Max. Once they'd ordered their meals Arlo needed the toilet and he left the table with Max. Lily, who was colouring, put her crayon down.

'What should we do for Arlo's birthday, Ella? It's in May so a winter wonderland party like mine wouldn't really work. He loves animals and farms. Maybe Daddy could find someone to drive a big tractor round in the garden, like the horses and carriage.'

'I'm not really sure, Lily.' Ella made herself sound vague on purpose, thinking of spring at Halesmere when she would probably already be gone. 'You need to talk it over with your dad.'

'But you know more about parties than Daddy. Mine was amazing.'

Here it was. The bit of the conversation Ella didn't want to think about, much less have with Lily now. 'I'm sorry, Lily, I don't think I will be here in May. My job is only temporary and that means I won't be staying.'

'But couldn't you stay?' Lily's eyes were troubled, and Ella hated wounding her. If she needed another reminder why getting involved with Max was not a good idea, then she had one sitting right next to her with a curly red ponytail and looking adorable in her green winter dress and boots.

'Daddy likes you, Ella, I know he does. He laughs more since you came, and Mamie says that sometimes he's too cautious to know what's good for him.'

'She said that to you?' Ella's voice rose along with the flush on her skin.

'No, I heard her telling Stan when she didn't know I was there. Arlo and me were playing in her flat and Stan had brought boxes into the studio for her. She said it was time Daddy stopped thinking he'd always be alone and that he needed more people around him.'

'Lily.' Ella touched her hand gently. 'Sometimes people say things that aren't meant to be overheard or shared with anyone else.'

'But why would Mamie say that to Stan if she didn't think it was true or she minded other people knowing?' Lily made it all sound so very simple. 'I think Mamie's right. Daddy's not alone because he's got us but when I grow up, I want to be a dog trainer and he'll need someone to look after him. I don't want him to be alone all the time.'

'Oh, Lily.' Ella squeezed her fingers. 'You mustn't worry about that, your daddy won't want you to. It's going to be a long time until you leave home and he'll make his own decisions about who he might want to share his life with. And not everyone does want to share.' She smiled, trying to lighten the worry she saw in the little girl's face. 'And he will always love you both so much and want you to be happy, whatever he's doing.'

'Arlo doesn't remember Mummy.' Lily's bottom lip was trembling, and Ella wanted to gather her up and tell her everything would be okay. But she couldn't, it wasn't her promise to make. She settled for sliding an arm across Lily's shoulders, stroking one gently. 'I remember her, she was fun, and she made Daddy laugh. I want him to laugh and remember Mummy when I'm not there. But Arlo won't know how to do it.'

'Arlo will always know how to make your daddy laugh, Lily.' There was a tightness in Ella's throat clutching at her words. 'He's always getting into mischief and your dad will be fine.' She hadn't really wanted to leave home when it was time either, and it was only the thought of failing to live Lauren's dream for her that had forced her away from her family.

'But what if he doesn't want to be alone when Arlo's gone too? Will I have to stay home to look after him?'

'No Lily, you won't.' Ella gripped her shoulder, hoping to help her understand. 'Your daddy won't let that happen. He only wants you to be happy and safe, and if that means you leaving home to be a dog trainer, then he'll be there to cheer you on and watch you become the very best trainer. You're getting lots of practice with Prim already.'

Max and Arlo were back, and Ella saw the flash of concern in Max's expression as he settled Arlo, made sure he was comfortable and had a cushion to support his cast. 'Everything okay?'

'It is.' She nodded firmly, giving him an 'I'll tell you later' look, and he nodded back once.

'I've had an idea for our next kindness from the calendar, Daddy.' Lily's words were almost tumbling over one another in her excitement.

'What now?' Max was amused as he leaned back, holding his bottle of non-alcoholic beer. 'Does it involve getting anyone up early or dragging some poor unsuspecting person from their bed to make breakfast?'

'No, we've done that already.' Lily dismissed his question as though it were the stupidest remark she'd heard all day. 'I'm giving it to Ella as an invitation to our nativity at school.' She turned a pleading glance on Ella. 'Will you come? I know we have a spare ticket because I heard Daddy telling Ashley last night, as Mamie's gone away. I think Daddy would be happy if you came.'

'Lily, you hear an awful lot of things that sometimes you're not meant to. You two eating your lunch when it arrives would make me happy.' Max put his glass down

225

with a clatter. 'Maybe it's kinder to Ella, not inviting her to a school nativity play. Those things can be torturous.'

'Daddy! We're really good, we've been practising for weeks. Mrs Graham will be very cross if she hears you.'

'Well, she won't hear me, will she?' He gave Lily a prod and she giggled. 'And don't you go telling her, either.'

'That's fine if it's better I don't come.' Ella thought it prudent to offer Max a way out.

'Oh, I don't mind, Ella, if you're sure you can stand it.' He gave Arlo a sideways look. 'Arlo's been practising at home, and I found him the other day trying to whack Lily with the shepherd's crook Stan made him because she wouldn't let him pen her like a sheep. Absolutely anything could happen on the night.'

Chapter Eighteen

'Two lunches in two days, Ella Grant. People will be talking.' Max settled in his seat, thanking the young waiter who had brought over a drinks list.

'I've got a feeling they already are. Stan gave me one of his looks when I told him you were out with me and if he knows, then Pearl will know and...'

'Then the shop, the pub and the whole village,' Max finished. 'Does it concern you?'

'For me personally, no.' A waitress arrived with a menu, and they listened while she carefully outlined today's choices. 'But for you and consequently what the children might think, yes,' she finished when the waitress had gone.

'I know we have to be rational, Ella.' He leaned closer now. 'But I feel as though I've been holding my breath for two years and I'm gradually remembering how to let it out again.'

The first waiter was back, and they both ordered water. This was a working lunch, or so Ella had thought until the swerve in direction the conversation had already taken, and she tried to focus on the menu. It was Monday and they'd arranged to meet at the catering college in town. They'd walked up to the first floor, along the usual corridors and past teaching rooms, and turned a corner, finding themselves in a small bar with seats and a pair of sofas lining the walls. There was a comfortable and modern restaurant room next door, with Christmas decorations restricted to a large tree in a corner.

'How was Arlo this morning? Happy to be going back to school?' Ella moved their discussion on. She had decided on a starter and was thinking about mains. She wanted to have the full three courses and try the students' cooking, even if it was considerably more than her usual weekday lunch.

'Yes.' Max had his glasses on and he too, was studying the choices on offer. 'The head emailed over the weekend to say they'd done a risk assessment and arranged some extra support. It's only a few days until the end of term anyway and by the time he goes back in January it won't be long until the cast comes off.'

'So it doesn't affect him in the nativity? He can still be a sheep?'

'I think so. One with a broken leg, perhaps. They'll help him on stage and keep him out of harm's way. I don't think he'd have minded about sitting it out but changed his mind when Lily told him he'd be a wimp if he did.'

The waitress returned, along with a tutor who introduced herself as Leah, the course leader, who Ella had already been in touch with. She brought over the four students working front of house today, and Ella was interested to meet them and hear more. She had almost forgotten about Max sitting opposite until the students left to wait on other tables. Their meals ordered; he was watching her with a smile.

'Sorry, Max, but aren't they brilliant? So enthusiastic, and the opportunity to cook in a real environment with support while they learn is fantastic. I know you've got to head off after lunch but they're going to show me the kitchens and I'm so pleased to have the chance to meet the team before I come back in January. Most of their guest chefs are from restaurants and they really liked that I worked on so many different events.

'You'll see Katie and Ethan again on Wednesday as they're cooking supper with me,' she went on, 'and two students I haven't met are going to wait at table. It'll be amazing to work with them and show the local producers what they can do. I know it's my menu, but they'll be preparing a lot of it and I've kept it simple on purpose— Sorry, I'm getting carried away again. But isn't it lovely in here?'

Max glanced around the room and Ella assumed he too was admiring their surroundings until he reached across the table.

'You don't need to apologise.' His hand hovered close to hers and she closed the distance to touch the tips of his fingers. 'I was perfectly happy listening to you. The students were hanging on your every word, in awe.'

'Hardly. I think it was more that they couldn't get a word of their own in once I'd ambushed them.' His hand slid away as a young waiter approached and served a selection of delicious-looking bread rolls with salted butter. Max dived straight in.

'How did you get that scar?' She hadn't noticed it before, a pale line snaking to a knuckle on his left hand.

'Pruning saw slipped,' he said. 'Sliced through the tendon and ended up having surgery.'

'Ouch. So you like getting hands-on in your gardens then?'

'I do. I love the planning that goes into creating a garden, but I always spend some time working with the team on site, planting usually but sometimes building as well. I can knock up a retaining wall with the best of them.' Max was on his second bread roll. He grinned. 'I did flirt with the idea of becoming an engineer, but the lure of the outdoors was too great.'

The starters arrived and Ella thanked their waiter, giving him time and an encouraging smile as he explained the dish, aware he was slightly nervous of her. She had the impression he was relieved to have said his piece as he escaped.

'But not music, when you play so beautifully? When I heard you, I felt like I was going to cry happy tears, as though I understood what you were playing without really knowing why, if that makes sense.'

The fork in Max's hand halted halfway to his mouth and he laughed self-consciously. 'Probably just a spike of dopamine reducing your stress levels. But it's very kind to say you enjoyed it.'

'Why didn't you study music, go on to be a professional? You must have been good enough and I know you adore it. I hardly know a piano grade from a plant, but I don't think anyone who isn't amazing can play like you.' Ella knew she was pushing him, saw the lines deepen across his brow.

'So why aren't you a professional athlete then, someone who probably could've competed at the top if you'd carried on?'

'You know why.' She had to remember to think of the food, how the dish had been presented, if it matched what had been promised on the menu. It was excellent and when the waitress came over to check, she nodded her appreciation.

'I do, I'm sorry.' Max exhaled, picked up his glass. 'Maybe the simplest answer is that I didn't love music enough to push myself. Boarding school was a pretty lonely place, and I wasn't very confident back then. I didn't want somebody pulling me apart when I played, telling me I'd got it wrong, or I wasn't good enough. Music got me through a time I didn't enjoy, and it's mine, not something I'm good at sharing. I'm not brave like you, taking on someone else's dream and making it your life.'

His smile was rueful and this time it was Ella who reached for his hand. 'You are brave, Max. Incredibly brave and gifted, and you help Lily and Arlo to be braver every day too.' She let go reluctantly. 'I'm so very brave I've always run from any opportunity to get close to someone because I'm afraid I might lose them. It's always been easier to focus on my career and assume I won't have a family or make that kind of commitment.'

'Maybe you don't always need to be running.' Max offered the waitress a polite smile as she asked if she could clear their plates. Once she'd left, his voice became more urgent. 'Whatever's happening between us feels to me like it might be the beginning of something, Ella. I hadn't ever imagined being in this situation again and I'd be lying if I said I don't feel guilty about moving on from Victoria. It's complicated and yet already I'm scheduling my day to have coffee with you first thing and wondering when I'll see you again. And you're so amazing with Lily and Arlo. If you agree, then yes, we keep it simple and don't take risks in front of the kids. I don't think either of us can offer any more right now.'

'And what about when I leave?' Ella didn't voice her other thought: her fear of falling completely in love with him, and with his children. How she'd feel if something withered away to nothing after she'd come to love them all, and she was lost all over again. And more importantly, how Lily and Arlo might feel after they had included her in the everyday moments of their lives and she snatched all that from them and took off after something different because Max didn't love her.

'That's months away, Ella. And by then we'll know if it's more than a maybe.' There was only now in his eyes, and she knew neither of them could promise tomorrow unless they were both certain. She felt her stomach drop at the glimpse of hope he was offering as another little piece of her heart slotted into place.

–

'Budge up.'

'I can't.' Max grinned as Ella settled on the seat next to him. They were pressed together, crammed like everyone else in the school hall on chairs made for children. He tilted his head towards hers. 'If I move another inch I'll be on my neighbour's lap, and I'd rather not shower them with mulled wine. I already feel as though my knees are around my ears.'

'Better not, then.' She smiled as he leaned into her instead, his thigh warm against hers.

Judging by the number of people still trying to find space to sit, the nativity play looked like it might be one of the social events of the season. The school apparently liked to go all-out for the occasion; with mince pies and mulled wine for the adults, and a ticket to the New Year's Eve black tie fundraising ball was included in the price. Max had seen the children into the classroom converted into a dressing room for the evening and Lily had been almost beside herself with excitement.

Arlo was a little quieter, and Max had made sure he'd had enough pain relief beforehand. His arm was bothering him less each day as he got used to his red cast and enjoyed showing it off. He'd made them laugh in the car as he asked again why they didn't have tractors in Jesus' day and if the shepherds who'd seen the angels had brought their sheepdogs to meet Jesus as well because they weren't mentioned in the story he'd learned, and he was very sure they would have needed dogs. Max offered a smile or a nod to people he knew, and Ella was aware of curious glances directed towards her at his side. Ashley was chatting with a couple near the door. She'd kissed Max hello when they'd arrived and offered Ella a polite welcome.

An excited buzz swept through the crowd as a young teacher appeared and asked everyone to turn their phones to silent as the performance was about to begin. Moments later the children were shepherded into the hall, the littlest ones looking shyly for their grown-ups and waving while the elder ones walked in with a more nonchalant air and years of experience behind them. Teachers encouraged everyone into position on a low stage in front of a huge dark curtain adorned with gold stars. Phones were already being held aloft and the usual safety talk followed while the children fidgeted, impatient to begin.

Ella caught Lily's eye and waved, and she waved back merrily, keeping her crown in place with one hand. Arlo was sitting safely to one side in his costume, with his arm in its sling and his sheep's ears sticking up at strange angles. Another teacher hushed the children as the play was introduced and the crowd clapped a cheery welcome. Silence ensued, followed by some anxious whispers between the teachers and a growing sense of unease as the children shuffled nervously. There was a mild scuffle as one of the three wise men dropped his gift and bumped heads with another wise man, eliciting scowls and a squeal. Max chuckled and Ella gave him a nudge with her elbow, which only made him laugh again.

'Sorry everyone.' The head hurried out of the wings to stand at one side of the stage. 'We're having problems with the sound system; the speakers are refusing to play ball. So typical, everything worked perfectly when we did the dress rehearsal yesterday. We've got the words to the carols on the screen, so why don't we all help the children sing "Jingle Bells" while we sort out the problem? I'm sure we all know the tune.'

The children seemed relieved to have something to do and they were louder than the adults as they all launched into the familiar Christmas song. At the end the head, looking even more flustered, was back on the stage.

'I'm terribly sorry, it looks very much as though the problem with the speakers is not a temporary one. We're going to have to ask the children to sing without the music. Please do help them out – we'd all appreciate the support and I know they'll love the encouragement.' She clapped and the audience joined in, adding a rousing cheer for good measure. 'Oh, and if anyone has a sudden desire to accompany us on the piano – our usual teacher who plays is on maternity leave – then now's your big moment to say so.'

There was a collective silence and a few shrugs as people waited, looking around for a response as if waiting for the doctor in the room to make themselves known.

'My daddy can play.' Lily's voice from the stage was as clear as a bell and Ella felt Max stiffen beside her. He had his hands on his knees and his knuckles turned white as he gripped them. 'He can play other instruments too, but the piano is his favourite. He's really good,' Lily went on.

'Mr Bentley?' The head's voice rose as a hopeful expression replaced the tension in her face. 'No pressure of course, but you'd be helping the children out immensely.'

Ella's fingers covered his and she tilted her head to whisper into his ear, 'You're amazing and she'll be so proud of you.'

She felt him squeeze back, then he slowly stood up and the room gave a cheer. He made his way to the front of the hall, relieved clapping accompanying him. He gave Lily a smile as he settled at the upright piano, adjusting the stool and removing his glasses from his shirt pocket. Someone gave him a sheet and spoke a few words. Ella couldn't take her eyes off him as he quickly rolled his shoulders. He held out his arms, flexed his wrists and stretched his hands, then gave the head a nod.

There was a palpable sense of relief as the three narrators took it in turns to recite the beginning of the nativity story, sharing a microphone they passed between them. Ella was watching Lily and Arlo, but her glance kept sneaking back to Max, poised at the piano as the first song was introduced. She wasn't expecting the blast of emotion that rushed into her heart again as he began.

This time she understood some of what it cost him to play with others watching and she knew in that second, with absolute clarity, that she loved him. The knowledge hit her like a punch to her chest. It had been sneaking up on her for weeks: the hours they'd spent together with his children, the kiss they'd shared, the support and understanding they'd each offered the other. How could it be like this for her so soon when she was always so careful? And how was she going to make herself leave them if he didn't feel the same?

Max made the very ordinary piano sound as though it were soaring as the children sang their first carol, relaxed now they had someone to follow. He gave them enough volume to lead without letting the music eclipse their little voices, and at the end another cheer rose. Ella was trembling as the nativity moved on and nearly missed the moments when the manger was upended and Mary dropped the doll playing baby Jesus.

Lily was a brilliant wise man, making sure to offer her gift carefully and say her lines clearly. Arlo's sheep had had enough, and refused to get up for any more singing, despite some words from his teacher that Ella assumed were encouraging.

'Rockin' around the Christmas Tree' was a fun and very lively part of the finale, another reminder of dancing with Max in the cottage and Lily challenging them to a dance-off. The last song was a resounding 'We Wish You a Merry Christmas', and Max played it again as an encore. Then the performance was over and the children bowed as they accepted the loud clapping and cheers from their audience. There was another roar as the head thanked Max for stepping in and he was surrounded by parents wanting to shake his hand as the children were shepherded offstage. Ella lingered at the back of the crowd, still trying to organise her feelings into order and wondering anxiously how she had managed to fall in love with her employer.

'Daddy, you were brilliant.' Lily rushed across. She was out of her costume and back in leggings with a skirt and boots, a Christmas top beneath her coat. People were leaving and the crowd surrounding Max had finally thinned enough for Ella to catch him up. Arlo was with

Max too, still in the sheep costume, which he was refusing to take off.

'Everyone said so,' Lily went on. 'And Mrs Graham said if you ever wanted to play at school again, she'd invite you like a shot. She also said something about your glasses, but I didn't hear all of it. I think she likes them.'

'Oh, does she?' Max was still wearing his glasses, and he took them off with a wry smile. 'How you hear half the stuff you do, I've no idea, Lily Isabelle Bentley.'

She clutched Ella's hand, tugging her towards the exit. 'Can we have snacks at home? I'm hungry and you said we could have hot chocolate and brownies afterwards, Daddy.'

'I also said you had to go to bed without any messing about, so I'll keep my part of the bargain if you two keep yours.'

'*Oui*, Papa, *ça va*.'

They were home in ten minutes, Arlo too tired for hot chocolate, so Max lifted him carefully from the car to take him straight upstairs. It made sense for Ella to offer to make Lily's drink, to avoid delaying her bedtime any more than necessary.

'You sure?' Max paused in the hall, Arlo's head on his shoulder. 'Lily will probably have you counting how many sleeps there are until Christmas and asking whether Santa's bringing a hutch for the guinea pigs or if Stan will make her one.'

'I don't mind,' Ella murmured, bending down to stroke Prim, released from the kitchen. 'And my money's on Stan for a hutch; I think Santa will have enough to do with just guinea pigs.'

'We'll have to see about that. Stan's looking more elusive every day, I'm sure he's got something up his sleeve.' Max headed off, Arlo grumbling quietly in his arms.

Lily had finished her hot chocolate before Max reappeared, so Ella encouraged her to go up and they shared a hug before Lily went off in search of her dad. Prim was settled in her bed beside glittering Christmas lights. Ella collected her coat and called a cheery good-night from the bottom of the stairs.

'Are you going?' Max stuck his head over the banister. 'You don't want to stay for a drink?'

'Better not. I've got an early start and Ashley's coming to decorate the house.'

'Remind me what time everyone's arriving tomorrow evening?'

'Six thirty for drinks. Maybe you could come over before then? I was hoping you might let the photographer take your picture.'

'Oh, were you?' His grin was merry. 'Actually, I've rearranged my calendar so I'm all yours for the day. In between school hours anyway,' he clarified. 'You'll have enough on your plate, if you'll pardon the pun, without my two slowing you down.'

'That's thoughtful, thank you.' Ella felt her pulse jump, liking the anticipation of spending the day with him. 'I can give you lots to do. And it was a terrible pun.'

'Sorry.' He winked, letting her know he wasn't. 'I'm certain you've got it all under control, but I thought you might appreciate an extra pair of hands. I've borrowed Ashley's babysitter for the evening so we're good to go, in theory. I've promised the kids they can come over and see the house when it's ready.'

'Perfect. I think it's going to look amazing.' Ella fastened her coat against the rain. Max ran downstairs to follow her out, pulling the door across without closing it.

'Hey.'

'What?'

'Just this. I don't think I've got two minutes; one will have to do. Lily's still awake.' He placed his hands on Ella's shoulders, dropped a light kiss on her lips. 'Thank you for supporting us tonight, it meant a lot.'

'My pleasure. You were wonderful, truly, the way you played. You have such a special gift.' She slid her hands beneath his jacket, her heart filling up with love for him. 'I'd so like to hear you again.'

'Then you shall.'

'Do you mean it?'

'Yes. I'm sure you'll get bored before I do.' There was a shout from upstairs and Max grinned, touching his forehead to hers. 'Time's up.'

Chapter Nineteen

'You look lousy.' Dylan, on her phone screen, was grinning and Ella pulled a face at him. She was in her pyjamas and cosy in her comfortable bed.

'So would you if you were working half as hard as I am. I bet you're the laziest ski instructor in town.' Despite the late hour, she was glad they were finally catching up in person. He looked typically gorgeous, blond hair tousled and messy, blue eyes teasing in a suntanned face. She was joking; she knew he'd be working every bit as hard as he partied. 'Shouldn't you be in bed too?'

'I was, an hour ago. But she kicked me out and I'm back at the chalet.'

Ella rolled her eyes. 'Kicked you out? That's a first. Anyway, I've got a big day tomorrow and I need my rest. Why have you called me so late?'

'I've got some news and I haven't seen you properly for ages. And it's not like you'd have gone to sleep early. How do you fancy a house guest, I'm packing in the skiing gig. I've been offered a job in Copenhagen, and I've got a few days to spare before it starts. I thought I could come over and see your place.'

'Dylan, that's brilliant, congratulations. Doing what exactly, in Copenhagen?'

'Head chef in a start-up on the waterfront in Nørrebro. Private investors, big ideas, big budget. Check it out, it's a great district, really cool. I'm still in shock if I'm honest, it's an incredible opportunity. I start first week January and we open in February.'

'I'm so pleased for you, that's wonderful.' Ella wished she could hug him in person. But she also felt another thread to her old career snapping; like her, Dylan had always loved a challenge, refused to stand still, and now he was moving on again, returning to the work he loved, without her. 'Your first head chef. Wow. Totally deserved. We need to celebrate!'

'Thanks, Ells.' There was a casual note in Dylan's voice as the laughter fell away. 'I'd ask you to come with me if I thought you'd say yes. We're gonna need a brilliant sous chef and you're the best. But you don't, do you? Want to come?'

'I can't.' She knew he'd understand the quiet regret in her voice, the finality of realising they were unlikely to work together again. 'There's so much going on and I can't leave in January. I have to see it through and make sure Max has the support he needs to carry on.'

'Okay. It was a long shot but if you ever change your mind the offer's there.' Dylan shrugged and she was certain his wry smile revealed he knew she wouldn't. 'So have you got room for me in this country mansion then?'

'It's not a mansion. And I can probably find you a corner with a mattress, I just need to run it by Max.' Even saying his name made Ella feel happy. 'Send me the dates. You'll love it here. No skiing though.'

'Doesn't matter. I've had enough of snow and trying to teach people to stay upright all day. Let's just chill and watch Netflix.'

'In that order, right? Not the other one?' She was laughing at Dylan's merry grin.

'Well…'

'Forget it. You might be halfway to being gorgeous but you're a much better friend than you are a boyfriend. I've got more sense than to fall in love with you.'

'You're pretty much the only woman who's ever said that to me.' He pulled a sad face, and she rolled her eyes. He always cheered her up and he always had her back. She'd miss him, heading back to Europe, but Copenhagen would be great for visits. 'I'll text you my flight when I've booked it.'

'Dylan?' Ella's voice softened. 'I've missed you. It'll be so good to see you.'

'I know. Me too.'

—

Ella's alarm went off at six on Wednesday morning and she recognised the knot in her stomach as one of anticipation with a hint of anxiety. It was often like this before she cooked for a big event and today already felt different, especially after the evening with Max and the children. She went for a run early, lapping the tarn twice, before heading back to the house for a shower. Ashley was due at ten and Ella had orders to collect before then. Stan had got the largest of the Christmas trees they'd chosen into the hall and there was another smaller one in the drawing room. She had enough experience to know to also line up a small team of cleaners, who would restore the house to pristine glory once the guests had left.

She was filling the fridge when Ashley and her assistant arrived, and quickly outlined her plans. Every fire was to be lit and the colour palette was warm cinnamon and nutmeg with lots of winter foliage, and a huge copper wreath threaded with evergreens above the fireplace in the hall. Highlights would be jewel colours of scarlet and gold, and Marta's candles in each room. A drinks station would be set up so guests could help themselves after champagne cocktails had been served. The photographer was due at five thirty and Pearl was capturing the preparations on her phone and uploading everything to social media, creating more engagement and interest.

One order was delayed, and Ashley was pouring a glass of water in the kitchen as Ella hit voicemail on speaker on her phone after missing a couple of calls. She was expecting an update, but it was Dylan's voice she heard first.

'Hey Ells, it's me. Flight's sorted, I'll email you. I'm all yours for three days, Netflix and chill, remember. Save me some of your mum's Christmas pudding or else. Just kidding, love ya.'

Ella played the other message and was relieved to hear her order was due any minute. Then the third-years from the catering college, Katie and Ethan, arrived and she welcomed them. Max soon followed and made everyone coffee while Ella ran them all through the menu. The evening would begin with damson gin Royales, the gin infused with locally grown fruit. She had chosen just two canapés: pear crisps topped with creamy blue cheese and toasted hazelnuts, and tiny toad-in-the-hole parcels filled with caramelised onion relish and cranberry sausages.

The starter would be locally caught brown shrimps served with spiced butter, or sheep's milk cheese from Marta's farm baked with sesame and honey, and Rowan's sourdough bread, toasted. The main course was roasted pork rib with crispy crackling or truffle-roasted celeriac for the vegetarian choice, with seasonal brassicas, and fondant potatoes instead of roast.

It had taken Ella a long time to choose dessert, but she'd finally gone for individual rum custard tarts with gingerbread pastry. There was lots to do, and she set the students to making the pastry and preparing ingredients for the canapés. Her years of experience kicked straight back in, and she enjoyed hearing more about the careers they were planning.

Max had offered to source the drinks and he stuck his head through the kitchen door. 'I've got the champagne. Want to see?'

'Love to. Give me two minutes?' Ella left Katie preparing the pork rib, then washed her hands and went to find him. He was in the hall, a large case at his feet.

'What do you think?' He held up a bottle and she recognised it as a classic and elegant blend she had enjoyed before.

'Gorgeous, thank you. Perfect for the cocktails.'

'We'd better get it chilled, it's cool but not quite there yet.' Max slid the bottle back into the case. 'My parents-in-law sent it for us. They're wine merchants and wanted to offer a gift for tonight.'

'How lovely of them.' Ella caught the quick press of his lips at the reminder of Victoria.

'It is, very much their style. You'll probably meet them over the holidays,' he said casually. 'We're going to spend a few days with them and then they're coming back up to take Lily and Arlo away for New Year's Eve. We've postponed their longer holiday in the lodge until half-term as Arlo can't do much with his arm in a cast.'

'Ooh champagne, I'm looking forward to a glass when we're done.' Ashley emerged from the drawing room; her arms full of foliage. 'Max, do you mind if I use your place to get ready later? I've brought everything with me, it seems pointless to go home again as the girls are staying with James.'

'That's fine, long as you don't mind two small distractions getting under your feet.' Max hoisted the case into his arms. 'Ella, I'll chill these at home, save taking up more space in the fridge here.'

'Don't be silly, you know I love your two chasing around.' Ashley was still looking at Max as her assistant hovered with a box of gold baubles. 'What time would you like me to be ready?'

'Six thirty okay? We'll be serving the cocktails then.' He was on his way to the front door.

'Perfect. I'm so looking forward to it, I think it's going to be such a special evening. I haven't booked a taxi yet, I thought I'd sort that out later.'

'You sure?' Max hooked a foot round the door to pull it wide. 'I wouldn't leave it too late, Ash, you might not get one. You don't want to get stuck here.'

Ella returned to the kitchen and as the day moved on, she was thrilled with Katie and Ethan. They were coping beautifully under her supervision and everything was going exactly as she'd planned. The rum custard tarts were almost ready, just needing to rest. The pork rib would be seared before roasting in the oven, and the blue cheese dressing for the pear crisp canapés was ready to be piped into place and dusted with toasted hazelnuts and honey.

The photographer was due soon and Ella went to get changed, feeling the usual spike of adrenaline kicking in. She was used to being on the other side of events and making sure the food was perfect; not so much putting on a dress and hosting. She chose her go-to evening outfit, a black pencil dress with a ruched V-neck that she teamed with ankle boots. Make-up was her normal routine, and she applied lipstick in a flattering shade of blackberry for a little more drama, then checked her appearance in the mirror. Her hair was growing, the lilac highlights fading and a strange glimpse of her natural colour emerging.

The house looked magical as she walked down the staircase, her fingers brushing the garland wound round the banister. She knew they'd got it exactly right, thanks in no small part to Ashley's skill with the decorations. Flickering flames highlighted the stunning Christmas trees, every glittering bauble was a jewelled highlight among natural green foliage, and the scent of supper drifting into the hall promised more delights to come.

The drinks station was good to go, filled with craft beer from the pub, local gin and liqueurs, and whisky distilled in Cumbria. Ella had tasked Max with creating a playlist, the same in every room: Christmas carols, some classical and a few old favourites, to enhance the atmosphere. She wasn't expecting to see him already waiting in the hall, changed into an indigo blazer with a white shirt and dark jeans. He was watching her, and she took her time, liking the smile lingering around his mouth and the intensity of his gaze.

'Wow.'

'That's my line,' she joked. 'You look wonderful. But thank you, whether you're referring to me or the house.'

'I was absolutely referring to you, but the house looks incredible too. I can hardly believe it's the same sad old place I bought.'

'Ashley's done a wonderful job.' Ella joined him, aware of the students in the kitchen and the work she needed to do tonight. There were a dozen thoughts running through her mind, but for just these few moments while they were alone, she could allow herself to put them aside.

'She has. But none of this would be happening without you and I wasn't thinking about her while I was watching you walk down those stairs.'

'May I ask what you were thinking?'

He dipped his head to speak softly against Ella's ear. 'This might not be the right moment to tell you. I'd hate you to be distracted, I'm really looking forward to eating supper with grown-ups and you might spoil it if your mind's not on the job.'

'I'm an excellent multitasker, Max.' She placed a hand on his chest as he drew his head back, felt the warmth of his skin through the thin cotton beneath her palm. 'I promise I won't burn anything, whatever you might say.'

'I don't doubt it.' He smoothed a thumb across her cheek. 'Your hair's different tonight. It suits you. I didn't know you were blond beneath that crazy colour.'

'I think I'd forgotten as well.' Ella tried to shrug away her reply, and swallowed. 'It's been a while.'

'Since what? You had blond hair?'

She nodded slowly. Maybe it was finally time for acceptance, to see herself as the woman she was now, not the girl she had been. 'Twenty years, to be exact. I haven't been blond since Lauren died. We were identical, even down to our hair.' Ella took a breath. 'It hurt too much to see Lauren every time I looked in the mirror. I started dyeing my hair the day after her funeral. You should have seen me in my goth phase.' She hoped that last bit sounded funnier than it felt.

'Ella.' Max took her hands. 'You're beautiful just as you are, inside and out. You're completely your own person, and I think you're amazing.' He lowered his head, and she felt the soft pressure of his lips skimming her cheek. 'I'm so glad you're here.'

'Sorry if I'm interrupting. I am a little early.' Ashley's laugh seemed brittle, and Ella knew it was too late to hide what their body language had been suggesting. Ashley was stunning in a fitted plum-coloured floral dress. She hovered on the other side of the piano, her gorgeous brunette hair caught in an elegant chignon, revealing smooth shoulders.

'Not at all,' Max said easily as his hands fell to his sides. 'I was just complimenting Ella on everything she's done. And you too, Ash, of course. The house feels wonderful. Lily and Arlo will be over any minute and then we really should have champagne.'

'I'll go and check on Katie and Ethan.' Ella was already on her way to the kitchen. 'Let me know when the photographer's here, Max.'

–

Supper had been a huge success and Ella was overjoyed with how her carefully planned menu had been received by their guests. By the time they moved on to coffee and petit fours in the drawing room, gathered around the fire with the Christmas tree glittering in a corner, she had a firm agreement from each of the producers to supply Halesmere. The community shop would play an important role in how this was to be achieved.

The four students supporting her, particularly the two young chefs, had excelled themselves, and they received a huge cheer when Ella brought them into the drawing room to receive the praise they were due. Tonight was something they could share on their social media, and she had found working with them a thrill. She planned to email their course leader as soon as possible with her enthusiastic feedback. The photographer had captured everything, including Lily and Arlo scampering down the stairs in their pyjamas and Max waiting with open arms, and Ella couldn't wait to see her images.

Stan and Pearl spoke about the house and its history, of the family who had loved and lost it after the Great War and Pearl's own connection to a young wife from those days. Stan had plenty of folk stories to share and everyone was quiet as he recited the spooky tale of a monk who had supposedly cried himself to death on the shores of Windermere for love of a woman, and the medieval king killed in battle whose crown had been thrown into a tarn and still lay waiting for him to reclaim it. Ella hoped it wasn't the one at the bottom of the garden.

Pearl had uploaded more images to Instagram and new followers were increasing, along with enquiries about when the house was available to book. Ella was growing used to it now, familiar with the floorboards when they creaked, or her bedroom door when it rattled in the wind, or the house seemed to sigh. Tonight it felt alive, warm, glowing, and she almost didn't want it to end, despite the tiredness she knew would follow the exhilaration.

A couple of people left, and she and Max went with them to the front door to thank them and say goodnight.

'What do you think?' His hand drifted to the grand piano in the hall, and he touched the black gloss lovingly. 'Feels like it might be a nice moment.'

'Do you mean it?' Ella's smile was suddenly wide. 'Because there's absolutely no pressure or expectation – not everyone knows you play. You don't have to.'

'I know I don't.' He slipped off his blazer, draping it on the back of a chair. 'But I promised I'd play for you again and it just feels right, now, with the house like this. For everything you've done to help me, and Lily and Arlo, looked after them.'

'For me?' Ella's throat felt tight. The door to the drawing room was closed, their guests talking in low voices behind it. 'That would be amazing, Max, truly. I'd love it. But it doesn't have to be now, in front of the others.'

'Maybe it does. Playing at the school felt okay once I got going. I was thinking about the children, not who was watching. I love how the piano makes me feel and I should be a bit braver, not hold myself back and let the moment pass when it comes. Like now.' He pulled out the stool, flexed his hands as he sat down. 'Any requests?'

'Whatever makes you happy.' Ella saw how he touched the keys with his long fingers, already giving himself to the pleasure he knew would follow. She went to stand behind him, resting her hands on his shoulders as she reached round to kiss his cheek. 'Thank you.'

She couldn't tell him the rest, that she loved him and wanted nothing more than to curl up, close her eyes and listen. To be alone with him as the fires faded away, lights were dimmed, and morning followed night. He began with 'The First Noel', and it was only a few moments until their guests joined them. The students and cleaners came out of the kitchen to listen too as Max moved onto 'Silent Night', playing with an instinctive ease that to Ella seemed effortless and incredibly beautiful.

He lightened the mood with 'Jingle Bells' and everyone joined in, singing loudly, then carried on with 'Santa Claus Is Coming to Town' and a rousing rendition of 'We Wish You a Merry Christmas'. 'Joy to the World' came next, and he finally stood, to a round of loud applause and calls for an encore. His gaze found Ella's for a second and she knew her own was revealing her pleasure and pride. He was still smiling as he sat down again.

He finished with 'O Holy Night', and she knew she'd never be able to hear the carol again without thinking of him. He played as though he and the piano were one, soaring together as he found the notes with graceful ease, and the music was both simple and profoundly moving. No one sang this time; they could only listen, and she was certain she couldn't be the only one whose eyes were shimmering. She hadn't moved, couldn't seem to put one foot in front of the other or think about what should come next for their guests.

'Well.' Stan seemed stunned into as near silence as he ever got as Max rose, trying to shrug off handshakes and praise. 'You're a dark 'orse, boss. Never 'eard playin' like that before.'

'Max, you were wonderful!' Ashley found her way to his side and slipped her arms round him. 'It's been so long; I haven't heard you playing in for ever. You really have to do it more often.'

'Thanks, Ash.' Max was looking around at the guests as she let him go. 'Who's for whisky? Ella's chosen some amazing dark chocolate to go with it.'

Once the last of the guests had complimented Ella and Max on a wonderful evening and disappeared into the night, she saw the cleaning team out and thanked them for all they'd done. The four students had already left and only she, Ashley and Max remained. Stan and Pearl had left after the first whisky, tottering down the drive, Stan promising he'd be back at work first thing to hang the new barn doors with Pete's help. The fires had burned themselves out and Ella switched off the lights in the dining room, emerging into the hall just as Ashley left the drawing room. Max was outside, chucking empty bottles into the recycling.

'Thank you for today, Ashley, the decorations are perfect. They make such a difference and I'm sure the photographs are going to be stunning.'

'My pleasure. It's been a wonderful evening, I think the house is going to be huge hit with guests. I just hope Max can find the right person to take good care of it for him.' Ashley was fiddling with her phone and her voice was light. 'You're giving him a lot to think about with all your ideas, Ella, and he really doesn't need any more pressure or work landing in his lap once you've left.'

'That's the last thing I want, Ashley. I'm here to support him and the family as much as possible and if he decides to make this role permanent then I'd be happy to help him explore all options.' Ella was equally cool. She wondered if her feelings were plastered all over her face. Had Ashley recognised that Ella was already in love with Max and thought he loved her back? Or worse, did she know he didn't and never would?

Ella had no idea if there could be a future at Halesmere for her and very much hoped she hadn't revealed to Ashley that she might want to find a way to stay. She switched off the lamps in the hall, leaving the Christmas tree lights flickering over the grand piano, wishing Ashley's taxi would turn up. Max would be back any minute and Ella wanted to be alone with him, even for just these final few moments before he had to relieve the babysitter.

'Thank you.' Ashley accepted the sumptuous winter coat Ella was offering. 'I'm sure he'll appreciate that before you go. He was only telling me the other day he hadn't realised how much work was involved in running a holiday business and was looking at what a management company could offer.'

'Hell, it's perishing out there.' Max was in his shirt, without the blazer, and came in blowing on his hands. 'You two look very serious. Ash, your taxi's arrived. That was well timed.'

'Wasn't it?' Ashley's laugh was sharp, and she reached up to hug him and kiss his cheek. 'Thanks both, for a fabulous evening. Ella, I'd love to get your advice about a dinner I'm planning for friends after Christmas? Your menu was stunning.'

'Of course, if I can help at all.' She registered the quick nod Ashley gave her, still trying not to reveal the shock that Max was thinking of outsourcing her role and hadn't thought to discuss it with her. But she didn't want to dwell on that now. Their evening was almost over, and thoughts of work could wait. He saw Ashley to the car, then he was back in the house, closing the door and looking at Ella.

'What an incredible evening, thank you for everything. I think we could give Stan another job as resident storyteller, he was in his element with all those folk tales.'

'My pleasure.' Ella wondered if Max knew how much she wanted him to stay as she watched him pick up his blazer. 'That's not a bad idea about Stan, he was brilliant. Maybe we could get him to do a few tales at the Christmas open day.'

'Sure. You ask him, he likes you more than he does me.'

'Oh, he likes you, Max, he just doesn't want to show it too much because you're his boss.'

'He might say I'm the boss, but you're the one he comes to.' Max shrugged back into the blazer. 'So when do you need me to sign the contract for the website?'

'Tomorrow. Marcus has emailed it over and we should have images from tonight by early next week. I hope this is okay – I've asked the photographer to come again on Saturday for the open day. She's already got a booking, but she can give us an hour.'

'No, that's fine, good idea.' Max covered a yawn. 'Sorry. I suppose I'd better go, those two alarm clocks will be set bright and early. And I can't keep the babysitter hanging around all night.'

'I understand. I'll see you tomorrow, after school. I'm out in the morning, remember? No coffee.'

'Oh. That's a shame. Am I allowed to say I'll miss it?'

'Me or the coffee?' Ella followed him to the door, hoping she'd hidden her disappointment that he had to leave.

'The coffee for sure.' He was laughing as he stepped down into the porch, his eyes on a level with hers as she stood in her boots. 'I think you know which, Ella. Make sure you lock up. I've already checked the other doors, it's just this one. Will you be all right?'

'I will. I'm slowly getting used to being on my own and it's okay, most of the time.'

'Good. I'm happy you're more comfortable here.' Max reached to hold her hands. 'I feel as though I'm on a first date and trying to make the goodbye last as long as possible.'

'And how would you normally say goodbye on a first date?'

'It's been a very long time since I had one, so I'm out of practice.' His eyes dropped to her mouth and her breath caught. 'How would you end a first date?'

'It would depend on who the date was with and how it had gone.' The pulse in her throat was rushing and Ella felt desire stirring in her stomach. 'If it was bad then I'd make my excuses and leave before the end. If it was okay, then it would be thanks for a nice evening.'

'And if it was good? Or better than good?'

'Good... then I'd end it maybe like this.' She leaned forward, left a light kiss on his cheek.

'Nice.' His hands tightened on hers. 'And better than good?'

'Like this?' She drew Max close, close enough to place her hands on his face, and tilted her head towards his. She saw his eyes darken and heard the quick catch in his breathing as she kissed him, letting her lips linger against his mouth. 'Will that do?'

'What do you want me to say, Ella?' His voice was a muttered groan as his hands slid up her arms to grip her shoulders. 'I don't think I've ever ended a first date with something that felt as incredible as you kissing me like that.'

One slow finger inched across her collarbone towards the V of the dress, and it was her turn to gasp as he let it slide beneath the material, his eyes idly watching its progress.

He removed his hand, a smile regretful. 'I'm going, before it's too late and we rush into something I'd much rather we took our time over.'

Ella's nod was reluctant and her pulse slowly began to return to normal. Max was right; he couldn't keep the babysitter waiting until all hours, and if he came back into the house now, she knew they'd both find it impossible for him to leave. 'So, go.'

'I'm going, I really am. Still okay to collect the kids tomorrow?'

'Of course. I've promised Prim a run and I'd swear she understands every word.'

'Yeah? Pity she doesn't understand the "behave yourself" ones quite so well.'

Chapter Twenty

By seven a.m. on Saturday Ella was beginning to seriously wonder what she'd set in motion. She'd been up for two hours already, and the first creatives were due from eight to finish setting up for the Christmas artisan day, which was going to be open to visitors from ten until four p.m. Snow was forecast and when she'd mentioned to Stan that she was concerned people might struggle to get down the drive in it, he'd told her not to worry.

He'd rolled up early too, in a tractor he'd borrowed from a mate, and Ella hugged him gratefully. He seemed to make it his mission to find solutions to everything she threw at him. They'd already drawn their Secret Santa and she'd got him; she was planning to be as creative as possible with her gift.

Thanks to Pearl's brilliance on Instagram, they could have given away twice as many tables as they had room for in the barn. Ella already had a list of artists and other creatives who'd emailed asking to view the studios, and she'd been delighted when Marta had claimed one. She was ready to expand her candle-making business and as the studios were close to her farm, it would give her another outlet beyond the community shop and online orders without having to travel too far. Ella had also emailed the college to give feedback on the students who'd helped with the supper and the course director had invited her to a Zoom meeting next week to discuss her guest chef day in January.

The thought of leaving Halesmere was starting to seriously worry Ella. She'd come here with little idea of anything more than a fun and interesting role doing something different while she worked out what her future might look like. But already she had made friends, connected local producers to the house, and was helping Max find his way into the community. She loved the landscape, the sense of adventure waiting every time she went for a run or took her kayak out. The new website was under construction and the house's email in-box was filling up with booking requests. And then there was Max, and his children. She loved them all, but she knew she could say nothing of that to him, at least not yet. She understood some of what he must be feeling about Victoria and the guilt associated with moving on. She would have to give him time and pray it wouldn't run away with her.

She had arranged to meet Ana, a yoga and mindfulness instructor who also created beautiful jewellery from recycled silver, after the holidays with a view to setting up a weekend retreat to test the water for interest and what activities they might offer future guests in between classes. It would need catering this first time and Ella was already thinking she'd ask the students to work with her again. Noelle, painting in France, was in regular touch, calling the children on FaceTime every afternoon and promising them a holiday in her tiny seaside cottage in the spring.

Lily and Arlo had just broken up from school and were getting ever more excited about Christmas. Ella had managed to dissuade Lily from suggesting to Stan that it would be a kindness from her calendar to ask him to make her a hutch for the guinea pigs Santa was supposed to be bringing. Ella explained that Stan had quite a lot to do, and a better kindness might be for Lily to bake for him instead, with Ella's help. Lily had decided on cupcakes, and yesterday after school she, Arlo and Ella had delivered them to his workshop. A delighted Stan had been almost speechless with glee. He'd invited them in, cleared space on the battered old armchair in the corner, and showed them all the clever tools he used to make his little animal carvings. The new barn doors looked amazing now they were hung, and Pete's apprentice had painted them sage green to match the woodwork around the studios.

Ella had ordered all the refreshments for today through the community shop; they'd be serving mulled wine and a non-alcoholic Christmas punch alongside the food. Sandy's ceramics studio was open and the one next door for refreshments was being manned by two volunteers from the shop and a student from the catering college looking for extra Christmas cash. Stan had asked Ella if she trusted him to provide a surprise and she'd told him she absolutely did and to go on ahead. Now she halted her dash to the barn, her arms full of empty gift bags, when she saw a group of carol singers in Victorian dress warming up around a violinist.

'Stan! They sound amazing, thank you.' Ella had thought of offering entertainment but had run out of time to set anything up. 'How did you manage to find them so late on? No, don't tell me, you have contacts in all the right places.'

'Aye, young Ella, I do.' He winked. 'Right, better get me hi-vis on, there's people arrivin' already.'

'Thanks to Pearl.' Ella gave him a grin as she carried on to the barn with her bags. 'She's been brilliant on social media; I think we're going to be busy.'

Within a couple of hours the car park was full and a mate of Stan's, in charge of it, was operating a one-in, one-out system. The refreshments were going down a storm and Ella was very glad of the extra help as she made another bowl of Christmas punch. Sales were encouraging and she made sure to keep the artists supplied with food and drink. The carol singers drew crowds of admirers whether they were performing inside the barn or standing around the Christmas tree in the courtyard. Stan was giving her sideways looks and making sly comments about what she was planning to do to top this for their next open day and how did she expect him to do his job if she wasn't there to organise him as Max was nowhere near as good at it as she was?

Ella laughed it off, telling Stan she had enough plans for work to see him through until next Christmas and he'd better keep out of her way if he didn't want a list as long as his favourite chisel. But his remarks were very close to her own thoughts about leaving and she hadn't missed how Max had got stuck in, emptying bins, nipping down to the shop for more supplies and making himself useful. He'd asked Ashley's babysitter to keep an eye on Lily and Arlo and take them back to the cottage if they got bored. Arlo got fed up before Lily did, and disappeared back to his beloved tractors, while Lily stuck close to Ella and learned how to take payments on the new card machine and helped with gift wrapping.

At three the crowds finally began to thin. The sky was grey, laden with the snow Stan had told her would fall in the next twenty-four hours. Ella hoped it would hold off until Sunday evening at least; her parents were visiting tomorrow and as it was the only time she'd see them over the holidays she didn't want the weather keeping them away. The open day had been a big hit, and she now had more artists interested in studios than they had space for. The carol singers and violinist finished with a session around the Christmas tree, with everyone joining in to sing 'We Wish You a Merry Christmas'. Ella almost didn't want it to end, even though her feet were starting to ache.

'So this was why you ordered a dozen Christmas puddings on our account from the shop.' Max was at her side, watching Lily handing out parcels to everyone who had helped. 'That's a really nice idea.'

'Thanks. I just wanted something to let them know we appreciate all they've done.'

'Another successful event, Ella Grant.' He was smiling and she felt his hand reach for hers. 'Thank you, it's been fantastic. I heard Pete say he was going home for a lie-down after you reminded him about the flat being finished for the end of January so we can accept guests in the house.'

'He did look a bit perturbed.' Ella loved the amusement in Max's voice, how his gaze lingered on hers, the warm touch his fingers. 'But the studios aren't that far off being done now, which is good – Marta wants to move in straight after New Year. I've arranged to email all the artists for feedback on the open day and see how we might improve for next time.'

'Next time? When were you thinking of doing that?'

'I really don't know but the artists are going to need days for opening the studios to visitors. But obviously you need to be on board with that. It's your home and you can't be overrun with people every day.'

'Okay. We can talk about it.' Max casually let go of her hand. 'So are your parents still coming tomorrow?'

'Yes, before they fly out to New Zealand on Wednesday.' Ella was still trying to get her head around Christmas Day without her family. Now the open day was almost over she could think about the lunch Max was planning to host here. Her brother and his husband were calling in too on their long drive back from the Highlands after Hogmanay, so at least she'd see everyone, even if they wouldn't be together on the day itself.

'And your mum and dad definitely don't want to stay over? You know they're welcome to join you in the house.'

'Thanks, Max. But they're heading back in case the weather becomes a problem. I think my mum just wants eyes on me to make sure I look okay before they go.' Ella's smile was sad.

'Sure I can't persuade you all to join me and two overexcited kids on a Santa steam train? We're booked for tomorrow afternoon. I could probably add three more if we're quick.'

'No thanks.' She wished she could accept. Arlo would love the train, she was certain, and she'd be sorry to miss seeing him enjoying it. 'I think Mum and Dad would love it but it's probably better we spend the day separately. I don't want them to think there's more to you and me than there really is.'

'I guess that makes sense.' Max glanced across the courtyard. The Victorian carol singers were leaving with their Christmas puddings and Lily was showing Stan her empty basket. Max returned his gaze to Ella. 'I have a suggestion for our first date, though, if you'd actually like to go on one with me.'

'I might.' Ella liked the fun hovering in his face. 'Is it a good suggestion?'

'I hope so. You know I have two tickets to the school's New Year's Eve ball?'

'Is that a rhetorical question?'

'I suppose it was. Would you like to come with me?'

'I'd love to. But don't you think people might start talking? If Stan suspects something then that's it. And what would happen afterwards?'

'Well.' Max's grin was mischievous, and he glanced over at Lily to make sure her back was turned, then brushed Ella's cheek with a thumb. 'The kids will be away with their other grandparents. I can think of at least one way we might spend time together.'

Ella's pulse jumped as she caught his intent. 'I'm sure you can.' They'd be alone, truly alone, for the first time and the thought was a delicious distraction from practicalities. 'But you know I was referring to what might get back to Lily and Arlo about us being seen together on a date.'

'Come with me, Ella, I want you to be there.' His voice was urgent as Lily turned and skipped towards them. 'We can play it safe, say you're my plus one because I had a spare ticket and it would be a shame to waste it. Most people are used to seeing you at school now with the kids. We can have a nice time and no one else need know any different. And afterwards, that's private and up to us to decide what we want and how we feel.'

'But we have to be careful. We can't give them false hope.' Ella prayed she wouldn't regret this later. She already loved Max, but what if for him, she was only a first step? A flirtation he was enjoying after all he'd lost, and it was only her future here, her heart, that hung in the balance. He seemed to be reading her mind when he spoke again, removing the intimacy from his voice now that Lily was almost upon them.

'What's to say you won't stay here, Ella?' His eyes narrowed on hers. 'Unless you've already made other plans?'

'Of course I haven't. I would tell you if I had.'

'So you could stay, if you wanted to?'

Not if you don't love me, she longed to say. But it would be madness to confess that now and hear him laugh it off. Have him tell her it was far too soon to say such things and a date at the ball was only the very beginning of something that might never happen. He loved his wife still, Ella was certain, and however much they were enjoying getting to know one another, he may never feel that way again about anyone else. Lily was at his side now, and he smiled as she took his hand.

'Ready to go?' he said to her. 'I bet Prim's missed you.'

-

Ella introduced her parents to Max, Lily and Arlo before they had to leave for the Santa train experience. Lily was excited to reveal Prim's latest trick of holding up a paw on command, and Arlo wanted Ella's mum and dad to meet the chickens and help collect the new eggs. Her mum was interested in the garden and Max walked her round, sharing his plans for redesigning it the next year. After he and the children had left for the train, Ella showed her parents the house before taking them to the pub for lunch. They had a lovely time, but the weather was worsening and her dad became impatient to get going. There was just time to exchange presents and thank her mum for the home-made Christmas pudding she'd brought. Ella hugged her dad and tried to persuade her mum to get in the car. The sky was grey, laden with snow, and her dad was running the engine.

'Max and those beautiful children are lovely, Ella. It's so sad, what they've gone through.' Her mum had both of Ella's hands in hers. She sniffed. 'And the way he looks at you. I can see what's happening, I'm not daft.'

'Mum, don't, okay.' Ella wrapped her in a tight hug. 'I like him, the children are adorable and his mum's a scream.'

'And?'

'And what? Nothing's going on.' There wasn't really, not unless her mum counted one exceptional kiss and a desire to do it again and again, and Ella wasn't telling her that bit. 'I don't know what I'm going to do when I leave here, and Lily and Arlo are far more important than doing something silly we'd regret later.'

'But what about your volunteering at the centre on the lake? You told me how keen they are for you to join them, so why bother if you're not going to stay? And then there's the college, I know you're talking to them this week.'

'Yes, and that will be to discuss spending a day cooking with the students, that's all. Stop running away with things.'

'Ella, my love, it's always been you that's done that.' Her mum held Ella's shoulders and her eyes were suddenly glistening. 'For once just let yourself stop running long enough to take a good look around you. You don't always have to be on the move, and you mustn't keep worrying that someone will find a way to hurt you if you stand still for long enough. Think about what you'd be missing if you left here.'

'And what would I be missing?' Ella was relieved her mum had let go and was finally getting in the car. Her dad flipped on the wipers to flick away the first snowflakes and gave her mum an impatient look.

'I don't think you really need me to tell you that, do you?' Her mum fastened her seatbelt and gripped Ella's hand one last time. 'Lauren's with us always and you've done it, Ella. You've achieved her dream and more, and you know she'd be the first to say it's time for your own dreams. Don't be afraid – you were always going to meet someone and fall in love. It just looks to me as though three of them might have come along at once.'

–

The Zoom meeting with the catering college two days later wasn't quite what Ella had been expecting and afterwards a new idea was ringing in her head. She needed to take some time to think it through, but as soon as the course leader had suggested teaching, it had seemed to make perfect sense. If Ella did decide to act on it, then there was a long road and more studying ahead. The course leader had offered the possibility of a place to teach the number of hours Ella would need to gain her formal qualification, and she felt as though another part of her life might just be falling into place. Much as she loved her developing role at Halesmere, thoughts of passing on her skills to other young chefs filled her with excitement. And she hadn't forgotten Ashley casually mentioning after the supper that Max was looking into a management company to take over Ella's role in the future. Marta got in touch to ask how she'd got on and Ella messaged to share the beginnings of the new idea.

After the success of the Christmas open day, all the studios were now provisionally filled, and she was excited to have Ana and her jewellery as well as a woman who created stunning fabrics and bags from Cumbrian wool joining Sandy and Marta in the New Year. Ella had also received an enquiry from a sculptor who was currently based in New Zealand but familiar with the area and looking to move. Stan wasn't the only one who liked the idea of returning to the days of having someone working with metal in the old forge. Ella had looked up Cal Ryan on Instagram and was seriously impressed with his brand of bespoke wildlife sculpture.

As Lily and Arlo counted down to Christmas their excitement and energy only increased. Lily had caught Max in a weak moment and persuaded him to volunteer at the local dog shelter for a day as an act of kindness. He'd tried to wriggle out of it, protesting that his and Ella's GoFundMe challenge to swim in the tarn on New Year's Day in aid of the shelter was enough – it was taking off as interest and donations grew – but Lily was insistent. Ella was so looking forward to their first date at the New Year's Eve ball, especially as she and Max managed to find very few moments alone. The end of the year was approaching, and she was clinging to the hope that the upcoming one might just bring a new beginning as well.

Chapter Twenty-One

By Christmas Eve Lily and Arlo were nearly demented with excitement and Stan had a pair of adorable brown and white guinea pigs he was keeping very firmly under wraps in a small shed. He'd made a run for them as Santa had apparently taken care of a hutch and Stan was planning to set everything up in the garden last thing before bed. Noelle returned from her cottage in France looking refreshed and was delighted to see the children, hugging them tightly and sweeping them off to her flat and reminding Ella gaily that she would need to sit for her again soon.

The house looked beautiful, the decorations still in place, but Ella was aware this might be the last time Max had the use of it for Christmas; they'd already received enquiries for next year after the images from the supper had gone online.

She was in the kitchen, helping Pearl and Max with preparations for lunch tomorrow. She'd organised the Secret Santa between the six of them and could only hope Stan hadn't got Pearl.

'You coming over later?' Max was peeling potatoes and Pearl had gone to set the table in the dining room. 'I'm doing my not-so-famous mac 'n' cheese and we're going to read *A Charlie Brown Christmas*.' He attempted a smile. 'We haven't done any of these things on Christmas Eve before. My mother's going to eat with us and tuck Lily and Arlo into bed. I know they'd like to see you too.'

'It's not that I wouldn't love to.' Ella was wrapping cocktail sausages in bacon and lining them up on a tray. She was picturing Lily and Arlo's elation over Santa coming that night, and their reluctance to go to sleep. 'But that sounds like a wonderful new tradition and it's probably not a good idea for me to be a part of it.'

'I suppose.' Max sighed. 'I just thought it might be nice, that's all. What are you planning to do then?'

Ella raised a shoulder. '*The Bishop's Wife* is on later and we grew up watching that with my mum and dad. They love black and white movies, and my dad was always trying to find something to surprise us with that we hadn't seen before.'

'You don't mind watching it on your own? If it's on after the kids have gone to bed you could watch it with me, I've never seen it. And we could probably stream it anyway.'

Ella's smile was quick. 'Would it sound silly to say let's not stream it? There's just something about catching an old movie in the moment it's on, especially Christmas ones, rather than when you feel like it.'

'Okay.' Max grinned. 'I'll take your word for it. So, eight thirty?'

'Think you'll have got them safely in bed by then?'

'I certainly hope so. Otherwise tomorrow could be a really long day.'

Once all the preparations for lunch were done, Pearl and Stan had left, and Max was in the cottage with Lily and Arlo, Ella had a crazy notion to make something festive to enjoy with the movie later. There was some whisky left from the supper and she whipped egg yolks with sugar and added double cream to make eggnog. She'd never had it at home before but had made variations on the theme for events. She always kept an emergency pack of puff pastry in the fridge and now she rolled it out and filled it with sausage meat, sage, and finely chopped onion for seasonal sausage rolls.

Anticipation at seeing Max without the children was fizzing and it felt like she was dressing for a date as she changed into a long-sleeved black and red floral blouse and jeans. She couldn't wait for the moment to arrive and was at the cottage a few minutes before eight thirty, tapping gently on the door and holding the tray of still-warm sausage rolls and eggnog. They would need finishing off with whipped egg whites and a little sugar folded into the yolks.

'Hey. You've got your hands full.' Max was whispering as he took the tray from her. 'It smells amazing, thank you.'

'Just some treats.' Ella glanced up the stairs. 'Are they asleep?'

'Yes, or at least they were. I'm in here.'

Instead of the kitchen as she had expected, Max opened the door to the sitting room. Ella had only been in here once or twice after school with the children and it was snug, with a real fire burning in a black grate beneath a chunky oak mantelpiece. A small, real Christmas tree stood in a corner near a window hidden by velvet curtains in pale green. There was a sofa to seat two, and a pair of wingback chairs were a pretty addition. It was a lovely room and Ella was sure she recognised Ashley's work in here too.

'What would you like to drink?' He kept his voice low. The kitchen door was open, and Prim found her way to

Ella's side before flopping on the rug in front of the fire. 'Glass of wine? I've got a nice Californian Pinot Noir?'

'Perfect, thanks.'

She arranged the sausage rolls on a low coffee table with the eggnog, so creamy it was almost a dessert. The television was already on, and when Max returned with their drinks he joined her on the sofa. He found the movie, teasing her about having to sit through ad breaks watching it live, but Ella shrugged it off.

'It's part of the romance,' she told him. The sofa was cosy, even for just the two of them, and their arms were pressed together. 'Stop complaining.'

'Sorry.' He'd brought plates and now he loaded them with sausage rolls as the credits began. It was a charming movie and even though she'd seen it so often, it had never lost its appeal; a handsome angel visiting a preoccupied bishop to remind him about the importance of family. There was sadness for Ella in watching it so far from her parents, but she couldn't deny her pleasure to be sharing the experience with Max. When it was over, he stretched out long legs and yawned.

'Well? Did you like it?' She put her empty wine glass on the table. The eggnog had gone and the few sausage rolls that were left could go in the fridge for the children.

'I really did, more than I expected. The ice skating was nice. That's something I could take the kids to do in the holidays. I don't think any of us miss London, just now and again some of the things we did there.'

'How was tonight, your new tradition with them?' Ella's voice had fallen as she pictured Lily and Arlo snuggled up to Max reading Charlie Brown, facing another Christmas without their mum.

'Yeah, good. I think it's something we'll do again. They loved the book and my mac 'n' cheese turned out okay. I was trying to give them something to hang on to that belongs here. Arlo's too small to remember that we used to eat cookies and read *The Night Before Christmas*.' Max sighed. 'I've still hung the stockings at the ends of their beds. I don't want to change everything, just mix it up a bit.'

Ella found his warm hand, resting on his thigh, and he lifted hers to kiss her fingers. 'It takes time, years really. I don't think you ever get over it, just used to it.'

'I'm sure you're right. So how was your new Christmas tradition, watching the same movie but with me?'

'Nice. One of those things that makes Christmas feel as though it's really here.' Better than nice, but she couldn't quite bring herself to say that out loud.

'Ella, what will you do, when you leave here?' He let go of her hand and his eyes were troubled. 'Have you thought about it?'

'Not much.' She hadn't mentioned the potential for becoming a teacher to anyone other than Marta. Ella still had research to do and a decision to make. If she wanted to teach young people at catering college then it meant she could at least stay on in Cumbria, whatever happened between her and Max. She hadn't forgotten her mum's words about always running away from anything that might hurt, and she was beginning to think she'd found a place where she could put down some roots. She'd enjoyed Brighton, but her flat was more of an investment once she'd been able to afford it rather than somewhere she envisaged living for a long time.

'What if your role here could be permanent and full-time? I've been giving some thought to a more substantial job managing the holiday business.' He shifted on the sofa to face her, and their hands separated. 'It's all your ideas we're implementing, and you know what you're doing with it better than anyone.'

'Max, I'm not sure the business warrants someone full time.' Ella wanted to share the truth fixed in her heart, about how much she already loved him and his children. But it wasn't right to rush ahead when he simply wasn't ready for more, and she found another reason, one which offered a version of the truth. 'I do love it up here but I'm not making any definite plans before the New Year. I'm still not certain about my career and it wouldn't be right to accept something until I am.'

'And what about us?' His eyes were sharp on hers.

'You and me?' Her laugh was light, gone. She had to leave a way out for them both. A way for her to leave in the spring with her heart mostly intact, her job done. And for him to let her go, not suspect the hurt she knew she would carry if that day ever came. 'We're just a maybe, aren't we, Max? Maybe one day you'll be ready for more and maybe I'll be ready for that family.' She stood up. 'I'd better go. At least one of us has a very early start tomorrow when Santa's been down that chimney.'

'So we're still on for our first date at the ball?' Max followed her to the front door and Ella raised a shoulder.

'Sure, seeing as officially I'm just your plus one. Merry Christmas, Max.' She reached up and kissed him lightly, felt his hands tightening on her waist as he kissed her back.

'Merry Christmas, Ella,' he said softy. 'See you tomorrow.'

–

When Ella woke on Christmas morning, she felt sad for a few moments, thinking of her parents so far away in New Zealand, their day over and evening about to begin. Her brother Jamie called, and they chatted for a bit, reminded each other of Christmas mornings at home and the long walks they'd take after lunch before flopping in front of the telly. Dylan had hooked up with someone in Chamonix and returned Ella's messages with the briefest of replies. She was thinking too of Lily and Arlo just across the drive in the cottage, opening their presents with Max and hopefully having a lovely time. The house was quiet when she wandered down to the kitchen in her pyjamas in search of breakfast, until a thumping at the front door had her going to see who was there.

'Flippin' 'eck, young Ella, thought you was never gonna let us in.' Stan crashed through the porch into the hall, his arms full of a huge roasting tray and a large turkey. 'Gotta get this in the oven sharpish.'

'I thought you were cooking it at home.' She watched him stomping to the kitchen and heard the clatter as the tray hit the table.

'Aye well, I was. Until Pearl told me you was on your own an' not spendin' the mornin' with the boss an' them kiddies, an' your mum an' dad away.' Stan huffed out an embarrassed laugh as his gaze slid away from Ella's. 'You gonna show me 'ow to drive this fancy oven, then? I was off sick the day we did physics at school.'

'Oh, Stan.' She went over and gave him a hug. He squeezed her back, letting her go just as quickly. 'And there was me thinking you were dressing up again, not coming in that old donkey jacket.'

'There's time yet, don't you worry.' He winked and she grinned at him before turning away to rearrange the trays in the oven and switch it on. 'Reckon I can trust you to keep an eye on this while I go back for Pearl, you bein' a chef an' all.'

'Ella! Look!'

She spun round as Lily flew into the kitchen, holding a squirming guinea pig. 'He's been, Santa's been! Look at my guinea pig.'

'Merry Christmas, Lily.' Ella bent down as Lily halted and held out her arms very carefully. 'Wow. She's lovely. Or is it a he?'

'She's a she, and she's called Lottie, after my favourite doll, the dog-walking one. Santa's brought the hutch, but Daddy said he must have had a word with Stan too cos Stan's made us a run for the garden.' Lily turned to him, her eyes shining. 'Thank you, Stan. Daddy said you must have known about the guinea pigs because you're such a good elf.'

'Well.' Stan was delighted. His chest seemed to swell as he puffed it out and he tapped his nose. 'I can't reveal my secrets or what Santa told me but long as you're pleased, Lily, then I'm 'appy too. Where's Arlo?'

'Getting dressed. He was cross because Daddy wouldn't let him come out in his pyjamas.' Lily looked at Ella. 'But you're still in your pyjamas.'

'I am.' Ella was on her way to the door. 'I'm going to shower right now, but I'll be back very soon and we'll go and see Stan's amazing guinea pig run, okay?'

'Okay Ella. Daddy and Arlo won't be long, and Mamie's coming too.'

'Don't you forget that turkey, chef,' Stan called, and Ella raised a hand as she ran across the hall.

It was a cheery morning with all seven of them in the house, a playlist of party music in every room. Noelle opened champagne and sketched the children as they played with their new toys in the drawing room, the guinea pigs chasing each other around their run. Arlo had named his guinea pig Herdy, after his favourite breed of sheep.

Everyone else was in the kitchen, helping with the lunch and trying not to get under each other's feet. A very different morning to the ones Ella had been used to with her family, but it felt lovely all the same. She teased Max about the amount of Toblerone he was scoffing whenever he thought no one was looking. She'd made a simple mushroom pâté for the starter, and it was all she could do to prevent Stan from finishing the lot when he tried it and declared it the best pâté he'd ever had. Pearl was busy with the vegetables and Lily's leek and mushroom strudels, and Ella was looking after the gravy.

They were a merry bunch when they sat down to eat, and the house was filled with noise as they talked and laughed their way through a fabulous lunch. Ella assured Pearl she had never tasted stuffing so good, and Pearl promised to email the recipe. Ella was suddenly glad her mum and dad had made the decision to do something different and force them all to find a way to create new traditions for the future. Had she gone home then she would have clung to the loss of Lauren instead of carrying her adored sister into this new life.

Ella's mum's Christmas pudding was a hit and Stan said it was even better than his beloved sticky toffee one. Ella snapped him on her phone tucking into his second helping and sent it to her mum with a laughing emoji. She only remembered to save a scrap for Dylan at the last minute.

Lily and Arlo had been given gifts by Stan and Pearl and, after dessert, escaped from the table to play as it was time for Secret Santa. Max turned down the Christmas playlist and their own gifts were handed round. Ella couldn't wait to see Stan open his. Max could only shake his head and laugh when he unwrapped a plain white mug with THE BOSS splashed across it and a single sachet of instant coffee for 'if you ever get a notion to visit me in me workshop, boss', from Stan, who was guffawing. He'd rolled up, not in fancy dress again as Ella had expected, but neat and tidy in a shirt and tie. She loved the tie. It was bright red, covered in white sheep with a single black sheep in the centre, and she'd told him it suited him more than he knew. Pearl received a ceramic yarn bowl, and Noelle roared with laughter when she opened her gift to discover a colouring book and pencils.

So it was just her and Stan left, and he persuaded Ella to go first. She opened her gift, and stared in wonder. It was a small paperback and, turning it over, she saw it was a collection of poetry and prose, a reminder to celebrate and live in the moment and to look at what was around her. It was beautiful, profound, and she was certain it could only have come from Max. She raised her head to find his eyes waiting, understanding, sharing the moment almost as though they were alone together. But it was Stan's turn now and she would thank Max properly later. She dragged her gaze away.

'Now then, oo's got me?' Stan tore at the paper, and it was his turn to be astonished as he removed the present from its wrapping. 'It's a pencil,' he muttered eventually. 'Never seen one like it. It's got a spirit level in it. Look Pearl, look at the level.' He sat back in his chair, holding the pencil in his hands as though it were a gold clock.

''Spose I've got you to thank for this, young Ella,' he said gruffly. 'I were expectin' a clean mug.'

'I couldn't possibly say, Stan, it's meant to be a secret,' she replied casually. 'But I'm sure whoever's chosen it for you is very glad you're pleased.'

'Aye, I am. I'll be usin' it later.' And for now, he tucked it lovingly behind his ear.

They gathered around the piano in the hall to sing carols and afterwards Noelle disappeared to catch up over Zoom with friends in France – or, as Max called it, have a couple more sneaky glasses of champagne before a snooze. He persuaded Stan and Pearl to stay longer, and they insisted on doing the very last bits of clearing away. He and Ella settled in the drawing room to watch a family movie, and she gave the children the gifts she'd bought for them. Lily was thrilled with her tiny pink handbag shaped like a dog's face, and Arlo was over the moon with a toy tractor and trailer he could build and take apart with a little drill. They were already starting to tire from the excitement, flopped on cushions on the floor with Prim nearby.

'So how was your day? I know it won't make up for not being with your family, but I hope you're enjoying it.' Max's arm was behind Ella on the back of the sofa, and she smiled as she felt the touch of his fingers.

'I have, it's been different but really wonderful.' She covered his other hand with hers, raising her knees so the children couldn't see if they happened to turn round. 'Thank you for including me today.'

'My pleasure. Our first Christmas at Halesmere. And it's been good – better than good.' Max was trailing a finger along her neck. 'Stan was over the moon with his gift. I don't think I've ever seen him so happy – or stumped for something to say.'

'Bless him, he and Pearl are brilliant. They've gone out of their way to help and make me feel at home. You might want to think about offering Pearl a part-time role if she'll take it, managing your social media. She's ace at it. Better than anything I could do.'

'I'll talk to her in the New Year. I'm too full of Christmas lunch and Toblerone to think about it now.'

Already the end of the holidays was in Ella's mind. Tomorrow Max and the children would head off to his parents-in-law and when he came back it would be New Year's Eve and the fundraising ball, then their charity swim in the tarn the morning after. The days were hurrying by, and she wanted to hold them still, draw out these last few hours before they went away to see her through the coming ones without them, despite the prospect of Dylan's merry company.

'Will you be okay, while we're gone?' Max's voice was soft, and she appreciated his concern.

'I'll be fine; I've got lots I can do, and my friend will be here for a bit.' Arlo and Lily were giggling at something from the movie and Ella and Max were smiling at the sound. 'We've had so many enquiries about the house and Pete's threatening to go on holiday in January – apparently his mate has a place in Tenerife, and he's said he'll book a flight if I find him any more work. He was laughing when he told me, but I do need to persuade him to hang back until February. I need to be in the flat by then so we can officially welcome our first guests.'

Lily jumped to her feet and Ella quickly removed her hand from Max's. 'Daddy, we forgot the mistletoe.' She darted from the room and returned moments later with a few stems fastened together with a red ribbon. 'Mamie brought it earlier, she said it would be nice to have in the house.'

'And what do we need with mistletoe, Lily? I've already hugged and kissed you both a million times today.'

'Not me, Daddy.' She shook her head very slowly, as though explaining something so simple that even her father ought to be able to understand. 'It's for you and Ella.'

'We don't need that,' Ella said hastily, inching away from him. 'Thanks all the same, Lily.'

'But Ella, it's Christmas and people always kiss at Christmas, don't they? That's what mistletoe is for, Mamie told me. She told me not to forget it and I nearly did.'

'Oh, did she?' Max was amused. He turned to Ella with a shrug. 'I don't mind if you don't?'

'I guess not. As it's Christmas.'

Arlo was oblivious, watching the movie, and Lily skipped across to hold the mistletoe over Max and Ella. He was holding back a grin as he tilted his head and his lips made contact with hers. She'd been expecting him to kiss her cheek and had to resist the urge to open her mouth beneath his, let the kiss linger. Instead, she smiled and drew back as Lily dropped the mistletoe and it fell to the floor, mission accomplished. Pearl and Stan came back into the room, and Pearl started unpacking her knitting from a bag she'd left beside a sofa.

'That's good news about the college, Ella,' she remarked, laying a ball of wool on her lap. 'I was down at the farm yesterday to pick up our order and Marta told me about you planning on being a teacher and them offering you a placement to get your hours in.'

Chapter Twenty-Two

Ella froze, feeling the weight of Max's stare suddenly fixed on her, anxiety running through her limbs. 'Marta said that?'

'Something along those lines, I think. She did say the college is very pleased to be getting you.'

'It's not decided. I haven't made up my mind, I have to do more research, look at the courses available.'

'So you're planning to stay in Cumbria then?' Max's tone was level. Ella heard the cool note as he returned his gaze to the television.

'I don't know. It was just a suggestion from the course leader and I'm thinking about it.'

'Seriously?'

'Yes.'

'I see.'

Ella felt him edge away, and misery set in as the movie progressed. She'd seen it before and she laughed in all right places, offered Lily and Arlo cheery smiles whenever they turned round to share a funny line or their favourite scene. But there was a new rigidity in Max's frame, and she wasn't surprised when he stood up the moment the film finished and said he was taking the children back to the cottage.

'But Daddy, *Frozen*'s on later and we want to watch it here.'

'You can do that at home, Lily. And you don't even like it.' He lifted Arlo into his arms and held out a hand to his daughter. 'You're both very tired after an exciting day and we've got a long journey tomorrow.'

'I like *Frozen* today,' Lily grumbled, and ignored Max's hand to go to Ella and wrap her arms round her. 'Bye Ella, thank you for our presents, I'm taking my bag to Granny and Grandpa's tomorrow. Will you come and wave us off when we go?'

'I doubt Ella will be around, Lily.' Max's gaze on her was sharp over Lily's head. 'We may as well make the best of you both being early risers and get away in good time. I think it's her turn for a lie-in, don't you?' He looked over at Stan and Pearl. 'Thank you for everything you've both done today, you've made it very special for all of us. I really appreciate it.'

'Our pleasure,' Pearl said, knitting needles still flying as she smiled at the children. 'You two have a lovely time and we'll see you back on New Year's Day, okay?'

'In time for Daddy and Ella's swim!' Lily grabbed Max's hand and swung his arm. 'The dog shelter's going to be so happy, Daddy. Please will you talk to the guinea pigs and the chickens while we're away, Ella? I don't want them to be lonely without us.'

'Of course I will. I'll see them every day.' She felt bereft as she trailed out of the room behind them, Arlo's head resting on Max's shoulder.

'See you when we get back,' Max said as Lily scampered off ahead, Prim trotting beside her. 'Thanks for all you did today.'

'You too.' Ella wanted to delay him, explain somehow. 'It really helped.'

He nodded once and set off.

'Max?' She darted after him and caught his hand. 'Nothing's decided, and I didn't want to tell you until I was sure.'

'Right.' He hesitated and she saw the questions, the doubt following. 'At least I know now you'd have turned it down if I'd offered you a job here.' Arlo was grumbling and Max put him down so he could follow Lily. He waited a few seconds, until Arlo was in the cottage. 'You're going to leave, that much is clear, Ella. Us, if not Cumbria. My children and me.'

'And if I didn't? Leave you all?' Her voice was a whisper and she'd never been closer to confessing what she felt for him, and Lily and Arlo too.

'Do you mean it?' There was a yell from the cottage and Max sighed impatiently. 'Look, I've got to go, those two should be in bed. Let's just take some time to think and I'll see you when we get back.'

'Okay.' Ella knew she couldn't delay him, not when his children needed him. 'I'd offer to help but...'

'Better not.' The briskness was back, and he was already walking away.

'I hope you have a lovely time.'

'Thanks.'

Ella didn't wait to see Max bang the cottage door behind him, instead trailing back to the drawing room.

'I'm sorry if I've spoken out of turn, Ella, and said something I wasn't meant to.' Pearl's look was sympathetic. 'Marta just mentioned it in passing because she thought I already knew.'

'It's all right, Pearl, really.' Ella dropped onto the sofa. The fire was still warm and she felt suddenly exhausted, ready for bed herself. 'I needed to tell Max about the college at some point. I do love the idea of teaching a subject that would put my training and experience to good use.' She bit her lip. 'I'd have to find somewhere to live as well.'

'Not stayin' 'ere, then, young Ella? Halesmere?' Stan was eyeing her beadily. She shrugged.

'Whatever I do, Stan, I don't want to work for Max for ever.' She didn't want to be his colleague with a professional distance coming between them again; she wanted so much more. But perhaps now, because she'd kept her thoughts about the future to herself, her chance had gone.

'Righto.' He shrugged. 'Reckon I'll still need you around to keep an eye on me, though.'

'You think?' Ella tried to laugh it off. 'We'll see.'

–

Ella was up early on Boxing Day but the black pickup outside the cottage was already gone, and she felt crushed. Even taking her kayak down to the tarn and having the most glorious hour on the water couldn't quite lift her spirits and she was glad of a long hot bath when she returned. The New Year's Day swim in aid of the local animal shelter was still attracting lots of attention online and Stan had promised to double his donation in the unlikely event of Max being able to beat Ella in their race. She hadn't swum once since she'd arrived at Halesmere, and she resolved to fit in a couple of practice swims while he and the children were away.

Noelle invited Ella over to her studio later, for drinks and another opportunity to sit for her. She wasn't really in the mood as she changed into the rose chiffon gown, but Noelle cheered her up, pouring glass after glass of champagne and abandoning her sketches to tell Ella stories about her modelling days. Noelle was also going away soon, to spend a few days with friends, and Ella felt relieved at the thought of Dylan arriving so she wouldn't be completely alone at Halesmere overnight. She could feel the effects of the champagne as she returned to the house and Zoomed her parents in New Zealand. They were having a wonderful time and she managed to convince them that she was too, leaving out the bit about the family being away.

Stan was seeing to the chickens and the guinea pigs every day, and Ella was very glad of Prim's company in the house. Prim stuck close to her side and Ella hated leaving her downstairs when she went to bed at night. But the dog wasn't allowed in the bedrooms in the cottage and Ella didn't think it fair to teach her habits she would find hard to break once Max and the children were back home. Stan and Pearl invited her to eat lunch with them and she had a lovely dinner in the pub with Marta and her partner, which also included Sandy, who had popped in to see about using the pub for another church meeting.

Dylan arrived that evening, bringing his usual energy and upbeat attitude, and she was very happy to see him and grateful for his company. They filled the three days with walking, a first practice swim in the tarn and a wonderful drive up to kayak at a glorious lake further north, which was almost deserted and so very different to the bustle of Windermere. High fells to one side, farmland and fields to the other. They ate in the pub a couple of times and flopped in front of Netflix each night. Sandy invited them for supper, delighted that Ella's mum was thrilled with Ella's present to her of a vase from her collection of ceramics.

Dylan headed off the day before New Year's Eve and Ella was sorry to see him go. She was glad to throw herself back into thinking about the first retreat, working out a rough programme of activities and a menu. They could accommodate up to eight guests, a number that would work well as it would probably attract a group of friends or couples. Phil from the pub put her in touch with a woman who ran workshops specialising in eating well, and Ella set up a meeting. Dylan had invited her to Copenhagen soon, and she had promised to visit once her time at Halesmere was over. She was expecting to be busy for her last little while here, settling the artists into their new studios and running the retreat, and hated the thought of taking time away from Max and the children before she had to.

He'd messaged a couple of times while they were away, sending a few images of the children that apparently Lily had wanted to share and casually checking in to make sure Ella was okay. His tone was cool, more business-like, and nothing of what they had shared or how they'd parted on Christmas Day was mentioned. She made sure to offer her own updates on the guinea pigs, chickens and of course Prim, who was missing her family, despite Ella's company. Every time Prim heard the front door open or a vehicle on the drive, she would leap up expectantly and tilt her head in hope, only to be disappointed.

On New Year's Eve Ella only realised that Max had returned when she was curled up on the sofa watching an old black and white movie and Prim shot to the door, whining and wagging her tail. At first Ella sighed and ignored her; she'd done this before. But Prim was insistent, and eventually Ella got up to let her out of the room. She charged to the front door and Ella's heart leapt when she saw the black pickup on the drive. Max wasn't alone; Ashley had somehow managed to time her own arrival to coincide with his. Ella guessed Ashley must have known when to expect him, which was more than she had.

He was unloading luggage and Ella watched as Prim hurled herself at him in joy. He put a bag down and bent to give her a cuddle as she bounced beside him. When Prim ran inside the cottage and back out, she almost seemed to be asking why Lily and Arlo were not with him, and Max gave her a wry grin and a pat. Ella was still standing in the porch and their eyes met for a long moment as he looked across.

'Hi. Good trip?' she called over, clearing her throat to hide her nerves. This evening was supposed to be their date at the black-tie ball and there hadn't been such distance between them since her first weekend here.

'Yes thanks. Kids enjoyed it,' he called back, watching Prim as she hurried over to rejoin Ella. She thought she knew why; there was a fire blazing in the drawing room and if Lily and Arlo weren't here to keep Prim company, she'd take the fire instead. 'It was good to spend time with Victoria's family. They're all at the hotel now, ready to watch the fireworks.'

'Sounds lovely. I'm glad you had a great time. Hi Ashley.'

'Nice to see you, Ella.' Ashley gave her a smile that didn't seem quite as warm as her words. 'I'm sure Max is grateful to you for dog-sitting.'

'Are you okay? Everything all right?' Max glanced at Ella before slinging a rucksack over his shoulder and reaching for a couple more bags.

'I'm fine. No problems.'

'Who was that gorgeous man you've had staying here, Ella?' Ashley's laugh was light as she raised beautifully groomed eyebrows. 'It's all over the village, you two going everywhere together. Surely it wasn't the incorrigible ex you were telling me about, the one who offered you a new job? Is he still here? Are you bringing him to the ball?'

'You had someone here with you?' Max's look at Ella was sharp.

'You know I did, I asked you before he came. Dylan. He's my best friend.' Ella's words were falling over each in other in her rush to explain, certain Ashley was enjoying her discomfort. 'He left yesterday, he's moving to Copenhagen for a new job.'

'Right. My mistake, I'd forgotten. Silly of me to wonder if you were okay on your own.' Max slammed the boot and Ella jumped. 'You not going with him? You seem to have had plenty of offers.'

'Of course not.' She was crushed; after their stolen moments together with the children around, Max was clearly not looking for more now they were alone – well, alone if Ashley and her smug little smile would just go away. He was obviously distracted and upset, and Ella couldn't blame him. However excited Lily and Arlo had been to see their grandparents, there must still be all kinds of memories and hurt hovering, for the loss of the young woman who had been responsible for bringing them all together.

'Max, shall we have that coffee I messaged you about? Some time on our client without the kids haring around would be good.' Ashley was already heading towards the cottage and Ella stared incredulously. He'd just driven two hundred and fifty miles, after being with his late wife's parents for the best part of a week, and Ashley wanted to him to think about work?

'Not now, Ash, sorry.' Max said, his arms still full of bags as she turned to meet his impassive gaze. 'The client will have to keep until the New Year.'

'Of course.' She offered him a beaming smile. 'I could make us a late lunch and you can relax before we go dancing.'

'Dancing?' He looked blank.

'The ball, tonight? Surely you haven't forgotten?'

'Not exactly.' He sighed, his glance sliding pointedly to her car. 'Let's leave lunch too, Ash. I'm going to have a kip and a shower before anything else if you don't mind.'

It wasn't a question and Ella registered the flicker of disappointment on Ashley's face. 'Of course not.' She finally took the hint and made a point of kissing Max and telling him how much she was looking forward to seeing him in black tie later. She and Ella shared a more distant goodbye and then she was finally gone as the car took off down the drive.

'What time is the taxi picking us up?' Anything to delay him, anything to discover whether going to the ball together might still mean as much to him as it did to Ella. She'd eventually confessed her feelings for Max to Dylan and he'd been sympathetic, told her to go for it and not wait for the opportunity of love to pass her by. Where might she and Max be tonight, on this very last night of the year? And what might follow for them at the beginning of a new one? Might he ever feel the same, and love her too?

'Six. That all right for you?'

It was a few hours away; she had plenty of time to get ready. She felt chilly suddenly, the delicious anticipation of time alone with him disappearing in the cool reality of his eyes. 'You still want to go... with me?'

'Do you? If it's yes, Ella, then let's keep it to you being my plus one, not my date. Simpler that way, nothing we need to hide.'

It was as though he wasn't really seeing her. She sensed his mind was full of something else and was almost certain it was his late wife. How could it not be, at this time of year, Christmas over and his children away, the time he had spent with Victoria's family bringing back the reality of his loss? He wanted to be alone with his memories.

And Ella knew then that she wouldn't be staying at Halesmere. Max didn't feel the same way she did. And she understood. It was madness to have hoped for something else and she would have to let them all go. She already loved Lily and Arlo too much to risk their happiness for a fling.

'I'm not coming with you.' The words were tumbling from Ella's lips and her throat felt scratchy. 'I know you're still angry with me for not telling you about the college and I'm sorry I didn't. I hadn't planned to let you down at the last minute, I'll obviously pay you for my ticket.'

Part of her was hoping he'd challenge her decision, insist she come with him, that he wanted her there, but she saw none of those words forming in the cool reality of his stare. 'Maybe it's for the best,' he said. 'And of course you don't need to pay for your ticket, it's my children's school they're raising money for.'

And there it was. His children, his school, his life. She couldn't push him, even though she wanted to hear the possibility of a future, a reason to stay, not another one to run.

'It's too soon, too much.' She tried to smile, make herself laugh it off. 'We can't risk Lily and Arlo for something that might never amount to anything.'

'You're right. You're the one who's leaving here, even if you do stay in Cumbria.' Max's eyes on hers were hard and he let the bags in his arms fall to the ground. 'You're the one who said family life wasn't for you because you won't risk your heart to love anyone else. You're the one who didn't think it important enough to tell me you were thinking of staying and find out what that might mean to me and my children. We barely get a minute alone because I'm almost always with them. That's my reality and it isn't going to change, but I can't expect it to be yours as well when it's something you never wanted. Lily and Arlo come first, and I think that maybe being alone is easier for all of us.'

Ella's stomach dropped. She wanted him, loved him, and loved his children too, and her heart was already breaking at the thought of leaving them. But if he would never allow himself to love her back, then she couldn't stay at Halesmere, whatever role she chose for her career.

'I understand, Ella, I do,' he went on. 'I know you don't want to be hurt again and neither do I, but I don't think we fit into your new future. What is it you actually want? A different job, another life somewhere else? A place where no one knows your story and you can keep on hiding in the shadows? Has it ever occurred to you that you're not actually living two lives?' His voice became gentler as the resentment disappeared. 'What if you're only really living half a life, with half of your heart?'

'And what if I stayed?' Her voice was a frightened whisper. Something in his words told her he was right, that she had been living only a half a life before she came here.

'Do you mean it? And for what? How do I know we'll be enough for you when all your decisions seem to be based around your career?' He took a tiny step back. 'I can't offer more than a maybe on you and me if I can't trust you to stay, Ella, much as I want to.'

'That's not fair, you're suggesting I stay for a maybe! That I change my entire life and hang around here on the off-chance that maybe someday we'll find a way to commit. I've already turned down every approach I've had because I dread the thought of leaving you all. But I need a job when I'm done here, Max.' Ella's voice hardened. 'Ashley told me you were looking into a company managing the house.'

'She said what?' His words were sharp, and his eyes narrowed. 'I had one meeting so I could create a valid job description to suit Halesmere. I don't even remember telling her.' He shook his head. 'Ashley's a friend, Ella, or I thought she was. And that's it. I wanted to make your role permanent, find a way for you to stay. But you didn't tell me what you were planning, and I'm frightened I'd wake up one morning and you'd be on your way because you've had a better offer, a shiny new career somewhere else. I can't do that to my children, and I don't want it for myself either.'

'It seems neither of us is great at sharing what we're thinking.' Ella's eyes were glittering, and adrenaline was racing through her limbs, leaving her trembling as the truth escaped in a rush. 'Falling in love with you hasn't completely ruined my reason; I know you're right to be cautious and I'm not crazy enough to expect you to be on one knee at the ball or making some grand gesture. But I can't risk more of my heart for a maybe if you won't trust me. I need to know it's something we both believe can last if I stay here for you, and Lily and Arlo, regardless of what job I do. I need to know your children aren't going to be hurt again.'

Too late, she wanted to take it back. She had let spill what she felt for him, and shock was chasing across his face as the colour drained from it. His mouth opened but no words came. He shut it again and Ella laughed sharply.

'It's okay, Max, you don't have to say anything. I'll see out the job here – unless you want me to go before. Whatever's best for Lily and Arlo; I don't want to risk upsetting them unnecessarily.' She hesitated, blinked back the tears threatening. At least now he knew what was in her heart and she could think about her future – one without him and his family. She turned towards the house, and a second later his voice, shaky and still urgent, followed.

'Ella, wait, please. We need to…'

'What? How can we make this fit if we can't find a way to share what we feel?' She couldn't look at him. 'Happy New Year, Max, truly. I wish you all the best.'

Chapter Twenty-Three

'Ella? Are you in there? I need you! Ella!'

Ella gritted her teeth. She was curled up on a sofa in the drawing room, but she knew Noelle well enough to recognise that tone and that Noelle wasn't going to be dissuaded. Ella got up and trailed over to open the door. At least she hadn't borrowed Max's keys and let herself in, although Ella wouldn't put it past her if she hadn't replied.

'Hi Noelle, what can I do for you?'

'You can sit for me, that is what.' Noelle grabbed her arm. Ella's laugh was almost a splutter as she found herself being towed across the drive and through the arch.

'Noelle, it's dark and getting late. It's New Year's Eve. Surely you're not painting? I was just planning a nice quiet evening and I'm really not in the mood.'

'You do not need to be in the mood, Ella, I do. I am the artist.' Noelle was surprisingly strong, and Ella rolled her eyes. She'd had a bath and changed into her pyjamas and a long, lonely night beckoned. She sighed, she supposed she might as well sit for Noelle, it would see out the last hours of the year and at least she wouldn't be alone. She had no idea if Max had gone to the ball. Maybe he would take Ashley instead and she would be a better fit for him, after all. She already had children, she lived here, they worked together. Maybe that would be enough for him.

Once Noelle had Ella in the studio, the rose chiffon gown waiting, she finally seemed satisfied that Ella wasn't going to escape. Ella took off her pyjamas and changed into the gown, the fabric seeming to sigh against her skin. As she emerged from behind the screen, Noelle pointed to a pair of beautiful high-heeled sandals in palest pink.

'Wear those,' she instructed. 'Today I need you taller. They will fit. You have small feet.'

Ella put the heels on obediently, already feeling more elegant and slightly less balanced. Noelle arranged her as before, one hand up to her face, holding the gown off the floor with the other. She glanced at a clock on the wall, picked up a pencil, her brow furrowed.

'Ella, you are distracted. Concentrate please, you must not look quite so dismayed.'

She pursed her lips, thinking about the charity swim with Max tomorrow. From what Pearl had told her, now the dog shelter had put it on their own social media lots of people had taken an interest as well as donated, and a crowd of locals was expected. She would just have to grin and bear it after that crazy confession of love to Max.

'How long will this take, Noelle? You know we've got the swim tomorrow; I can't be in bed too late.'

Noelle ignored that to continue sketching, her hand flying over the easel. Ella's arm, held up to her face, was already beginning to ache. She glanced at the clock. She'd give it ten more minutes and then she was out of here and getting straight back into her pyjamas. Somehow another fifteen minutes inched by and she rolled a shoulder.

'Noelle, I'll have to stop, sorry.'

Noelle sighed and checked the clock again. '*Bon*, Ella, we have done enough. You may go.'

'Thanks.'

Dismissed as quickly as she'd been summoned, Ella bent to unfasten the sandals, and jumped as Noelle cried: '*Non*, leave them on. They suit you; they look perfect with your gown.'

Ella straightened, surprised to see Noelle holding her cosy pyjamas. 'Thanks, but I think I'll get changed. I've got to go back outside and it's freezing.' She held out a hand for the pyjamas, but Noelle backed away.

'So? You are young, you will hardly feel the cold.'

'May I have my pyjamas please?' Ella inserted a firm note into her voice, but Noelle shook her head.

'*Non*, Ella. Go home in your gown. Max is waiting for you in the house.' Noelle's face softened in a smile. 'Just know that he has loved and lost, and he is cautious, it has always been his nature. But if you think I do not know what is going on, you are mistaken.'

'Noelle, what are you talking about?' Ella's heart was racing, and her skin was beginning to tingle. 'There's nothing going on between us.'

'Nonsense, it is perfectly simple. You are in love with him, and I know my son well enough to know he is in love with you. Now go. Out, before I throw these terrible pyjamas from my window, and you will never see them again!'

'Noelle, you really are mad.' Ella wanted to rush across the room and hug her, but didn't dare; she'd probably slip on the wooden floor in these heels. 'You've practically kidnapped me.'

Noelle threw back her head and laughed. '*Oui*, lovely Ella, life is so much more fun that way. And Max needed you out of the house. I cannot work in this light, it is abominable.'

Ella managed the stairs in a series of cautious steps. Outside, snow was falling, landing on her skin, melting as it met the goosebumps forming. The chiffon gown was almost nothing and could do little to prevent her from shivering as she hurried across the gravel. She pushed open the door to the house and the warming notes of classical music being beautifully played was the first thing to hit her already heightened senses.

Her eyes raced over to the piano to see Max, not playing as she had expected, but standing by it. Now Ella understood why Noelle had been so insistent she keep on the beautiful gown. He was in black tie and looked devastating, the white shirt sharp against the elegance of his beautifully cut jacket and trousers. Ella recognised a glimmer of nerves behind the smile hovering on his lips.

'If you weren't beside the piano I'd think it was you playing.' Now she was here, apprehension, anticipation, desire were all tumbling through her stomach and her voice was a croak.

'It is me. I recorded it and made a playlist. I couldn't think of another way to play for you and dance together at the same time.' He was walking towards her, and she swallowed as she saw him taking in the gown she was wearing. One very thin strap had slipped in the dash across the courtyard, and she went to pull it up.

'Let me.' His eyes were blazing on hers as he slid a finger beneath the strap and inched it back up her shoulder. Ella very nearly told him it was the wrong direction as he placed his other hand on her bare back. 'You are going to the ball, Cinderella.'

'That's a terrible line.' She was already melting like the snow on her skin as Max fitted her against him and she felt the silk lapel of his jacket next to her chest.

'I know, I'm sorry,' he murmured, his mouth against her temple. 'I promise I've only just thought of it. Dance with me?'

'Is this a waltz?' She could only whisper as she tried to follow him across the wooden floor in the unfamiliar heels.

'It's the "Waltz of the Flowers" from *The Nutcracker*. Do you like it?'

'I love it, mostly because you recorded it for me. I'm sorry for stepping on your feet.'

'That's okay, you'll get better with practice.'

'I really don't think I can dance all night in these shoes.'

'I wasn't thinking we'd dance all night.' He dropped his head to speak against her ear, his lips drifting to her neck. 'I have other things beside dancing planned for our ball.'

'Such as?' Ella had never been swept across a floor quite like this and she was finding it almost impossible to think of anything other than his body against hers, his hand on her back holding her up as her knees started to give way.

'Champagne. Frozen pizza. I hope you'll forgive me for that.'

'I love frozen pizza.'

'Yeah?' Max smiled as Ella faltered in her heels, then drew them both to a halt to stare into her eyes. 'That's not what you told Lily and Arlo.'

'It's a bloody nuisance to make pizza from scratch, just don't tell them I said so.' She giggled. 'I know, that's another pound for Lily.'

'Ella, this is me, sharing what I feel. It's not always easy but you need to know.' Max gripped her hands, the nervous smile back as the music soared through the speakers to its end. 'I'm sorry about before. I ended up telling Victoria's parents about you while we were away

298

and they told me to go for it, not waste time if it felt right. All the way home I practised how I was going to ask you not to leave, beg you to give us a chance if I had to. Then Ashley was there, I panicked when she mentioned your ex and the words just fled.' He shook his head. 'When my mother found out we weren't going to the ball she roasted me, said she'd never taken me for a fool and hadn't ever met a bigger one if I couldn't act on my own feelings, and how often did I think a woman like you would come into my life and love my children the way you do. I thought she was going to give me a black eye to go with the black tie.'

Ella was caught between crying at his words and laughing at the image he painted of Noelle. Ella could just image her livid, eyes flashing, waving a fist in Max's face as she told her own son exactly what she thought of him. 'Oh, Max.'

'I didn't ever think I'd love anyone again, not like this. I tried to convince myself not to, that you wouldn't stay, didn't want a family or a reason to risk your heart, but none of it worked.' He squeezed her fingers. 'I think I fell in love with you the moment I came through the door that first night after school and you were dancing with Lily. I felt as though I'd come home again and suddenly the four of us seemed to make sense. And then before, when you told me you loved me. Did you mean it?'

'Of course I did.' Ella was staring at him, reading the passion, the promise, a future in his eyes. 'I was the same. I didn't want to fall in love with all of you the way I did, and I don't want to go, to leave you. I was afraid you wouldn't love me back and I knew I couldn't stay if you didn't.'

'There's no maybe about this for me, Ella. I can only hope it's the same for you.'

'You know it is.' She paused. 'Lily and Arlo, they're everything.'

'They are, almost. Then there's you and there's me.' His smile was widening as his hands drifted up her arms to her shoulders. 'And we're completely, utterly alone.'

'Max?'

'Mmm?' His lips were inching along her neck to her ear, and she was breathless as she clung to him.

'My strap's fallen down again.'

'I know. I might have had something to do with that.' His gaze fell to his fingers on her shoulders. 'I was thinking we should dance again but now I'm not so sure.'

'Dancing's overrated,' she whispered, reaching for his bow tie as the other strap of her gown slipped away. 'I've never understood how you tie these things.'

'Then let me help you.'

'You can't, I need you to hold my gown up.'

'Actually, Ella, you really don't.' Max shrugged out of his jacket, draping it on the piano stool, and slid his arms round her. She laughed as he swung her up and the gown fluttered to the floor. 'As stunning as you look in it, I prefer you like this right now.'

'You're wearing far too many clothes,' she grumbled, finally managing to get the bow tie undone as he carried her to the stairs.

'It's a black-tie ball. What did you expect?'

'Not cufflinks! That's totally cheating; how am I supposed to get this shirt off in a hurry?'

'I'm not sure you can. You'll have to be patient.'

'That is not fair.' Ella wound her arms round his neck instead. 'Happy New Year, Max,' she whispered against his lips. 'I love you.'

'I love you too, Ella Grant. Happy New Year. And it's not even midnight. We've got hours.'

'Oh?' They were on the landing now, and he shoved her bedroom door open with a foot. 'What will we do with all that time alone?'

'Have a very long, uninterrupted lie-in tomorrow, for starters.'

'We can't.' She laughed, loving the kiss they shared as he stood her up and removed his cufflinks. 'We've got to swim in the tarn in the morning, or have you forgotten?'

'Why do you think I brought you up here?' He was looking at her as he hurriedly unbuttoned his shirt and Ella went to help him. 'The only way I'm going to beat you in a race is if I've exhausted you first.'

'Go ahead,' she said innocently, drawing in a breath as he dragged the shirt off. 'If you really think that will work, give it your best.'

'I intend to.' He gathered her against him, walking her back to the bed. 'Until next year at the very least.'

–

'Please tell me that's not a photographer over there?' Max looked astonished by the number of people waiting at the tarn, who raised a cheer at the sight of him and Ella arriving. Her adrenaline was already bubbling at the thought of the challenge ahead and how it would feel to be in the water. She checked the trees on the far side, assessing the conditions with a practised eye. There would be no wind today; everywhere was still, layered in white after the snowfall, the tops of the high fells clipping the clouds.

'Okay, that's not a photographer over there.'

'Bloody is,' he muttered, dropping his bag to the ground. 'How did…? Pearl. Of course.'

'Yep. And people are getting to know you now, Max. You're part of the community here.'

'Thanks to you.' He pulled his neoprene hat from his bag. Ella's smile was full of love and happiness as she caught the look he was giving her. She'd never spent a New Year's Eve quite like the one they'd shared last night and was certain it would never be bettered.

They'd eaten pizza and drunk the champagne in bed at midnight, and now they were both bleary-eyed and getting used to their very new, very different relationship. Every touch felt like their first, every kiss a promise for the next. And Ella didn't doubt, however much change lay ahead and what her new career might look like, that she loved him, and he her. They both had too much hurt behind them to risk a relationship based on less. Of course, there was Lily and Arlo to tell before anyone else.

Noelle, who was here, swathed in a huge coat, her Cossack hat and enormous sunglasses, hadn't needed an explanation to read the new light in Max's eyes as she came over to kiss them both. Ella and Max had already agreed that Ella would remain in the house until the first guests were due before moving back into the flat. They would be able to spend time together as a family and give Lily and Arlo more opportunity to get used to the idea of Ella living with them later on. It also meant no more nights together for now, and neither she nor Max had been in a hurry to get up this morning until they couldn't put it off any longer.

The snow had stopped falling but the air was still bitter, and she was glad they'd changed into wetsuits at the house before jogging easily through the garden to warm up. Phil from the pub had brought his partner and Marta was there with Luke, giving Ella a cheery thumbs-up. Sandy the ceramist was chatting with Mrs Graham from the school and one or two other parents had turned up to offer support, along with a couple of staff from the dog shelter. Ashley was busy and had sent her apologies and an online donation. Stan stamped his feet, sporting another woolly bobble hat and decidedly excited.

'Way to go, boss,' he shouted happily. 'Young Ella's gonna beat you 'ands down. I've got money on it.'

'I think your plan backfired and Stan's right.' Ella, doing a few stretches, raised her arms. 'I don't feel at all tired.'

'Is that right?' Max, adjusting his goggles, looked up to let his eyes linger on her mouth instead. 'Maybe now's a good moment to take your mind off the swim then.'

'And how will you do that?' Her pulse was already hurrying, and he was right, she wasn't thinking so much about water temperatures and if she'd remembered her Dryrobe in the dash from the house. 'With so many people watching.'

He raised an arm as though he was discussing their swim, what to expect once they were in the water. Only Ella heard his low words as he told her how much last night had meant to him and exactly how they might like to spend their next evening alone. The photographer was snapping away, and Ella was thankful she was the only one who knew the heat on her face hadn't come from the cold.

'Daddy, Ella! We're back!'

They whipped round to see Lily charging across the meadow with Prim on a lead, Arlo following more slowly with their grandparents, returned from their night away.

Lily was being towed along so fast she was almost skiing, and Stan made a grab for Prim's lead before Lily hit the deck. She was breathless when she reached Max and he swung her up, spinning her round and making her laugh. 'We had a brilliant time, Daddy, but I'm glad we're home. I can't wait to see Ella win.'

'And happy New Year to you too, Lily,' Max said dryly. He put her down and she hurried over to Ella for a quick hug. Max lifted Arlo up for a cuddle too, then, after Ella kissed him, handed him over to his waiting granny. He introduced Ella to his parents-in-law and, lovely as they were to her, she knew it was going to take them a while to get used to her place in their daughter's family. It was time for the challenge and an air of expectation was building in the crowd.

'Ready?' Ella walked to the water's edge with Max. They were both wearing their neoprene hats and socks with gloves. She pulled her goggles down. 'Remember to think happy thoughts. You'll be buzzing for the rest of the day after this.'

'I'm already buzzing, and I don't need a bloody freezing dip to remind me to think happy thoughts.' He was grinning and she laughed back, feeling the shingle jabbing into her feet.

'We've nearly doubled the target for the dog shelter now so it's all worth it. And that's another pound to add.'

The water was shallow for a few metres as they slowly waded in and she relished the familiar chill around her thighs, rising to her waist. She liked to swim as soon as possible once she was in. She took steady breaths, heard Max doing the same. Then, as the ground fell away, she dropped her shoulders and settled into a comfortable crawl. They weren't really meant to be racing; they weren't properly familiarised to the conditions and injuries or worse could happen if they really went for it.

'Okay?'

'Yes,' he called back. 'I'm fine. You?'

'It's perfect. Cold but perfect.'

The water felt so different from the rolling waves of the sea at Brighton, and she was aware of the rising fells enclosing them in the landscape, making her surroundings seem smaller and more intimate. She increased the pace, feeling the familiar pleasure as she sliced through the water with the efficient stroke that was nearly as natural to her as walking. Max, beside her, called again: 'Short race, to satisfy Stan?' They were doggy-paddling to stay afloat in the deeper water. 'To that birch over there?'

Ella followed where Max was pointing. It wasn't far, about thirty metres ahead and they'd be fine. 'Yes, but don't go mad.'

'May I have a head start?' He was grinning.

'You may not. You're taller and stronger than me so you already have an advantage. Go!'

She won, easily, her stroke much better than his. Treading water as they got their breath to turn for home, he kissed her quickly, wiping the wetness from her face. 'How the hell do you swim like that?'

'I'm competitive, that's how. And I have lots of experience. Come on, we should get back.'

They waded out of the water to loud cheers and the attention of the photographer as Pearl snapped them on her phone. Everyone was crowding around offering high-fives. Ella was delighted to see Stan had got a camping stove going and was ready with hot drinks as she and Max quickly wrapped themselves in their Dryrobes to change. Stan was frying sausages now, including some vegetarian ones for Lily, and most people, tempted by the smell, hung around for something to eat. Max thanked everyone for helping and sponsoring the dog shelter so generously.

'New Year tradition, boss,' Stan shouted, putting two sausages in Arlo's roll and smothering it in sauce for him. 'Reckon you an' Ella takin' a dip in the tarn is a good way to start every January.'

'I like the sound of that, Stan,' Max called back. 'You could join us, take one for the team.'

'No thanks. My idea of takin' one for the team is double 'elpin's of sticky toffee puddin' at our next meetin' down the pub.'

Lily and Arlo were sat in between Ella and Max, and he slid an arm round Arlo's shoulders. 'I've got something to tell you,' Max said softly. 'And I think you're going to like it.'

'Are we getting another puppy, Daddy?' Lily bounced to her feet, knocking her last bits of bread roll to the ground. Prim leapt up too and Max reached out a hand, stroking her head as he rolled his eyes. 'Because this time I think we should get—'

'No, Lily, it's not another puppy. Or a kitten or a pony.'

'Sheep?' Arlo said hopefully. 'And a sheepdog?'

'No. Not yet anyway.' Max gave an exasperated shake of his head and Ella giggled. 'Actually, you're getting more of an Ella. As in, we thought it might be nice if Ella spent more time in our house, with us. Like a family.'

'Do you mean you're in love with each other?' Lily tilted her head and Ella held her breath. 'Because I think you probably are.'

'Well, I suppose that's one way to explain it, yes. Ella's staying at Halesmere because she loves all of us, not just me.'

306

'Mamie too, even though I heard you say she's trouble?' Lily sounded in awe that Ella might even love her tricky grandmother.

'When did I ever say Mamie was trouble?' he questioned with a grin. 'Yes, even Mamie. So, are you both okay with that?'

'Yes!' Lily flung herself onto Ella's lap. 'It's even better than getting a pony. That means we can get another chicken, so we all have one each.' Ella's arms were tight around Lily as she looked up. 'Mamie said you'd be good for us, Ella, and she was right, wasn't she?'

'Yes, Lily my love, she was.' Ella swallowed. 'And I think you're all very good for me too.'

'Does that mean we can have pizza for tea tonight please, Ella?' Arlo seemed to have forgotten about the sheep for now. She reached across to smooth his hair back. 'If we're going to be like family then it won't always be up to Daddy to choose what we have for tea, will it?'

'I don't suppose it will, Arlo, we'll share. And yes, you can have pizza for tea tonight. I'll even see if we can try a bit of chocolate on it. Just this once,' she added hastily as a look of glee flew across his face. 'Otherwise your daddy will be roaring.'

'None of that,' Max said firmly, looking at his children gathered around Ella. 'No more roaring.'

'Or swearing?' Lily sounded disappointed. 'The dog shelter won't like it if you stop, Daddy.'

'Well, we can just give them a donation instead and I'll try not to swear any more, okay? Come on, it's freezing. Let's go back and celebrate Ella's victory with hot chocolate and a movie at home.' He held out an arm, his grin wry as his children took her hands instead.

'Ella, what should we call you now that you're staying?' Lily stopped skipping and her eyes were suddenly serious. 'Not Mummy, because ours went to heaven and I don't want another Mummy. But my friends at school all have mums and I like that.'

'I like that too, Lily,' Ella murmured. 'In fact, I love it. But there's no rush, you can call me Ella until you're ready to try something else.'

'Okay. Will you be there to read me a story and tuck me in tonight?'

'If you'd like that?' Ella had to swallow back the emotion so tears didn't start sliding down her cheeks.

'Yes please, it's called *Guess How Much I Love You*. My mummy used to read it to me, and I'd like you to do it. Daddy tried but it made him cry and I didn't want him to be sad when he read to me. I don't think he's so sad now. He laughs more, especially when you're with us, and I saw him giving Prim a cuddle and telling her how good she was when he didn't know I was there.'

Lily's fingers were tight inside Ella's, and she saw Max brushing at his eyes and giving her a tremulous smile. He settled Arlo on his shoulders and held out an arm to Ella. She led Lily to his side and wrapped her other arm round him as his slid across her back.

'We're going to be okay, aren't we?' He touched his lips to Ella's temple as they began the walk back to the house, Prim lolloping ahead.

'I know we are.' They were her family now and she loved them. This was her place, and she was home.

Acknowledgements

Cumbria is a county I know well, and I've long wanted to write about it. *Love in the Lakes* is inspired by the most beautiful landscape and an outstanding arts, crafts and food culture. There is always something new to discover and I pictured Halesmere in the heart of the Duddon valley, with all the fabulous walking and climbing this area offers. Like Ella, I want to stop and stare, and being on foot is a wonderful way to see it.

Thank you to Susan Yearwood, Emily Bedford, and all at Canelo for giving me the opportunity to write a second series. I very much appreciate your support and encouragement and continuing to work together is such a pleasure.

To readers and bloggers who share the books they love and do so much to support our genre, thank you. I'm very grateful to be finding readers who love romance as much as I do.

I must thank Graeme, the team and the students in Hospitality and Catering at Kendal College for a superb three-course lunch and answering all my research questions so thoroughly. These young people are very dedicated and talented, and a catering college plays its own part in the book. Cumbria is a fantastic place to begin a career and I'm looking forward to the tasting menu when I return to the college restaurant.

Thank you to my family for the love and support you give me; it makes all the difference to the time and space I have to write, and I appreciate everything you do. Stan and Pearl are two characters I'm really fond of and love to write, and thanks go to Jo and Harper for suggesting their brilliant and well-suited names. Thank you to Garth for lending Stan a fabulous array of ties, and Claire for helping me choose. Stan's going to need another one soon... To Becca, who loves Christmas and Cumbria, thank you for joining me there for those few days in summer when this book was first begun. We must plan another retreat...

It's said that friends are the family we choose and I'm very thankful to have wonderful and loving friends who are part of our family. Ella and Max's story is one about family, holding those we love close and finding moments of joy in every day. And to Piper and Betty, who mean more than they'll ever know.